MISS BISHOP

Other titles by Bess Streeter Aldrich available from
the University of Nebraska Press

Journey into Christmas and Other Stories
The Rim of the Prairie
Spring Came on Forever

MISS BISHOP

Bess Streeter Aldrich

University of Nebraska Press
Lincoln and London

First Bison Book printing indicated by first digit below:
1   2   3   4   5   6   7   8   9   10

Library of Congress Cataloging-in-Publication Data
Aldrich, Bess Streeter, 1881–1954.
Miss Bishop.
I. Title.
PS3501.L378M5 1986   813'.52   86-6969
ISBN 0-8032-5909-3 (pbk.)

First published in 1933 by Appleton-Century Company, Inc.

Reprinted by arrangement with E. P. Dutton

MISS BISHOP

I

IN 1846 the prairie town of Oak River existed only in a settler's dream. In 1856 the dream became an incorporated reality. Ten years later a rambling village with a long muddy Main Street and a thousand souls welcomed back its Civil War boys. And by 1876 it was sprawling over a large area with the cocksure air of a new midwestern town fully expecting to become a huge metropolis. If all the high hopes of those pioneer town councilors had been fulfilled, the midwest to-day would be one grand interlocking of city streets. As it is, hundreds of little towns grew to their full size of two or five or ten thousand, paused in their growth, and admitted that none of them by taking Chamber-of-Commerce thought could add one cubit to its stature.

So Oak River, attaining the full strength of its corporeal self some years ago, has now settled down into a town of ten thousand, quite like a big boy who realizes that the days of his physical growth are over, and proceeds to look a bit to the development of his mind and his manners.

The chief source of the big boy's pride is the school,—Midwestern College. It stands at the edge of town in a lovely rolling campus, sweet-smelling in the springtime from its newly cropped blue-grass and white clover, colorful in the autumn from the scarlet and russet and gold of its massive trees,—a dozen or more pompous buildings arranged in stately formation, a campanile lifting its clock faces high to the four winds, a huge stadium proudly gloating over its place in the athletic sun. Concrete driveways and sidewalks curve through the green of elms and maples, and young people walk or drive over them continually,—a part of that great concourse of Youth forever crossing the campuses of the world.

Until last summer, an ancient brick building known as Old Central Hall stood in the very middle of the group of fine modern structures, like a frowzy old woman, wrinkled and gray, surrounded by well-groomed matrons. A few mild-spoken people referred to the building as quaint, the frank ones called it ugly—but whenever there was talk of removing it, a host of sentimental alumni arose *en masse* and exclaimed: "What! Tear down Old Central?" And as the college board consisted one hundred per cent of alumni, Old Central continued to sit complacently on, year after year, in the center of the quadrangle, almost humanly impudent in attitude toward the rest of the buildings.

To several thousand people it was so familiar, so much a vital part of their lives, that when, last spring, a regretful board guiltily sounded the death knell, many more alumni than usual arrived on the campus at Commencement time, quite like children called home to see a mother on her deathbed.

Those who had not seen her for several years found her worn and cracked and disgracefully shabby, with her belfry half removed and extra pillars placed in the dismantled auditorium for safety's sake. But, even so, there were two or three present who recalled that like any other aged soul who has outlived her usefulness, she had once been as strong and bright and gay as a bride. That had been in 1876, when Oak River itself was still young.

On the sixth of September of that year, so important to the thirty-two young people entering the new hall for the first time, the building rose like a squatty lighthouse on a freshwater lake, for it stood in the center of forty acres of coarse prairie grass bent to the earth with the moisture of a three-day drenching rain.

It was still raining dismally at eight o'clock on that Wednesday morning—a slow monotonous drizzle that turned the new campus into a sea— a Red Sea, for that matter, as the brick dust around the newly erected building made of the soggy ground a rust-colored mud. Wheelbarrows leaned tipsily against the new walls. Mortar boxes held miniature chalky pools. The approach to the big doors, unpainted as yet, was up an incline with wooden cleats nailed on it, upon which the girls in their flowing ruffled skirts tottered so perilously that their long thin hoops quivered up and down in rhythmic sympathy.

Inside, a few potential students stood about in the hall, which was almost too dark for any one of them to get an enlightening look at his neighbor. The newly plastered walls were scarcely dry, so that the atmosphere here was seemingly as moist as that without.

Chris Jensen, a young Dane, just starting out on his janitor duties, stood solemnly at the doorway with a broom, and after the entrance of each young neophyte, brushed out puddles of muddy water with the air of having swept a part of the River of Sorrows out of the infernal regions.

The first comers all watched him soberly. No one said anything. Everyone was cold, the huge coils of pipes around the rooms having as yet no intimate relation to any heating plant. All was as merry as a burial service.

Then a young girl opened the door and blew in on a gust of rain-filled wind. An expansive smile from a wide cheerful mouth greeted the assembled mourners as she gave one sweeping glance toward them all.

Chris Jensen, with broom poised for her entrance, grinned cheerfully back, his pale eyes lighting with responsive mirth.

"Velcome to school," he said in Danish accent and lowered the threatening weapon. It was the first word he had uttered during the whole moist morning.

With the girl's coming some new element entered the room, as though a bright pigment had suddenly been used on a sepia picture.

She was not pretty. One could scarcely say what it was that set her apart from the others,—humor, vitality, capability, or some unknown characteristic which combined them all. It was as though she said: "Well, here I am. Let's begin."

Removing shining rubbers and a dripping brown cape with a plaid hood at the back, she placed them in the hallway that gave forth a strong rubbery odor, and came up to the other students.

She had on a long plaid dress, brown and red, over narrow hoops, with ruffles curving from the bottom of her skirt up to the back of her waist, and a tight-fitting basque brave with rows of brass buttons marching, soldier-like, four abreast, across the front. Her hair was piled high in the intricate coiffure of the day and drawn back into curls.

She gave one look at the funereal expressions

of the assembled embryonic collegians. One girl, highly overdressed in a green velveteen suit, was shedding copious tears into the expensive lace of a large handkerchief.

"What are we waiting for?" the newcomer said with some asperity. "Let's go on in."

Like sheep, the whole group, under the new bell-wether's leadership, tagged meekly after her into the assembly room—a room so huge that the wildest optimism of the most progressive of Oak River's citizenry could scarcely conceive a day when it would be filled with youth.

A young instructor sat at a desk just inside the door, two others were consulting by a window. Everything about the young man at the desk was thin. He had a thin body, a high thin forehead, a long thin nose, a thin mustache of recent raising straggling over a thin-lipped mouth. A blank book, very large and very white, was open in front of him over which he held a pen poised for action.

He appeared so timid in the face of the situation that when he managed to emit, "Will some one please start the enrollment?" the girl looked about her inquiringly and then marched sturdily up to the sacrificial altar as it were.

"Your name?"

He looked so embarrassed that the merry eyes of the girl half closed in crinkling humor and she stifled silent laughter.

"Ella Bishop," she said demurely.

He wrote it with great flourishes, his hand making many dizzy elliptical journeys before it settled down to an elaborate "E" with a curving tail as long as some prehistoric baboon's.

When he had finished the lengthy and intricate procedure, he paused and asked shyly:

"Your age?"

"Sixteen."

As this was executed in the less spectacular figures, it did not consume quite so much time.

"Residence?"

"Oak River, now . . ." And in further explanation, "We just moved in from the farm—my mother and I—and settled here."

"I see. On what street, please?"

"Adams Street—half way between Tenth and Eleventh."

He looked up as though at a startling piece of news. "Why . . . why . . . that's right across the street from *me*." And flushed to his thin forehead.

The green velveteen girl, who had been weeping continuously, suddenly tittered, a bit hysterically.

By this time the timid one had been joined by another instructor, evidently for monetary reasons, so that immediately there was a flutter of pockets and bags,—one big-boned German boy extracting gold coin with difficulty from the lining of his homemade coat, while a freckled girl of apparent Scotch lineage turned abruptly to the wall and deftly removed a roll of bills from some unknown source in the region of her left lung.

When the last name had been entered by Professor Samuel Peters' agile pen with much shading of downward strokes and many extra corkscrew appendages, the president called the students to order in the church-pew seats of the huge assembly room, in which immensity the little company seemed lost.

The faculty consisted of four instructors besides President Corcoran. They were Professor Loren Wick, mathematics, brown-whiskered and paunchy, with a vague suggestion of his last lunch somewhere on his vest,—Professor Byron Carter, grammar and literature, small and nervous, with gray goatee, eyeglasses and a black cord,—Miss Emmaline Patton, geography and history, a solid appearing woman, both as to physique and mentality,—as though an opinion once formed became a necessary amendment to the laws of the Medes and the Persians,—and the thin, embarrassed Samuel Peters, he of the coquettish pen, who was to teach spelling and the intricacies of the Spencerian method of writing.

These now with President Corcoran, who was to teach a mysterious subject called Mental and

Moral Philosophy, filed up on the rostrum and sat down in a solemn row. Evidently the transmission of knowledge was to be a melancholy procedure. The girl, Ella Bishop, felt her heart pounding tumultuously with the formality of the occasion. The green velveteen girl mopped seeping moisture diligently.

A new reed organ with many carved cupids and gingerbread brackets stood at one side of the rostrum. President Corcoran, a short plump man whose kindly face was two-thirds hidden behind a duck-blind of beard, indicating the musical instrument, asked if any one could play, whereupon the green velveteen girl, having foreseen the possibility of this very prominence (and hence the velveteen) dried her eyes and volunteered with some alacrity.

Shortly, the assembled students were singing "Shall We Gather at the River?" and any one glancing out of the high Gothic windows with prairie adaptations, where the rain splashed and ran dismally down, could have answered honestly, "No doubt we shall."

There was prayer, in which the president informed the Lord of the current events of the morning, including the exact number of matriculations, and then, suddenly, abandoning statistics, asked fervently for divine love and light and guidance in the lives of these young people, which

II

latter part of the petition seemed somehow to reach immediately the place for which it was intended.

When he had finished, there was an announcement or two, a reading of many and stringent rules with penalties attached thereto for nonconformity, and another song of such dry characteristics as might counteract the moisture of the first one:

> "*. . . In deserts wild*
> *Thou spreadest a table for thy child.*"

Then classes,—and Midwestern College was fairly launched.

CHAPTER II

THE girl, Ella Bishop, entered whole-heart-edly into this first convocation of the new college,—as indeed she would have entered into anything, an auction sale or an Irish wake.

Morning classes for her followed one another in rather sketchy fashion. With a surreptitious flour-ish of many cold chicken legs, lunch at noon was consummated in a room politely termed the phys-ical science laboratory, but whose apparatus con-sisted largely of a wobbly tellurian, a lung-tester, and a homemade air-pump which gave forth hu-man-like sounds of torture. One group sat in the recitation seats, one on the edge of a long table, and a few girls under Ella's efficient management gathered in a friendly arrangement of chairs in a far corner. The instinct to run to cliques settles itself in the breast of every female child at birth.

Afternoon saw Ella in Miss Patton's class re-citing a little vaguely concerning the inhabitants of South America, and in Professor Peters' class watching with fascinated wonder as he executed a marvelous blackboard sketch of a fish never known to any sea, with the modest assurance that they too could be in time as proficient as he—although once it did briefly occur to Ella to question what specific importance could be attached to the resultant accomplishment.

The close of day saw her at home in the modest wing-and-ell house "on Adams between Tenth and Eleventh," where her widowed mother was attempting to settle the furnishings.

She removed her wet things and slipped into another dress which strangely enough was made of the same plaid goods as the one she had worn to school. A mystified onlooker could not have known that Ella's father, before his death, had taken over two bolts of cloth from a merchant at Maynard in payment for a horse—and that for several years now Ella's wardrobe had consisted entirely of red-and-brown plaid trimmed with blue serge, or blue serge trimmed with red-and-brown plaid.

"Shall I wear the pork and beans to-day, Mother, or the beans and pork?" she sometimes asked facetiously.

At which joking her mother's expression would become hurt and she would answer: "Oh, Ella . . . you shouldn't make fun . . . Father . . . the cloth . . . like that. . . ."

Mrs. Bishop seldom finished her sentences. She was so uncertain about everything, so possessed by a sense of helplessness since her husband's death, that at sixteen Ella had assumed management of the household and become the dictator of all plans.

Just now she accomplished more in the first half-hour of her brisk labor in the unsettled home than the mother had done in the whole day. She whisked things into place with marvelous dexterity, chattering all the time of the greatest event of her life,—her first day at the new college.

She could give the names of practically all the other thirty-one students. The big-boned German boy was George Schroeder. He had been a farm-hand and could scarcely speak English. The small weazened-face boy who was so sharp at mathematics that Professor Wick had spoken about it was Albert Fonda, a Bohemian boy. He had told Professor Wick he wanted to study astronomy, and that nice Professor Wick had said he and Albert would have a class if there was no one in it but they two. The Scotch girl was Janet Mc-Laughlin and she had made them all laugh by saying that she thought the day would come when cooking and sewing would be taught in schools. Imagine *that*,—things you could learn at home. The girl in the velveteen dress was Irene Van Ness, the banker's daughter, and she had cried because she didn't want to go to this school, but her father was one of the founders of it and had made her go. Irene was half-way engaged to Chester Peters, brother of the penmanship teacher, who went east to school,—the brother, she meant, not The Fish,—though how any one could be *half-way* engaged was more than she could understand.

Indeed, half-way measures were so unknown to Ella Bishop, that carried away by her own entertainment she was now imitating the instructors, describing her fellow students, impersonating Irene playing the organ so vividly that her mother laughed quite heartily before suddenly remembering there had been a bereavement in the family the past year.

The wing-and-ell house into which the two were moving sat behind a brown picket-fence not far back from the street. Two doors at right angles on the small porch opened into a dining-room and a parlor; the porch itself was covered with a rank growth of trumpet-vine. Inside, there were sale carpets tacked firmly over fresh oat straw, the one in the parlor of dark brown liberally sprinkled with the octagon-shaped figures to be found in any complete geometry, the one in the dining-room of red with specks of yellow on it looking like so many little pieces of egg yolk dropped from the table. The parlor contained an organ, a set of horsehair furniture of a perilous slipperiness, a whatnot, and in the exact center of the room a walnut table upon which Ella had arranged a red plush album, a stereoscope with its basket of views, and a plaster cast of the boy who is never quite able to locate the thorn in his foot. A plain house but striving to be in the mode of the day.

As Ella went now to the parlor door to shake out the crocheted tidies that belonged on the backs of the horsehair pieces, she glimpsed a young man walking slowly past the house in the rain and gazing intently at it. At the noise of the opening door he turned his head away suddenly and started walking faster down the street. "There he goes," she told her mother, "the young man whose pen is mightier than his swordfish." And laughed cheerfully at her own wit.

She watched from the shadow of the doorway and saw him cross the street, turn into the large yard with the two cast-iron deer, and go up the steps of the big red-brick house with the cupola on one corner.

"That's Judge Peters' house," Mrs. Bishop said, "the woman next door . . . was telling . . . The other son . . . She said . . . medicine or law . . . or something. . . ." Poor Mrs. Bishop, slipping through life, always half-informed, never sure of any statement.

"Yes, that's what I told you, Mother. Don't you remember? That fits in with what Irene Van Ness said—that she is half-way engaged to Chester Peters who is away at school and is coming home in a few years to go in his father's law office. This writing teacher's name is Sam, and

Irene Van Ness says you never saw two brothers so different."

Ella's first day at school had been one containing many and varied bits of information. Keen, alert, the young girl was interested in every human with whom she came in contact.

On Thursday the rain had ceased, so that the short walk to school was a thing of delight. The college building sat so far back in the prairie pasture that at least half of Ella's journey was through the grass of the potential campus. It lay to the west of Oak River, near a winding prairie road running its muddy length at the south of the pasture and beyond. Oak Creek was to the north, a wandering gypsy of a stream, that after many vagaries of meandering, joined the river.

All of the keen senses of the girl were alive to the loveliness of the day and the joy of living. To her sight came the wide spaces of the prairie whose billowy expanse was broken only by clumps of trees which indicated the farmhouse of some early settler, and by the far horizon where the sky met the prairie like a blue-china bowl turned over a jade-colored plate. To her ears came the drone of Oak River's sawmill, the distant whirring of a prairie grouse, and the soft sad wail of mourning doves. To her nose the pungent odor of prairie grass and prairie loam after their drenching rain, and from the direction of the creek-bed the faint fragrance of matured wild crab-apples and hawthorn.

Plodding along through the lush grass she could see many of the new associates ahead of her wending their way up to this new Delphian oracle—this Greek temple with lightning-rods—the big-boned George Schroeder and the weazened little Albert Fonda and the Scotch Janet McLaughlin. A two-seated open carriage with prancing bays and jangling harness and swaying fly-nets came across the uneven ground and drew up beside her. An old colored man in a high silk hat was driving; Irene Van Ness was in the back seat.

"Come, get in," Irene called pleasantly. And Ella picked up her long ruffled plaid skirt and clutching it with her books, climbed up on the high seat beside her. Irene had on a blue silk dress with white pearl buttons and a flowing cape to match.

As the carriage bounced over the ground they passed a cow grazing near the building and when it snatched a greedy mouthful of the damp luscious prairie grass, Ella said: "That's Professor Wick's cow—and see how much like him she looks."

It set Irene to laughing—the cow gazing placidly at them over a great mouthful of grass, for all the world like Professor Wick looking calmly over his bushy whiskers.

Men were building the new wooden steps to-day, but placed the board with the cleats over the open framework for the two girls. Chris Jensen stood at the top and caught each one by the hand as she went teetering and giggling up the incline.

The day was something of a repetition of the first, without any of its depressing effects. Professor Wick conducted a class in experiments in which the human-voiced air-pump was the leading character, Professor Carter made an heroic attempt to initiate the novices into the mysteries of Chaucer, Miss Patton, coolly rearranging the year's outline to suit herself, moved deliberately out of South America into the British Isles, and young Sam Peters added a flourish of fins to his aquatic vertebrate.

And the evening and the morning were the second day.

CHAPTER III

ELLA BISHOP, healthy, country-bred, alive to every fresh sensation, enjoyed her studies in the new college immensely, but to say that they were the least of her pleasures, is to admit that it was not that she loved her classes less, but that she loved her classmates more. Peculiarly a lover of human contacts, she brought to every day's work an exuberance of spirits, a zest for living, a natural friendliness toward every one in the little school, from President Corcoran to Chris Jensen.

Toward the new neighbors she felt also the same healthy curiosity and friendly spirit. On Friday morning of that first week Sam Peters caught up with her as she was leaving home and carried her books up the long straggling street and across the coarse prairie grass to school. For his shyness she had only sympathy, and when he confided to her that he was not particularly pleased with teaching but that his father had wanted him to try it, her heart quite ached for the unhappy appearing fellow.

On Saturday for the first time she saw Judge Peters leave the big brick house with the cupola on one corner like a stiff hat over one eye.

And to see Judge Peters leave the house and start down to his law office was almost like seeing an ocean liner leave dock. Swinging a cane without change of beat, he walked with a long slow gait as rhythmic as four-four time in music. He was tall, pompous, solemn. Black side-whiskers formed the frame for his face, a wide black cord connected his glasses with some strategic spot on his coat, black gloves added their share to the ensemble, a bit of red geranium in his buttonhole completed the work of art.

By October, when the Indian summer days had come, the judge and his wife, in the neighborly fashion of an early day, came one evening to call.

Mrs. Bishop had been making apple butter a little messily and inefficiently in the back yard all day. She had stirred the concoction in the iron kettle hanging by a chain over the fire, using a big wooden paddle, until, as she said, she was too tired to think. Having burned the last batch, she had left it in the kettle until Ella could come home to clean up the disagreeable mixture.

So when Judge and Mrs. Peters arrived, she was completely upset at the unexpected coming of so much grandeur. She fluttered about, removing her apron, pushing chairs a few inches from their original positions, picking at imaginary threads on the floor. Even at sixteen Ella was far more poised than her frail mother, undaunted by the pompous entrance of the Judge with his meek little wife in tow. Mrs. Peters wore a Paisley shawl and a black velvet bonnet with pansies outlining the rim and satin ties under her patient looking face.

"We came to pay our respects to the newcomers in our fair city," the Judge announced with pompous formality.

The little wife nodded meek assent—and Ella saw then how like his mother was the shy penmanship teacher.

The entire call was made in the manner for which the judge set the pace. So clothed was he in formal phrases, it seemed to Ella that he said everything the hardest and longest way. To remark that the weather was mild was really all he meant when he said that there had been a noticeable lack of inclemency in the activity of the elements.

Once he turned to Ella with exclusive attention: "You have no doubt made the acquaintance, at least in the capacity of student to instructor, of my elder son, Samuel?"

"Yes," Ella said, "oh yes, sir." Mercy, she thought, he is making me feel frightened, too. No wonder his little wife is cowed.

"You have no doubt heard ere this that I have a younger son, also." And before Ella had a

23

chance to reply, he went on proudly: "A younger son, Chester, studying law at Winside—a bright scholarly lad—I may even go so far as to say brilliant. He will make of the law a thing of truth and beauty and justice."

"That's certainly nice, sir." One was not required to say much in his presence. He needed only an audience for his own bombastic speech.

"Chester and Sam are very different," he stated with no apparent loathness in comparing the two openly. Ella was sure she saw the little wife flush and draw back as though struck. "Chester has none of Sam's backwardness and timidity,— has much that Sam lacks."

And she felt an embarrassment for the mother she could scarcely control when he added: "Sam is his mother,—Chester very like me. I am very proud of Chester. He will make a great lawyer, —yes, indeed,—a brilliant lawyer."

Ella was to remember that proudly reiterated statement years hence.

"I am very happy to hope, also, that Chester will some day bestow his hand and heart upon the daughter of my banker friend, thus uniting the old families of Peters and Van Ness."

So that was it, thought Ella—perhaps Irene's "half-way" engagement to Chester was merely an understanding between the families.

"I wouldn't like that," she thought. "When

I'm engaged I want the man to love me for *myself,* and not for any other reason." Then she looked around the simple little parlor with the sale carpet and the cheap curtains, the horsehair furniture and the home-crocheted tidies and laughed to herself, "I guess he'll like me for just myself, all right."

After the call the man's egotism so lingered in her mind and the bald comparison of the two sons made such an impression upon her, that in the weeks to come she found herself forming a dislike of the younger Chester even before she had seen him,—feeling a relative compassion for the shy young instructor so earnestly teaching the swinging arm movements of his Spencerian writing.

A half dozen times that October he walked home from the college with her, so timidly, so self-effacingly, that in spite of laughing silently at his unattractive shyness, she felt a renewal of sympathy for him.

Her mother asked her about it: "This Sam Peters, Ella . . . do you . . . how do you . . . ? You see, he seems . . ."

"My word, Mother," she could always translate her mother's halting thoughts, "you don't think I especially *like* him, do you, just because of walking along the same way home?"

Her mother's eyes filled. "I don't suppose

. . . I won't be staying with you . . . long, Ella. I'd like . . . if you could get settled . . ."

Ella ran to the frail little woman and clasped sturdy arms around her. "You're going to stay with me a long time, Mother. And I don't have to get settled yet for years and years."

Mrs. Bishop wiped her filling eyes with the corner of her apron. "Just so . . . you won't . . . an old maid . . . I wouldn't like . . ."

Ella threw back her head and laughed her hearty laughter. "Don't you worry. I won't be an old maid." Suddenly her voice dropped to a husky sweetness. "I have too many dreams for that, Mother. I think sometimes it is as though I am weaving at a loom with a spindle of hopes and dreams. And no matter, Mother, how lovely the pattern—no matter how many gorgeous colors I use,—always the center of it is . . . *you* know, . . . just a little house in a garden and red firelight and . . . the man I love . . . and children . . . and happiness. For me, Mother, that's the end of all dreaming."

CHAPTER IV

ALL that fall life in the young college was a never-ending journey of adventure for Ella Bishop. Full of vigor, her keen mind grasping for every advantage of her new surroundings, each morning with eager anticipation she donned either the blue-trimmed-with-plaid or the plaid-trimmed-with-blue and ventured forth upon the search for her own particular Holy Grail. But school life to this girl from the country was not only an avenue of approach to knowledge, but to that larger experience,—contacts with her fellow humans. She never lost interest in the most insignificant of her classmates,—held open house for them all in the chambers of her heart. "There isn't one of them but has some likable qualities," she told her mother.

"You're like your father, Ella," Mrs. Bishop would say with moist eyes. "I declare—he seemed . . . his friends . . . he knew every one . . . and then, to think . . ."

"Friends!" Ella always disregarded her mother's depressed attitude. "Do you know, Mother, I'd rather have *friends* than any amount of money."

Her mother managed a wan smile. "I guess
. . . your wish, Ella . . . you'll get it . . .
with Father gone . . . leastways, there'll never
. . . there's no money now . . ."

So with an exuberance of spirits Ella went happily to school each morning through the lovely
Indian summer of the midwest's October, with a
few wild flowers still colorful in the prairie grass,
—through the chilling rains of November when
the mud-puddles on the way held white rims of
ice,—and through the heavy December snows
which sent the young Danish janitor out with a
horse to break a path that the girls with their
flowing skirts might get through the field.

At Christmas time Chester Peters came home,
and Ella admitted with something akin to regret
the superiority of the younger brother's charm.
There were several social events of the community to which she was invited,—a masquerade
party in the town hall, a more select one on New
Year's Eve at Irene Van Ness's big home on Main
Street, and a bob-sled ride to the town of Maynard, including an oyster supper while there.
Chester Peters was Irene Van Ness's escort, although Ella told herself with reluctance that
Chester did not appear to be a very ardent lover
inasmuch as he paid far more attention to a holiday guest from away than to Irene. It was true
that Irene was not pretty,—she was sallow and

scrawny, and attempted to cover these discrepancies with a continual change of fine clothes. Poor Irene, with all her nice things she never appeared very attractive. No wonder she was merely "half-engaged" to Chester.

Ella went to the party at Irene's with Samuel Peters. And while he did not attract her in the least, in all honesty bored her, with her usual effervescent spirits she managed to have a grand time in spite of his rather depressing presence.

The big snows of winter melted, huge chunks slipping off the college roof so that every dash up the wide new wooden steps was a gamble with the back of one's neck the object in peril. Spring came on, a gorgeous creature, with the prairie campus turning to lush green as though a lovely new dress had been made for her, with wild roses trimming the green of the gown, with wild haw-thorn buds for her hair, wild crab-apple blossoms to perfume her, and prairie larks to sing for her. Chris Jensen set out young elms and maples in two curving lines toward the door of the building, a huge half-ellipse of little switches a few yards apart, around each of which he placed a small barrel for protection. George Schroeder and Albert Fonda worked with him after school hours in order to help pay their tuition. When the three had finished, the tiny trees looked almost ludicrous, mere twigs hidden by a half-hundred pickle-kegs on the broad expanse of the prairie campus.

Spring turned to summer with the meadowlark's voice stilled in the torrid heat and the prairie grass curing for the hay barn. All vacation Chris Jensen hauled water to the tiny trees, so that President Corcoran said to him: "Chris, when future generations sit under the great branches of towering elms and maples, they ought to think of you."

"Vell, py golly," Chris beamed with the praise, "I'll be den as old as Met'uselah, an' ve'll all be pickin' dill pickles off de trees."

The summer ended and school began.

While life for Ella the first year had been largely one of adjustment to the new conditions and getting acquainted, the second year proved to be one of greater growth with several constructive plans taking shape. For no sooner had a young men's debating society been formed, than Ella was champing at the bit. In her belief, no masculine student could tread paths over which his feminine colleagues might not go, and so largely through Ella's efforts in which she found her Man Friday in one Mary Crombie, the Minerva Society came into being.

They met once a week in the small room on the third floor into which President Corcoran allowed them to move,—and it was not noticeably surprising to any one that Ella was made the first president.

With Ella, six others composed the personnel of the charter membership—Irene Van Ness and Janet McLaughlin, the Scotch girl, homely and lovable, and Mary Crombie, frank and efficient—one Mina Gordon, little and lithe and gypsy-like, Emily Teasdale, the college beauty, and Evelyn Hobbs, soft-spoken and shyly humorous.

For several months the seven charter members composed the society in its entirety, but with the growth of self-assurance in speaking, in perpetrating their essays and original poems upon each other, came a desire for new worlds to conquer, and the exclusive bars were let down to admit six more Daughters of Wisdom.

Lusty debates were indulged in, which settled so far as they were able, the burning questions of Equal Suffrage, national party accomplishments, and the brighter effulgence of Rome or Athens.

On Friday afternoons when the secret business meetings were over and the doors opened to the proletariat, the small room on third which was the rendezvous for Minerva's handmaidens became the mecca for those outside the pale. Other girls arrived to listen to the pearls that dropped from the lips of the chosen few. Sometimes a group of the young men came also and caused much confusion as to the bringing in of extra chairs, and the fluttering of feminine pulses,—feminine pulses being as they were of a far more fluttery type in the late seventies than those of recent years.

Ella Bishop was in her element at these meetings. Whether she had the management of the entire program or the mere duty of slipping one-half of the black calico curtain across the rather shaky rod to meet its other half, she performed her task with deep fervor. Whether in the chair as president, handling with dictatorial power the noisy wooden potato-masher she had brought from home to serve as a gavel, or sitting humbly in the cold outside the door as sentinel, like some little Rhoda at the gate, she put all her energy into the duty. Her rival in managerial capacity was Mary Crombie whose high-powered energies took the form of a deep belligerency toward anything masculine. That woman would one day vote,—that woman would sometime hold office, —would compete with man,—this was her battle cry. The girls agreed with her in most instances, but the Friday afternoon on which she declared with widely sweeping arm gestures that some day a woman would sit in the cabinet at Washington, they all burst out into high girlish laughter at the absurdity.

A library was formed that year, and while it consisted in its entirety of *Pilgrim's Progress,* the plays of one William Shakespeare, *Uncle Tom's Cabin, Swiss Family Robinson, Plutarch's Lives,* Fox's *Book of Martyrs,* and the highly romantic and therefore thoroughly dog-eared *Barriers Burned Away*—it was indeed the nucleus of what eventually became a library of many thousand volumes.

The students were for the most part serious, studious, almost over-zealous. President Corcoran threw himself heart and soul into the building of a great college. If at times he became discouraged, if the worn-out apparatus of the laboratories, the half-furnished classrooms, or the small number of students worried him, he did not show it, but placed the whole of his energies with those few students and the people who had so enthusiastically founded the school.

In that second year there descended upon the authorities the terrible knowledge that young men and young women of the college were paying romantic attention to each other. When the worthy board found out this crime of the ages, they straightway made a ruling which was printed and passed out to all forty-six students. The ruling set forth: "While it is expected that the ladies and gentlemen of this institution shall treat each other with the polite and courteous civilities, there is a condition which transcends the proprieties of refined society. Anything like *selection* is strictly forbidden. Private walks and rides at any time are not allowed. Students of the two sexes by special permission of the president can meet privately, for the transaction of business and for that purpose only."

Be it said to President Corcoran's credit, that he labored faithfully with the board for several hours, attempting to explain that world-old human philosophy, that the apple which is strictly forbidden, becomes straightway the one fruit every Adam and Eve desires. But the committee on rules and regulations was adamant, and for two years the ruling stood on the college books, until that most potent of all weapons, ridicule, caused it to become obsolete.

At the end of the second year Sam Peters was dropped from the list of instructors. In spite of his marvelous dexterity with a pen, Sam and his exotic-looking fish and the elaborately constructed hand with its protruding index finger which he could draw so skillfully were not considered of enough importance as aids in mounting the ladder of success to warrant their continuance.

Judge Peters and President Corcoran thereafter avoided each other assiduously, due, it was rumored, to Judge Peters having turned the full weight of his extensive vocabulary upon the president, using in addition to the words found in his dictionary, a choice selection of those that were not.

Poor Sam's life under the withering criticism of his father was far less comfortable than before. He went to work soon in a grocery store where he kept the books with his fine Spencerian penmanship, somewhat embellished with intricate figures of hands whose long protruding index fingers pointed to the various commodities, but as he had to wait on trade in addition to the bookkeeping, and as trade in the seventies and eighties bought much salted mackerel and kippered herring, he rather lost his desire to do the fish.

At the first increase in his bookkeeping wages, he dressed in his best, crossed the street, and with almost as much formality as his father might have employed, asked Ella to do him the honor to marry him.

"Oh, no, Sam, I couldn't. I couldn't *think* of it."

"There's somebody else you like?" Sam's pale blue eyes blinked at the hurt.

"Yes," said Ella, and added hastily: "Oh, no,— I don't mean that, Sam. I wasn't even thinking of what I was saying when I said 'Yes.' I meant, I hope there will be some one some day that I can care for. I have an ideal in my mind. I can almost see him." She grew so enthusiastic that even Sam, as obtuse as he was, realized there was no hope for him. "I can see how tall he is . . . and broad-shouldered . . . and even though I can never see his face—in my fancy, you know—some way I just feel that I'll know him right away when I first see him."

"Then . . . he doesn't . . ." Sam swallowed with difficulty. "He doesn't look like me?"

"Oh, no." And at the sight of the flush on his thin drawn face she held out her hand to him. "I'm *so* sorry. You know . . . how it is. If you can't,—you just can't."

"I suppose not."

"But I'll be your friend, Sam . . . for all my life."

"I'm afraid friendship . . . doesn't mean very much, Ella."

"Oh, yes, it does, Sam—truly it does. Friendship is a wonderful thing—a perfectly wonderful thing. Let's make a promise. No matter what girl you marry,—and no matter what man I marry,—let's promise to be friends all our lives. Will you?"

Sam lifted his thin hurt face. "If you say so, Ella."

"I do say so." She spoke happily as though the whole question were settled with satisfaction to them both. "It's a promise. We'll always be friends. When I'm an old lady and you're an old man—isn't that funny to think about, Sam?—

we'll *be friends.*" It sounded as though she were bestowing an honor upon him,—that a young priestess was anointing him.

It was a persuasive way she had with people, even at eighteen—the art of getting them to see a thing from her viewpoint, to believe it was their own decision.

So Sam went away, stepping almost jauntily— taking Ella's promise of undying friendship. Poor Sam Peters, carrying away a friendship—who had come for love.

CHAPTER V

BY Ella's third year a teachers' course and a music course were launched—and she straightway began studying didactics. To clerk in a store, do housework, or teach school were the only three avenues open for any girl, and her mind's selection was immediate. To teach—well, at least until her Lochinvar came riding by, she admitted to that innermost recess of her heart where dwelt her real self. To have a home of her own—children—nothing could ever take the place of that. But she could not look at the lovely picture hanging there so sacredly in her heart and place therein any young man she knew now. The only one who had ever offered himself was Sam Peters—and Sam was unthinkable.

The college boys were all good young chaps. She admired their energy and their sincerity, but to her fastidious mind there was no one outstanding among them—George Schroeder with his big head of rough hair, his foreign accent and his constant praise of anything Germanic—little Albert Fonda with his obsession for the study of the moon and the stars—or any of the others.

So the last two years were spent in a frame of

mind as fancy-free as were the first two. Those last ones saw the faculty enlarged by the additional courses—Professor Cunningham for the didactics—Miss Susie McAlister for the music—the former friendly and humorous—the latter so devoted to the goddess Euterpe that she lived in a world apart, breathed the atmosphere of the upper strata.

Newcomers entered the young college, knowledge was disseminated, minds expanded, the Minerva Society waxed strong in numbers and oratory, the prairie grass was cut, the elms and maples looked superciliously down on their pickle-kegs from a height of five feet. Growth was in the air.

One might ride in state now to the very door of Central Hall in a public vehicle termed "the hack,"—but always with the precautionary measure of placing a newspaper or one's shawl on the seat so the red of the plush cushions would not identify itself too intimately with one's clothes.

The spring of 1880 came on and the first class was to graduate. Ella sent applications to the Oak River board, to Maynard, to Maple City, to every place she thought there might be a chance for a teaching position.

Janet McLaughlin was elected at Maynard, Mary Crombie at Maple City. Mina Gordon and Evelyn Hobbs and Emily Teasdale were all to be married. Irene Van Ness was to stay at home in anticipation of Chester Peters' sudden desire to become wholly and completely engaged. And still Ella had not secured a position.

The time for final examinations was in the offing. For harried days and sleepless nights, Ella and the eleven others comprising the first graduating class crammed for the fray. No dates for execution could have contained any greater element of dread than the June third, fourth and fifth marked with warning crosses in twelve almanacs. Ella grew wan-eyed, lost appetite and weight, and always among her worries was the realization that she had not yet been hired for fall work. Her one great wish had been to get a school near enough so that she could live at home with her always-frail mother. Sometimes in the night she awoke in a cold perspiration with the appalling thought that it looked as though she might not get any school at all. She would lie awake with tense nerves and think: "But I must. . . . I *have* to get a school. . . . Mother has put me through the college . . . she hasn't enough to live on. . . ." All of which was not highly conducive to a healthy physical condition or calm mentality for the figurative Ides of March on which the examinations were to be held.

And then,—the miracle happened. President Corcoran called her to his office and asked her how she would like to teach English Grammar in the college. The school was growing,—they were rearranging classes—

Ella thought she could not believe what she was hearing. She was dreaming,—would waken in her bedroom and laugh at the wild fancy. But no, President Corcoran was saying: "I have watched you for four years, Miss Ella. You have done good work in grammar. You have a keen mind, an open heart, an enviable disposition, and that something which seems to me the very soul of the teaching profession—a keen interest in your fellow man."

No one knighted by a king's touch ever felt so honored.

There was the formality of the written application, the waiting of a few days for the decision already made in board meeting,—and Ella Bishop was to stay on at her youthful Alma Mater and teach. To earn a salary, even though modest, support her mother, live at home,—the whole world took on brilliant roseate lights.

"What have I ever *done* to have so much good luck?" she said over and over to her mother.

"You're like your father, Ella. He . . . there was something . . . he was always . . ." Mrs. Bishop groped, moist-eyed, for the explanation. "You go into things . . . just the way. . . ."

The examinations ended with no fatalities.

Commencement was a reality, and under the bright glow of the knowledge of the new position, a thing of happiness and joy. Happiness and joy to Ella Bishop is meant, for to the towns-people, friends and relatives of the twelve graduates the merry-making had its difficult moments. On Sunday, President Corcoran gave a tedious, if earnest, Baccalaureate address,—on Monday, class-day exercises were held. On Tuesday, four of the twelve members of the class delivered orations, each of forty-five minutes' duration,—on Wednesday, four more held the rostrum for another three hours,—on Thursday, the last group spoke for three more hours to a wilted, perspiring, dog-tired audience of the faithful. George Schroeder, not yet over his German accent, gave a glowing tribute to his beloved Goethe. Albert Fonda spoke on "The Course of the Stars." Mary Crombie presented the case of Woman's Rights so forcibly that she half ripped out a sleeve of her navy blue silk dress. Ella gave all she had ever known or would ever know about "Our American Authors." Irene Van Ness, whose father had written her oration, presented a profound dissertation on "The Financial System of Our Country." "Across the Alps Lies Italy," "Heaven Is Not Reached by a Single Bound," and "Black the Heel of Your Boot" were conspicuous by their presence.

The long-drawn-out exercises were in the auditorium. The girls wore trailing silk dresses with camel-like humps in the rear over wire bustles. Long gold watch chains entwined their necks, coming to rest somewhere in the region of their padded bosoms. The windows were open to the stifling summer air, the June-bugs, and the sound of stamping horses tied to hitch-racks. The odor that penetrated to the farthermost corner of the huge room was a combination of June roses and livery barn. Palm leaf fans whacked vigorously against buttons and lodge emblems. There were instrumental and vocal numbers,—solos, duets, trios, quartets, and choruses. There were invocations and benedictions, presentations and acceptances. Never did it take so long to go through the birth pangs of graduation.

Twelve tables in the hallway, representing each graduate, were laden with bouquets of home-grown flowers, gold watches, pearl-handled opera glasses, plush albums, and many duplicates of cushioned and padded "Poems of Keats,"—or "Burns" or "Shelley."

Chris Jensen, resplendent in a new suit of purplish hue which gave his red face the appearance of being about to suffer apoplexy, guarded the treasures.

The sixth evening the Alumni banquet was held in the auditorium cleared of a portion of its pews, but luckily for the long-suffering public, the attendance was limited to graduates and faculty and faculty wives. The whole procedure had consumed as many days as the fundamentalists' conception of the genesis of the world. Small wonder that the entire community rested the seventh day and called it holy.

At this first Alumni banquet less than two dozen sat down to the tables. President Corcoran referred in his talk to the possible day when two hundred graduates would sup together. It did not seem possible to contemplate.

Ella felt that it was one of the happiest events in her life. Examinations passed, the nightmare moments of her oration behind her—nothing now but the friendly intercourse with those closest to her in school, and the warm glow of the knowledge that she had won the cream of the teaching positions. Life was all before her. She was young,—gloriously young,—only twenty. She could do with her life as she wished.

Happy Ella,—not to know yet for a little while that life is to do as it wishes to you.

CHAPTER VI

ELLA could scarcely wait to begin her work. Sometimes in the summer she would go over to school, tramping through the campus grass to where Chris was mowing, and get the key to the building.

"May I take the key to Central Hall?" she would ask when he had put down his scythe and come swinging across the newly-cut grass to meet her.

"Say . . . vy you alvays call her *Cendral* Hall," Chris asked once, "ven dey ain't but von anyvay?"

"Don't you see, Chris? Look around. Here, stand over here,—can't you see a lot more buildings there,—one over here and one there,—a calisthenics building there,—and a huge library,—and a science building,—and maybe a teachers' training one?"

But even though Chris, open-mouthed, looked and looked, he could not see a calisthenics building, nor a huge library, nor a teachers' training building,—nothing but a plain three-story one with a few straggling ivy vines clinging desperately to the hot bricks in the prairie sun. Only those who have dreams in their minds and courage in their hearts when they are young see such mirage-like things on familiar horizons.

Her classroom was to be on the second floor at the front, with a tiny inner room opening from it. "My office," she said under her breath many times a day to get the thrill which the words gave her. The potential office was a little room in the tower over which the bell hung. To hear the resounding clang of that brass-throated messenger directly over her was to feel its vibration in every nerve of her being. It was more than the mere ringing of a bell,—it was a call to knowledge,—a summons to life itself. Already pigeons had begun to nest in the tower and when the bell rang, they flew violently out like so many frightened loafers. Sometimes they tapped the swinging thing themselves in their turbulent activity.

There were windows on three sides of the little tower room. From them she could see the town to the east, four thousand people now—that was what the college had done for Oak River—the rolling campus to the south—well, anyway, the short prairie grass sloped down an incline—and farm land to the west as far as the eye could see, some of it cultivated, much of it still rough prairie land with no sign of road or fence, and with horses and cattle, herded in little bunches, grazing on its vast unbroken expanse.

Surprisingly, the September morning on which Chris rang the bell for opening classes was almost a replica of the rainy one on which Ella first entered four years before. Remembering the dismal reception to those half-frightened newcomers, she stationed herself near the big doors and greeted every freshman as though he were an honored guest arriving for a social event. President Corcoran, coming through the hall, smiled behind the ambush of his whiskers. "Whatever that girl does, she *does*," he said to Professor Cunningham in passing.

All fall, Ella Bishop taught grammar classes as though she had invented adjectives and was personally responsible for subordinate clauses. Papers she carted home in sheaves. Notebooks she perused so thoroughly that not an insignificant "for him and I" or an infinitesimal "has came" dared lift its head without fear of her sturdy blue pencil. Still so young, she made no effort to disengage herself from student activities. She was adviser for the now-flourishing Minerva Society. She helped start a tiny college paper called the *Weekly Clarion*. She was secretary of the modest little Faculty Family Club. "She's just about an ideal connection between faculty and students," President Corcoran told his wife. "Young enough to get the students' viewpoints, with a nice older dignity when necessary."

Sometimes a little daring crowd of students would plan to slip away in a hayrack or a bob-sled to Maynard to dance, and hearing it, Ella would try to think of some new entertainment to counteract the scheme.

Altogether life was full for her and very, very interesting, swinging along at a lively tempo for the times. The town was growing. Mr. Van Ness built a three-story bank building, renting out the upper floors to the Masons and the Odd Fellows and the Knights of Pythias. Every day Judge Peters walked pompously down Adams and Main Streets in four-four time, his gold-headed cane swinging out the rhythm. Sam slipped quietly down to the grocery store at daylight. Chester wrote home glowing accounts of his own activities over which Irene hung with tremulous hopes. Mrs. Bishop attempted to keep house, but the results were so confused and messy that Ella put her young shoulder to the wheel and did much of it over when she came at night.

The graduating class,—Class of 1880, the members always reminded their friends, as though there had been a dozen others,—had started a round-robin letter. Ella and Irene Van Ness were the only ones living in Oak River, so the package made trips to ten other localities before its return to the city of its birth. Mina Gordon and Emily

Teasdale and Evelyn Hobbs all had new names now and were almost maudlin in their wishes that every one else in the class could be as happy as they. Mary Crombie and Janet McLaughlin were enjoying their teaching, the former having started a little Woman's Suffrage organization which she hoped would expand and sweep the country. George Schroeder was teaching and anticipating saving enough money to go to Heidelberg to school. Albert Fonda's report for the most part read like a treatise on astronomy,—Albert having hitched his wagon to all the stars.

On a Friday night in November, Chris came into Ella's room with a noisy depositing of mops, pail and brooms. She sighed and prepared to gather up her work to leave. That Chris,—he seemed to haunt her this week with his jangling paraphernalia.

He kept eying her furtively, she imagined, with a large show of cleaning activity but not much progress. Was it possible that the big bungling fellow had something on his mind?

"Why does every one always pick on me to unload their troubles?" she was saying to herself, half in exasperation, when he began:

"Miss Bis'op, I got news for you." His fat face was red, his pale blue eyes winking nervously.

"Yes, Chris?"

"I be gettin' marriet next veek."

"Well, Chris—congratulations. I didn't know you had a girl here."

"Oh, s'e not nobody here. S'e come by Ellis Island to-day. Next veek s'e get here to Oak Riffer—den ve get marriet. I rent a leetle house across from school over der by Smit's."

"Well, that's fine. I'm sure she's a nice girl, too, Chris."

"Oh, s'e nice all right. I not see her, now, come six year. S'e vait 'til I safe money and send for passage. S'e healt'y and goot vorker. S'e he'p me safe money."

Dear, dear, thought Ella—how unromantic.

"What's her name, Chris?"

"Hannah Christine Maria Jensen."

"Jensen?"

"Yah."

"The same as yours? Is she any relation to you now?"

"No-o." He threw back his head and laughed long and mirthfully. "Denmark, s'e full of Jensens."

Ella was interested, as indeed she always was in her fellow man. She could not quite seem to keep a hand out of the affairs of every one around her.

"Where will you be married?"

"I don' know. By the Lutheran preacher's house, mebbe."

Suddenly, Ella had an inspiration,—one of those

enthusiasms with which she was eternally possessed. "Chris, would you like to be married at my mother's house? Wouldn't you like to have your—your Hannah Christine Maria come right to our house from the train . . . and have the ceremony in my mother's parlor . . . and then a little supper with us afterward?"

The blond giant's eyes shone,—his fat face grew redder with emotion. "Py golly, Miss Bis'op, I like it fine an' I t'ank you."

Now that she was launched on this new interest, she went into it, as always, with heart and soul. Several times she went to the little cottage at Chris's plea for advice. She took over a half-dozen potted geraniums—sent eggs and bread and fried-cakes for the first breakfast—would have taken the dresser scarf or curtains from her own room if necessary.

When the girl arrived, she proved to be apple-cheeked and buxom—her flesh hard and solid, her pale blue eyes and pale yellow hair contrasting oddly with the flushed red of her face. So in the parlor of Ella's home, Miss Hannah Christine Maria Jensen became Mrs. Hannah Christine Maria Jensen, after which the newlyweds and the Lutheran minister and his wife sat down with Ella and her mother to what the Oak River paper later termed "a bounteous repast."

When they were leaving for the cottage, Chris

said, "To my dyin' day I'll nefer forget dis kindness."

He talked to the girl a moment in Danish and turned to Ella: "S'e say s'e tink s'e can mebbe come vork sometime to s'ow you her respeck."

It touched Ella. It was always to touch her a little,—Chris and Hannah Jensen's dog-like faithfulness to her all the years of her life.

It was not an astonishing piece of news to any one to hear in the spring that Ella had been elected for another year at a five-dollar-per-month increase in salary.

"I'm afraid . . . Ella, . . . you'll be an old maid," her mother said plaintively, "that way . . . teaching . . . kind of . . . seems like . . ."

"I can think of lots worse things, Mother," Ella laughed. "Marrying a worthless man, for instance, and having to take in washing or be a dressmaker. I wonder if the day will ever come when a married woman can do anything more than those two things?"

But Ella knew she would not be an old maid. Something told her so—some singing voice down in the innermost recesses of her heart. As well as she liked her teaching,—to have a husband and home and children,—these were better. These were the things for which her healthy young body and warm heart were intended. She knew.

CHAPTER VII

IN that second year of Ella's teaching, Chester Peters, having finished his school work, was at home and in the law office with his father. Judge Peters took occasion to tell any one who would listen what a brilliant chap Chester was and how he would make of the law a thing of truth and beauty. He never said much about Sam, eggs and flour and salt mackerel evidently not conforming to his ideas of either beauty or truth. Irene Van Ness had a new fur coat, sealskin with mink trimming, a long row of dangling tails around the shoulders and hips, and a mink cap to match. People thought surely Chester would marry her now that he was settling down, and Irene fully shared the desire.

Ella felt sorry for her, could not conceive of a half-hearted romance like that,—was soon to know more about one.

It was a cold Friday night in November. It had snowed all day and now the whiteness of the drifts lay over college and campus, town and prairie. There was a concert in the college auditorium given by the new glee club,—the Euterpeans, they modestly called themselves,—the proceeds to go to the library fund. But at the supper hour, Ella had given up going. "To have a sore throat any night is bad enough," she said irritably to her mother, "but to have it on Friday night with a concert on is a disgrace. This is the first thing I've ever missed."

But she would not listen to her mother's timid statement about giving up the concert too. "The Peterses will come for you as they expected, so you go just the same. I'll help you get ready."

Mrs. Bishop was only in her forties, but to have been forty-six in the eighties was to have been an old woman. She wore a heavy black wool dress, a thick black cape with jet-bead passementerie trimming, a black velvet bonnet with a flat crêpe bow on top and wide crêpe ties under her chin.

Judge and Mrs. Peters came for her, the high-stepping blacks tossing their manes and jangling their sleigh-bells vigorously the few moments they were forced to stand at the horse-block.

After they had gone, Ella took some medicine, gargled with salt and water, rubbed goose-grease and turpentine on her throat and pinned a wide piece of red flannel around that offended part of her anatomy.

For a little while she read in her bedroom by the warmth of the sheet-iron drum, then deciding childishly to make some maple candy, she descended to the kitchen. When she had carried the pan of melted maple sugar back upstairs, she opened her bedroom window to get a plate of snow upon which to drop spoonsful of the hot concoction. It was a favorite confection of the times— these hardened balls of maple candy. The cold wind blew in and the carbon street lights flickered. There was no snow within reaching distance and so while Reason told her that she was doing a foolish thing, Desire caused her to throw a crocheted shawl around her shoulders and step out onto the roof.

As she turned to go in, the window slipped down with a noisy crashing sound. She was at the glass in a moment attempting to raise it, but it would not budge.

At first she worked frantically at the sash, and then when she realized the seriousness of the situation, with more dogged deliberation.

The cold was penetrating and she drew the shawl tightly about her and tied it in a knot in order to work with the stubborn window. When it still would not yield, she thought of summoning some near neighbor. But there were no lights at either house.

She walked gingerly to the very edge of the slippery roof and considered jumping. "Yes, and break my ankles," she thought, "and then faint away from the pain and be covered with snow when Mother comes home. She'd think I was the woodpile." She grinned nervously and shivered.

So this was the way they all felt, was it—Babes in the Woods—Princes in the Tower—and she on the kitchen roof?

Something clammy lighted on her nose. It was beginning to snow again. She let out a lusty and prolonged "Hoo-hoo-oo." No answer came from any source on the deserted street but a mocking echo. She began to shiver again and a cough strangled in her throat.

She hurried back to the window and beat with her fists but the glass would not yield. If she had only left on her sturdy shoes instead of wearing the soft woolen homemade slippers, she could have sent one flying through the pane.

But even as she grew desperate with genuine fright she could hear some one coming up the street, crunching along over the snow-packed sidewalk. As he passed under the carbon street-lamp she could see that he carried a valise.

"Hoo-hoo," she called loudly, "will you please stop a moment?"

The man slowed immediately, and when she called again, he came across the street and then through the snowdrifts of the yard, stepping along with high striding walk. "What is it?" he asked. "What's wanted?"

Ella could not recognize him in the semidarkness, and decided that he was a visiting stranger, but in her desperation would have accosted President Arthur himself.

"I'm terribly sorry to bother you—and highly ashamed of my predicament—but I'm trapped out here on the roof for doing such a silly thing as stepping out here to get a pan of snow. The window slipped down behind me. I've tried to break the glass—I thought glass was supposed to be fragile—and I'm certainly not a weakling—but I can't even crack it."

The young chap laughed and put down on the steps the valise he had been holding all the time. By the faint glimmer of the street-lamp he looked big and substantial.

"Where can I get a ladder?"

"There's one in the barn, just inside the door on the wall to your right."

He strode off to the barn and Ella could see the flare of a match against the darkness and hear Polly snort and rise to her feet. When he returned, he was holding the ladder balanced across his shoulder. With no word he placed it in a snowdrift by the kitchen wall and held it firmly.

"Come on," he called. "But be careful."

When she was half-way down, one of the slimsy cloth slippers dropped.

"See here," he said suddenly, "you can't walk in this deep snow. I'm going to carry you around to that porch."

"Oh, no—thank you. I'll manage." She felt shy, ashamed of her loose, flapping wrapper now that she was part way down and near the strange young man. "Besides, I have goose-grease and turpentine on my throat,—and it's smelly. . . ."

At that he threw back his head and laughed good-naturedly, and for answer picked her off the ladder with no comment and rounded the corner of the kitchen where he set her on her feet in the porch between the cistern-pump and a washtub. For that short distance, she had not been able to see his face distinctly. There had been only time for a fleeting impression of his big cold overcoat and his muscular strength,—and a certain queer sense of liking his personality. She wondered vaguely with swift questioning if it were true— that one radiated personality like that—so that another could tell—even about a stranger—and in the dark—

"Thank you so much for your trouble."

"It was a good thing I happened along or you might have had a sorry time. Even yet, you'd better go take a sweat," he advised solemnly.

"And quinine and white pine and tar and molasses and onions and sulphur." Her voice cracked a little. And they both laughed.

"Now that the rescue is accomplished, can you tell me hurriedly where Judge Peters lives?"

Ella pointed out the big brick house where the

iron deer stood on frozen guard in the snowdrifts.

"I see. Chet has been my roommate—and I'm here to go in the law office with him and his father."

"Oh, how nice," Ella said almost before she realized. Nice for whom, Ella? It gave her a warm friendly feeling toward the young man.

"Well," he held out his hand, "Delbert Thompson is the name of the gallant fireman."

"Ella Bishop," she gave him her own cold one, responding cordially: "I teach in the college here —Midwestern."

"You?" He was incredulous. "I thought you were a little girl—with your hair in a thick braid down your back that way."

"No." And she sang slightly:

> *"The heavenward jog*
> *Of the pedagogue*
> *Is the only life for me."*

They both laughed—it seemed very easy to laugh with the pleasant young man—and then he was gone, crunching along the snow paths with his valise. And Ella went into the house quite distinctly aglow with a peculiar new sensation.

When Mrs. Bishop came, Ella told her all about the funny experience, and Mrs. Bishop was terribly upset,—the exposure to the cold and the trusting of her girl to the clutches of an utter stranger that way. But try as she might in her little fluttered and frightened way, she could not seem to arouse her daughter to the enormity of the danger in which she had been. Indeed, when that daughter was dropping to sleep later, all swathed up in a fat pork poultice after a mustard foot bath, she was thinking she wished she could have seen the young man's face. "I could see how tall he was . . . and his broad shoulders," she thought, "but try as I would, I couldn't quite see his face." And then, suddenly, the familiarity of the words were so startling that all drowsiness left her. For a long time she lay staring into the darkness of the night, thinking of the rest of the prophecy she had made to Sam: "But some way I feel sure, Sam, that I will know him right away when I first see him."

When finally she was dropping off, she dreamed of weaving a tapestry on the kitchen roof, but she was so cold that she must weave in the center of the picture a great deal of red firelight—and—a little cottage—and children—

CHAPTER VIII

THERE was now a freshly painted sign over the door of an office next to the new Bank of Oak River which said "Peters, Peters and Thompson." And the strange and wholly informal meeting of Ella and the firm's new young partner had taken upon itself a bright and shining halo of romance. And life had begun to hold new experiences.

Inherently honest, Ella grew cunning and sly with her own self that month,—would not admit that she was dressing for the new young lawyer, —that she was attending every gathering of college and town in the hope of seeing his big broad shoulders and ready smile. She grew sensitive to his entrance into a room, knew through some peculiar psychic information without turning her head that he had arrived. Gradually she grew to feel that he was looking for her, too.

So immediately mutual was this attraction that by the holiday time he was her exclusive escort to all the social events of the community. In January people were teasing her. Even her students could bring the tell-tale color to her cheeks by an innocently uttered innuendo. Chester Peters seemed to have breathed a bit of the highly charged atmosphere also, for he was more attentive to Irene than he had ever been,—and Irene was glowing these days, her sallow face lighted by the first real hope of the culmination of her long liking for Chester. Chester Peters and Irene Van Ness—Delbert Thompson and Ella Bishop—it was a common sight to see the four tramping laughingly in single-file through paths shoveled in the deep snow or riding in Judge Peters' two-seated sleigh with the jet-colored high-stepping horses that matched the Judge's black side-whiskers. Sam did not figure in the gayety—went quietly to the grocery store where he kept the books in his flowing Spencerian hand, and handled the eggs that the farmers' wives brought in for trade. There seemed no great change in Sam's courteous attitude toward Ella, —except that his eyes now were not only wistful, but tragic. Sensing his shy longing for her, Ella sometimes felt a hearty impatience toward him. Why should the loveliest thing that had ever come into her life have a shadow cast upon it by the moon-calf attitude of Sam Peters?

By February, Ella was formally engaged to Delbert Thompson. It was one of those things she could scarcely believe true. It seemed all too sudden—too beautiful a thing to come to definite words so soon. Just a few months before and she had never seen him, save in her own girlish dreams. She had loved the courting, the imagining the possibility of what might come, the holding to her heart the delicate unfolding flower of romance. And now this February evening Delbert had her in his arms, was lavishing warm kisses on her cool lips, and she was saying, "Delbert—it's too soon. It has all happened too quickly."

At that he was throwing back his head and laughing his boyish ready laugh. "It's not too soon, Ella—nothing's too soon. We'll be married right away this spring."

"Oh, not *this* spring, Delbert. I should teach one more year . . . to get ready . . . and save money . . . and maybe *know* you better," she added, a bit shyly.

"You're a cool little piece, aren't you, Ella?" He held her off and asked anxiously for the dozenth time, "You do love me, don't you?"

"Oh, yes, yes, Delbert. I do love you . . . *so* much. But . . . wait a little . . . I must be so sure . . . it's such a big thing . . . to understand just what this love *is*."

"It's *this*." Delbert laughed and crushed her to him until she nearly cried out in the strength of the embrace.

But Ella knew better—Ella Bishop knew her love was something more than that—something

63

more deeply beautiful,—something infinitely more delicate.

So in a whirlwind of courtship it was settled. Ella was to resign and they were to be married in June as soon as school was out.

When Irene Van Ness heard it, she cried a little. It did not seem quite understandable to her, —she had gone with Chet Peters ever since their High School days. The whole town knew she was Chet's girl,—no one else paid any attention to her. But he had never once mentioned marriage. She bought goods for two whole new outfits and took them to Mrs. Finch, the best dressmaker in town.

All spring Ella lived in the rarefied atmosphere of her romance. But instead of detracting from her work, it merely accentuated her fidelity to it. Every class brought her nearer to the end of her teaching and so she told herself she must give her best to that teaching while she could. This roseate happiness which was hers bubbled over into thoughtfulness for others, a warm kindness toward her students, an energy which sought to make the most of every opportunity to be helpful.

"I am teaching under the assumption that every young person in my classes has to learn from me *all* the English grammar he will *ever* know," she explained laughingly to Delbert. "By pretending that what I can't teach them now in the few remaining months they will never know, I hustle and make the most of my time."

"You're a bundle of energy," Delbert would say proudly, "so different from most of the girls with their kittenish ways and their silly little talk."

"I thought men were supposed to like that kittenish kind," Ella would suggest a bit jealously,—for the **very** feminine reason of getting him to disagree.

"Oh, they may be all right to flirt around with, —but for a wife, who wants a coquette?"

Delbert was to move into the Bishop home. It was a feature of the marriage which gave him some chagrin.

"It doesn't seem quite the thing to do, Ella. It ought not be that way," he would sometimes protest.

But Ella, practical as always, would laugh his humiliation away. "We bought the house after Father died and it's all paid for. I'm an only child . . . Mother has to live with us anyway— no matter where we would go. So what difference does it make?"

The last of March she spent her spring vacation doing the work of two women, for her salary, not any too large, had by necessity to stretch over many things. So, up on a sturdy stepladder, she papered the bedrooms with dainty flowered wallpaper. She washed and ironed the curtains, scrubbed and painted and cleaned.

"If it would only stay so until June." She surveyed her handiwork with the guilty acknowledgment that her mother was not much of a housekeeper. "I wish I could afford a hired girl just to stand guard and keep it nice."

April came in, soft and gentle, with the martins coming and the pussywillows over on the campus creek bursting into gray fuzziness—with time flying on such golden wings that Ella must even begin to think of her dresses now. Dresses in the eighties being, as they were, massive architectural works of pleats, flounces, panels, panniers, bustles and trains, she intended to have but two—a white silk one for the ceremony and a navy blue silk. "But no plaid," she grimaced.

"Do you think I should be so extravagant as to have a white silk one made, though, Mother?" She always went through the routine of asking her mother's advice although she knew the decision would have to be her own.

But almost to her amazement, her mother said definitely: "Yes . . . oh, yes. I had . . . the pale blue one, you know. Your father thought . . . He said I was so pretty. . . It's just one time. . . . When you're old . . . you live it all over."

Each of these days was filled with happy tasks.

Students must be helped tirelessly over the rough places, the house kept in order, her mother assisted, some plain sewing done at home, all her plans for the little June wedding perfected. Sometimes Ella stopped a moment to analyze herself. "What is there about me that is so different from other girls?" she would think. "When I stop to think about it, no one ever does anything for me. I always see to everything myself. Wouldn't it be nice sometimes to have some one else,—Mother, for instance,—take some responsibility? Even Delbert . . ." She felt a momentary disloyalty at the unspoken thought— "Oh, well," she laughed it off. "I'm just one of those people who get about and do things myself, I guess."

On the third of April, she started home at five o'clock. The campus grass, now in its sixth spring, was beginning to look almost like a lawn, the old prairie coarseness of the first two or three years having given place after continuous mowing and the sowing of blue-grass and clover to a fairly pleasing green sloping sward. The hard maples and the elms, planted in their curving horse-shoe formation up toward the building, were actually beginning to seem like real trees, although the barrel-staves around their bases for protection from wild rabbits still detracted not a little from their looks.

As she went down the long wooden sidewalk, she could see Chris in the distance burning leaves. Wild geese flew north, robins dipped low in front of her, sap on the sunny side of a soft maple was dripping clammily on the ground. All the signs of springtime had come,—*her* springtime. There was so much to do,—so many places to go, Irene was having a party in a few days, she and Delbert were driving to Maynard soon where he had business for the Judge,—he had said it would be a regular honeymoon trip with Judge Peters' team and shining new buggy. She was going to look at material for the white dress and compare it with the silk she could get here. Life was so full,—so joyous. How could there be unhappiness in the world?

"There just *isn't* any," she said to herself with a gay little laugh.

But there was unhappiness in the world. She found it out the moment she entered the house, and saw her mother sitting idly, a letter in her lap, tears on her cheeks.

"Mother, darling," she was at her side and down on her knees in a moment, "what's wrong?"

"My only brother is gone, Ella." And the tears overflowed again. "My Eddie—my little brother. One more sorrow for me, Ella." Then she added as casually as though it were not of great import, "And his daughter,—his little Amy

68

. . . she wants to come . . . here with us, you know, Ella . . . and live awhile."

With a cold feeling that life had played her a trick at the very time she wanted life to be most gracious to her, Ella picked up the letter.

It was true. Cousin Amy Saunders, eighteen now, wanted to come out from Ohio and stay with her Aunt and Cousin Ella.

I've nowhere to go, and I don't know what to do. Could you let me come a little while, just until I can get over my sorrow for dear Papa? And, Auntie, I haven't a cent. I don't want to be a trouble to any one but . . .

Ella finished in a daze of mind, conscious that she was deeply annoyed at that which seemed like an intrusion just now. Silently she put the little pink note back in its little pink envelope, and almost without volition raised it to her nose. A faint odor clung to it. For a moment she forgot the import of the message in the whimsical desire to place that elusive fragrance, so strangely familiar. Something in the woods. May-apples— that was it—mandrakes—the cloying fragrance of the waxy-white blossoms of the May-apple.

CHAPTER IX

MRS. BISHOP kept wiping her eyes and sighing. When Ella had stared at the little pink and fragrant epistle for a long moment, her mother asked helplessly: "Oh, Ella, what . . . do you . . . what shall we do?"

"Do?" Ella was suddenly all briskness and decision. "There's just one thing *to* do. Send her·some money and tell her to come on."

"Oh, Ella . . . with you going to get married. You're such . . . you're a good girl. First, you have me . . . on your hands . . . your newly married life . . . and now little Amy."

Ella's eyes wavered away from her mother's. "I was just thinking, Mother, now that it's turned out this way—Amy coming—maybe you and she could live here together. Delbert and I could get rooms—down town, in the building above Judge Peters' office. She'd look after you, you know, and I would be so close to come if I were needed."

That old childish look of fright came into her mother's moist eyes. "To leave Mamma, Ella? To leave me behind . . . when . . . I might . . . at best I may have only a year or two more . . ."

70

It moved Ella as it always did. Impatient she might feel, but one sight of that little delicate figure shrinking into its shroud of fear, and Ella was always on her knees, her strong young arms around it.

"Don't think about it any more, Mother. I'll manage you both somehow."

When she told Delbert about Amy's coming, he was not overly enthusiastic.

"Not that I should be the one to object, Ella dear,—your own house—and I just moving in. I can't quite swallow my pride yet about that. Some day, don't you forget, I'm going to be the one to furnish you with a new home. It will have colored fan-shaped lights over all the doors and windows,—and a black marble fireplace and this new walnut grill-work between all the rooms."

It pleased Ella. She loved that ambitious side of him,—those plans he always made for their future. It would be nice to have some one upon whom to lean. In all her twenty-two years she had never known the time when she could shift responsibility,—do anything but stand erect on her own two feet.

He caught her to him now, his flushed face against her own cool one, his kisses hot on her lips. "To think I'm to live with you . . . in the same *house* . . . the same *room* . . ."

71

"Delbert!" She drew back, a little shy as always. Never yet had she felt entirely responsive to those warm impulsive caresses. Just now he chided her for it. "You're an iceberg, Ella. You don't love me."

"Oh, yes, yes, Delbert,—I *do! How* I love you. You don't *know!* But . . . give me . . . time. Let me. . . ." She could not finish.

How could she tell him that love was such a fine thing, so exquisite, that she wanted to hold it in her heart awhile as one gloats over a pearl—or glories in the beauty of a rose—before wearing it? Sometimes—she wondered vaguely—if Delbert could quite understand that love was something infinitely more lovely, something far more delicate than the mere physical. Then in sheer anger at her disloyalty she would put the thought from her.

There was just time to get the third bedroom upstairs ready for the young cousin before her arrival. Mrs. Bishop's room was on the first floor, and there had never been any reason to furnish the third one upstairs which had been used as a storeroom.

But now Ella went back to the cleaning with only a few nights after school and one Saturday left in which to finish. She put the hat-boxes and her father's army equipment down in the cellar, papered and painted and hung up fresh curtains, and took her own best bedroom chair into the cousin's room.

As she worked, her interest in preparing for the guest overcame her resentment at that which had seemed at first like intrusion. "Poor little thing," she thought,—"left an orphan,—my own little cousin Amy . . . and I not willing to share a roof with her."

Irene's charade party was to be on Friday night, and it was just possible that Amy would get to Oak River in time to attend it, Ella thought, and decided it would be a nice way to initiate her into local society.

It turned out that it happened just that way. Amy was getting in on the four o'clock train from the east on Friday. Ella left school early. Delbert came and hitched up Polly and they were at the station long before the steam whistle sounded down the road. The train was a half-hour late— there had been cows on the track and the trainmen had been compelled to get out and extricate one from a trestle, the conductor said when he swung down from the coach. He appeared to show quite a solicitous attitude toward the girl as she came down the car steps. Evidently they had become rather good friends on the ride out.

Amy was lovely, Ella admitted that to herself. She was small-boned, softly rounded, the delicate pink of her flesh the texture of a baby's. Her wide eyes, too, were child-like in their blue candor. She wore a little gray dolman trimmed with baby blue, and a little stiff gray hat with blue cornflowers on it. It gave her the appearance of a soft little turtle dove, with a blue ruff. And she was fragrant with the scent of her letter—something that reminded Ella vaguely of the cloying sweetness of waxy-white mayflowers.

Also she was a helpless sort of little thing, Ella could see. She was not sure of anything,—her baggage, her checks, her way about. Delbert looked after everything for her and she thanked him so prettily that he flushed with pleasure.

"She makes me think of a kitten," he told Ella afterward, "a fluffy little kitten."

What was it Delbert had once said about kittens? Oh, yes, she remembered,—they were all right to flirt with— She put the thought quickly from her mind.

After supper, Delbert came for the girls and the three walked through the soft April night to the charade party at Irene Van Ness's home. The big house was bright from top to bottom,—hanging lamps with glass pendants and side lamps in brackets on the walls gave forth their limit of light. The heavy walnut furniture, the dark chenille portières, the thick-flowered Brussels carpet, and the Nottingham lace curtains, all looked rich in the night lights. Silver gleamed on the sideboard, and one caught whiffs of chicken and oysters when the kitchen door swung back. It was rumored that Mr. Van Ness had even ordered Sam Peters to send to Florida for a box of oranges.

Irene had on a new rich plum-colored satin— square cut in the front, from which her neck rose scrawnily, her dull complexion challenged by the purplish shade of the dress.

When Ella came downstairs with Amy, she was plainly aware of the admiring whispers that went around. Amy did look lovely—"bewitching" Chester Peters said before every one, so that Irene flushed a little. She wore pink silk, her plump form squeezed into the hour-glass shape which was the mode of the day, the low-cut front revealing the milky whiteness of her flesh. Her hair was a high mass of yellow curls through which a black ribbon was drawn, the one touch of mourning for her recent loss. Her wide blue eyes stared at the new-found friends with babyish candor. She had the merest suggestion of an impediment in her speech which certain of the young bloods there seemed to find quite entrancing, as they formed a little circle around her almost immediately.

At the end of the evening of charades and singing around the piano, a few dancing games, and the consumption of much rich food, there was no

little rivalry over seeing Amy home. Chet Peters high-handedly won her promise, but when he
was waiting at the foot of the stairs for her,
Delbert tried to put him off with a curt: "No,
you don't. I brought her and I'll see to her myself." Chet, however, won his point and carried
Amy off into the warm spring moonlight.

When they left, Ella could see that Irene was
making an ineffectual attempt to keep back the
tears.

In the days that followed, the whole crowd
knew that Chet Peters was quite mad about Amy
Saunders. It worried Ella to the depths, to a
great measure spoiled the days which should have
been so happy. Irene was her best friend and
was now too hurt to come to see her. It all made
an upsetting state of affairs.

"Oh, why did she have to come just now?" Ella
sometimes said to her mother.

But her mother was vague, uncertain what to
say, could only look to Ella for decisions on the
subject.

And Amy? Sometimes she went with him as
coolly as any woman of the world and sometimes
she clung to Delbert and Ella as though she were
a child and afraid of Chet's ardent wooing. Ella
could not read the girl clearly. Was she too
young and innocent to know her own mind? Did

she honestly dislike Chester? Or was she assuming a virtue when she had it not?

"I like him," she said one day to them both, her blue eyes wide and soft and child-like. And added with engaging candor, "But I like Delbert better." And to Ella, with a half-sad little smile: *"You're* the one I envy."

She said it so prettily that Delbert flushed with pleasure.

Ella scarcely knew what to say. Among all the girls of her acquaintance in her four school years, —among all the girls in the classes of her two teaching years,—she had not known one quite like Amy. She was so sweet, so guileless,—and yet,— This time, instead of vague Mrs. Bishop, it was Ella, herself, who could not finish a sentence.

CHAPTER X

ON the Saturday that Delbert was to drive to Maynard on business and to which Ella had looked forward, Amy remarked with her usual beguiling candor that it was such a lovely day she wished *she* could go too. There seemed nothing to do but to take her. One could scarcely conceive of leaving the young guest behind to sit in the house on such a spring day.

So the trip that was to have been almost a wedding journey became a rather different sort of thing. Ella felt cross as they started, chiding herself for having a beastly disposition, but on the long drive with the Judge's horses keeping up a steady swing, the scent of the spring day in the air, and Amy and Delbert gay and talkative, her unquenchable spirits rose too, and she felt such a magnanimity toward all mankind that her momentary disappointment was forgotten.

When they were ready to make the return trip, Amy placed herself in the middle of the seat. "I'm the littl'st," she said with her faint suggestion of a lisp. "I want to sit between you so I won't fall out."

Ella felt provoked at the absurd childishness, but Delbert laughed.

The horses were not so fresh as in the morning and the drive seemed longer. Amy quieted and fell asleep as they jogged along.

"She's like a baby instead of a young lady, isn't she?" he said to Ella—and with his finger tips touched the creamy whiteness of the curve under her chin. At which Amy sighed and moved in her sleep so that her head fell over against his shoulder.

At home Ella sprang as nimbly to the ground as her long skirts would allow, but Amy, rousing from her nap and yawning, made such hard work of it that Delbert helped her down carefully. As she put her foot on the carriage step, she slipped and would have fallen if he had not caught her. For a long moment she lay smiling in his arms until he set her hurriedly on the horse-block.

The first of May, Ella bought the goods for her dresses—twenty yards of lovely silk with nosegays of flowers strewn over its snow whiteness and sixteen yards of wide stiff blue silk and four dozen wooden buttons to be covered with the same material. She opened the packages on the bed in her room and could scarcely take her eyes from the beauty of the white one, the little bouquets of pale pink rosebuds and baby-blue forget-me-nots standing out in silken relief against the shimmering background.

Amy came in to see them, and went into such ecstasies over the white silk—her enjoyment of its loveliness so genuine—that Ella told herself she would forever forget all the impatience with her she had ever felt. The girl was merely immature—her joy lay in the material world almost entirely. As for the future, she would let that take care of itself for a time. Amy would not want to stay with them forever,—she would marry,—Chet, perhaps, as he was apparently infatuated with her. At any rate she was the type that married young. Never again would she let the actions of the girl displease her—now that she was assured of their naturalness.

In the late afternoon Ella took the package of silk to the little weather-beaten house where the dressmaker lived.

The woman was quite excited over the news that she could have the honor of making them. "I've heard of you, Miss Bishop, and saw you, and my neighbor girl here next door has went to you, and she says you're the best teacher she ever seen in her life. She says you make them students talk right. Well, gracious, I says to her, it's the Lord that gives you your talkin'—what can a mere teacher do about it? But I guess I got to admit maybe the Lord 'n you is in cahoots."

But it did not take Ella long to realize that maltreating the king's English had very little to do with the woman's natural knack for dressmaking. She brought out a lovely pale blue silk,—"for Irene Van Ness,"—glowing with pride at the name of her customer. "She has always went with that Chester Peters 'n while I wouldn't want any girl of mine to tie up with him—I guess there's plenty about him—there's them that must have their own ideas. But they say she's eatin' her heart out over jealousy of some girl here visitin'. The rich has their troubles the same as us dressmakers, I guess."

Ella said she must get right at the planning for it was growing late. So the woman brought out her "Colored Plates of Ladies of Fashion" and was immediately lost to the world of gossip.

In the days that followed, Ella made many trips to the little weather-beaten house in the far end of town. Having a dress made in the eighties was having a monument built.

On a Wednesday afternoon in the last of May she felt almost too tired to stand through the long ordeal of the fitting. School all day, doing her portion of the housework when home, then the fitting,—and still the day was not over, for she and Amy were going up the river with Delbert after supper.

"I wonder if the time will ever come that one

can walk into a store and buy a dress all made," she said to the woman down on her knees.

The dressmaker shifted two or three pins with the muscles of her mouth. "Good land, no. The' ain't no two sets o' hips 'n busts 'n shoulders in the world alike. No—that's *one* thing ain't never goin' to be invented by nobody. 'Til the end o' the world folks has got to have dresses made for ev'ry separate one."

When Ella arrived home, Delbert was there, and also there was word awaiting her to come to President Corcoran's office at seven-thirty to a hastily called meeting of the faculty over some Commencement difficulty.

"That settles going up the river," she said.

"Oh, no," Amy pouted, "I want to go."

Ella ignored it and turned to Delbert. "You know, Delbert, I wouldn't want any one to hold a single criticism against my work if I could help it. No one can say that I've not done my duty right up to the last."

"Of course not, Ella. It's right, too."

Amy's big china-blue eyes filled with tears. "I'm so disappointed. This beautiful evening—there's going to be a moon. I've counted all day on going. You see, Ella, you and Delbert are out all day." Her soft lips quivered, "But when I'm just here with Auntie, I look forward to little things like this."

"Where's Chester?" Ella was a little tart in tone.

Delbert answered that Chester was with his father who was having two men in the office for business—farmers who had made the date with him. Then he added: "I could take her, Ella— if she's so disappointed. We could walk over to school with you first and then go back down to the river."

Ella thought of her own self at Amy's age— she was nearly nineteen—remembered her self-reliance and self-discipline, and felt a disgust for her cousin's childishness and an annoyance at Delbert's succumbing to the soft little wiles of the girl.

She shrugged a lithe shoulder. "Oh, of course —she ought to be taken," she admitted dryly, and went for her own wraps.

Amy recovered her spirits then, chattered gayly all the way to Central Hall, left Ella with, "You're not mad are you, Ella?" Tired as she was, it took all of Ella's self-control to maintain her poise.

"How long do you think you'll be in the meeting, Ella?" Delbert was wanting to know.

"I haven't the least idea." To save herself she could not help an acidity creeping into her tones.

"I'll probably be waiting here in the hall for you."

"You needn't bother."

She went in to the office, thoroughly annoyed at her own annoyance. "Sometimes I think I'm my own worst enemy," she said to herself.

The meeting lasted late, involving as it did a necessary change of plans and their attendant preparations for Commencement. During the entire time Ella held herself to the line of duty, schooling herself in the concentration of her part in it.

When she came out, she looked about. But there was no one in the hall.

She walked across the campus with Professor Cunningham and Miss McAlister, scorning the idea that they accompany her on down Adams Street to her home, went into the house where the lamp was still burning for her and on up the enclosed stairway to her own room. There she undressed, got into her long white cambric nightgown with its embroidered yoke, and brushed her thick dark hair. When she was ready for bed, she took her lamp with its red flannel in the kerosene bowl and tiptoed down the length of the hall to Amy's room. Cautiously pushing back the door and holding her hand in front of the light in order not to disturb the sleeping girl, she looked in. Amy was not there.

A cold icy hand clutched Ella's heart and strangled her breathing. The gray deep river— a leaky flat-bottomed boat—or an upset canoe— or a fall from a rocky ledge—or—or—

She felt, rather than saw, her way back into her room, blew out the light to have the sheltering darkness, sat stiffly on the edge of the bed to stare into the enfolding blackness.

After a long time she heard the far sound of the outside door, the closer creak of the stair one, and the softly padded tiptoeing of the girl down the hall.

Ella lay back on her pillow. But for an hour or more she continued to stare into the engulfing darkness.

CHAPTER XI

MORNING and sunshine and the sweet May odors from the yard brought to Ella clearer vision and a mind swept of all doubts. Why should humans—decent souls who despised the perfidious—ever be besieged by disturbing and disloyal questions? It was not worthy of her,—was not trustful of the love which had been given her. As she dressed she made a little prayer to the God of Lovers,—and the humble request was: "Keep us both from unworthy thoughts."

She left the house cheerfully, before Amy had come down. All day long at school she was busy and contented. In the late afternoon at home she found Amy demure and gentle, slipping quietly about the house doing a simple task or two. Some May-apple blossoms drooped limply over the side of a vase,—mute reminder of the river trip.

"That's one flower should stay in its natural woodsy habitat," Ella said gayly. "Never pull a mandrake."

She did not notice that Amy's wide blue eyes looked up, startled and fearful.

Delbert did **not** come in the evening. Sometimes he had extra work and stayed at the office. Neither was there any word from him, for the telephone was but a new toy being **tried** out by a handful of people in the east.

Chester drove up in the new buggy with the prancing blacks, but when Amy saw him, she said hurriedly to Mrs. Bishop: "Tell him I have a headache"—and ran up the enclosed stairway.

Friday morning Ella went as usual to school, her active mind placing all the day's tasks in neat pigeon-holes: classes, a test on diagraming, see Professor Wick about Clarence Caldwell, meet with Miss McAlister and Professor Cunningham on a committee, go to Mrs. Finch's for a fitting, ask Irene about some music for the Alumni—the third banquet, now, with thirty-three graduates eligible to attend.

A busy morning—and then in the afternoon just before the one o'clock class was called, Chris Jensen came to Ella's recitation room, tiptoeing with noisy boots—squeak—squeak—all the way down the length of it. He grinned as he handed her a sealed note.

"Iss dis somet'ing you can use?"

"Thank you, Chris."

"Pleased to do t'ings for you, Miss Bis'op."

The note was in Delbert's handwriting so that Ella slipped into her little office to open it alone.

Sometimes he sent her these little messages by Chris,—about nothing at all.

She tore into the envelope with its *Peters, Peters and Thompson* in one corner.

But *this*,—this was different. Ella's heart pounded strangely at the queer letter and the same icy hand of Wednesday evening clutched at her throat.

DEAR ELLA:
Something has happened. I must see you this evening,—and talk with you.
DELBERT.

What—oh what had happened? Something that night. Why must Delbert talk with her? About something of that night. Why had he sent a note at all? He could come any time he wished. It was preparing her. For what? For something about that night.

Like the tom-toms of the jungle it beat its monotonous refrain: *Something that night.*

The one o'clock bell rang directly over her head with loud clamorous insistence, and the pigeons flew out in noisy response, their wings brushing the windows. The bell! The bell meant service to others. Oh, no, not now,—not this afternoon when something had happened. The bell meant obligations. No, no,—nothing was important but that something had happened,—

something vital,—something more serious than classes,—something to do with the things of the heart. The bell meant duty. Duty! One's duty had to be performed, no matter under what stress. Go on in there like a soldier. But something has happened, I tell you. Stop whimpering. *Go!*

Head up, Ella stepped into her classroom.

All afternoon she could hear the pigeons coo and their wings beat against the bell. And then to her tormented mind they were no longer softly cooing pigeons but great black bats that, like her thoughts, would not stay away. They swirled about her head, harassing and torturing her— the bats and the thoughts. They flew about her in all their ugliness, through the work of the three periods.

"The definition, please, for a transitive verb."

Something has happened.

"Name the principal parts . . ."

I must see you this evening.

"What type of clause do we prefer there?"

Something has happened.

CHAPTER XII

ELLA taught all her classes. She walked down to Mrs. Finch's and stood through a tedious and loquacious fitting. She found her mother not feeling well and put cold packs on her head.

When the bell rings, the Ella Bishops of the world answer the summons.

But she could eat no supper. She sat at the table and made futile little stabs at her plate, nibbling a saleratus biscuit, so her mother would not notice and worry.

Amy cast furtive glances at the two occasionally, her long thick lashes sweeping her cheeks whenever she looked away. Mrs. Bishop made plaintive and tedious remarks about the dull pain in her head. It was a tense meal.

"I'll wash the dishes," Amy volunteered with feigned lightness.

"No, I'll do them myself." Ella wanted activity for her body to deaden the constant questioning of her mind.

When she heard Delbert open the picket-gate and come up the board walk, she slipped outside and met him under the rank growth of the trumpet-vine at the edge of the porch. He stood and stared at her with no word. By the rays from the dining-room lamp, she could see that he was haggard, his lips drawn taut.

"What *is* it?" The thing was now frightening her beyond endurance.

"Let's walk, Ella. I have to tell you something. Let's get away . . . from the house." He threw a nervous glance toward the lamplight beyond the screen door against which a June-bug was thumping noisily.

"No." She heard her own voice as though coming from far off and detected the terror in it. "Tell it *now*. Right *here*." She felt that she was choking, so that she put both hands across the beating pulse of her throat.

"It's . . . about Amy." His voice sounded desperate.

She knew it. Something had been trying to tell her so for days. And she had refused to listen. Now in the flash of a split second she knew that she had sensed the thing from the first.

"You love her." She found herself saying it for him. In her whole life to come no one would ever accuse Ella Bishop of sidestepping the truth. Some sturdy element inherited from her pioneer father gave her strength to shoulder the hard part of the interview. Even now, in the crisis of the tense moment, she had a swift understanding of herself, a sudden fleeting premonition that she was always to do that for other people—assume their burdens.

"I . . . I . . . am afraid so." He was breathing hard,—was suffering. "Come over here . . . where we can talk . . ." He put his hand on hers to draw her to a bench in the yard. Ella pulled it back as from a striking reptile.

"Let me explain, Ella." His voice sounded as though he had been running. "When I went up the river with her, I *swear* to you . . ."

"*No* . . . that's enough."

She turned away.

He called her desperately: "Ella . . . come back."

But she had gone, in one swift flash, back into the house—the screen door clicking sharply behind her. Up the stairs with running feet—up to the darkness of her room—up to face despair—up to the black midnight of—

But in front of her own bedroom door Amy met her, barring the way to that dark haven.

"Oh, Ella, whatever will you say to me?" She tried to put her hand on Ella's arm, but pulled it back at the sight of the older girl's wild face.

Suddenly she began to cry, little, superficial, cowardly tears. "Ella . . . I'm sorry. I never meant to."

Meant to.

Ella stared, white-faced, at the soft pink features contorted into a baby-like expression of fear until Amy cowered before her.

"What are you going to do about it?" the young girl looked out between trembling fingers.

Do! Do!

"Ella, you aren't . . . you don't think you can still marry him, do you?" Genuine fright was in the soft voice.

Ella glared at the human who could conceive the thought. The young girl misinterpreted the long icy silence,—all the unanswered questions,— for suddenly she took her hands from her face and said dryly, with a little jaunty twitch of her shoulder. "Well, you can't. He *can't* marry you now. I'll have you know that."

It was with fascinated horror that Ella gazed now at the girl. What? What? Oh, what?

She wet her moist lips, tried to make the words come. Her knees were water.

"You mean . . . ?"

"Well . . . he has to marry me . . . now."

"You . . . you little . . . *animal*," Ella said. And crumpled to the floor.

CHAPTER XIII

ALL night and a day Ella lay on the bed in her darkened room without removing her dress. All night and a day she crushed her face into the pillow and prayed to die. "Don't let me live. Please don't let me live," was her constant petition.

Her mother tiptoed to the door at intervals,— plead plaintively with her daughter to see her. But there is no sharing Gethsemane with another. When one crosses the brook of Cedron into the Garden, one goes alone.

Toward evening there was a different voice at the door,—Amy's childish one. "I'm going, Ella." And in a moment: "Ella, . . . let me see you a minute before I go, won't you?" And when there was no answer, "Ella, don't be mad. Please don't be mad."

Ella wrapped the pillow about her head and moaned into its feathery depths.

At dusk she heard a buggy drive up. Her ears sharpened by distress conveyed the fact to her that there was more movement in the house than there had been all day. A door slammed twice, there was a sound of a man's low voice—Delbert's—the dragging of a trunk or box, a high childish call of "Good-by, Auntie." And the world had come to an end for Ella Bishop.

Toward morning, she pulled the clothes from her exhausted body and got into her gown. For the first time, then, she felt that she wanted her mother. Like a little girl, bruised and hurt, she crept down the stairs, felt her way through the darkness of the rooms, into her mother's bedroom, and crawled into bed with her.

"Mamma—comfort me." It was the cry of a wounded thing.

But her mother's heart was pounding so furiously from the shock, and she said her head was splitting so terribly, that in a few minutes Ella got up and dressed again and gave her medicine and wrung out cold compresses for her. So after all, it was Ella who did the comforting.

Sunday passed with tragic nerve-racking slowness. Once she threw out some dead mandrake blossoms and scrubbed the vase vigorously, as though she would cleanse it from all past association with the cloying odor of the waxy flower. Like a haunted thing then her mind would again travel in sickly imaginings up the river where an empty boat was nosed into the wet sand, drag itself up the bank and creep into the nearby woods where the May-apples grew in shady cloistered places— She would moan aloud in the agony of her mental illness and dark despair.

On Monday morning she dragged herself to her classroom. Duty—obligations—service. These await every one who comes out of the Garden.

"Oh, Miss Bishop, have you been sick?" a freshman girl asked.

"Just a Sunday headache," she answered with studied composure.

All day she taught with painstaking thoroughness. Not all the world's heroines are listed in the archives.

"Another use of the participle should be kept in mind."

Where did they go last night?

"Analyze it orally, giving attention to the function of the participle."

She's a cunning little thing—like a kitten.

Not a student could have detected any let-down in the detailed instruction. Ella Bishop's heartbreak was her own.

She stayed until five, assisting a pretty young girl with an outline for an essay. The student was only four years younger than the teacher, but to Ella, noting the girl's spontaneous smile, there seemed all the difference between blooming youth and tragic old age.

When the work was finished, she put on her hat and walked down through the June sunshine, redolent with the odors of Commencement, across town to Mrs. Finch's weather-beaten house.

The little dressmaker greeted her with: "Well, well, here comes the bride." And before Ella could respond she added: "The blue one is all finished to the last stitch, but *the* one has to have another fitting, so I'm glad you've came."

Ella held herself together with studied effort. There would be a great deal of this to meet now, and she must face it with composure. "You won't need to finish it, Mrs. Finch. I'm not going to use it."

"Oh—you'll wear the blue instead? But I *wouldn't,* Miss Bishop . . ."

"You don't understand. I'm not getting married at all."

"Oh, Miss *Bishop.* You don't . . . ?" But something formidable in Ella's face made her stop abruptly.

"Sometimes one just changes one's mind," Ella said quietly.

Mrs. Finch was embarrassed. She hardly knew how to proceed. "You'll take the blue one with you then?"

"Yes," said Ella.

"And how . . . about . . . ?"

"The white? I'll take it too."

"Just the unfinished way . . . with the bottom not hemmed . . . and the sleeves not sewed in ?"

"Yes."

She brought it out of an inner room—a shimmering mass of white with little bouquets of pale pink rosebuds and blue forget-me-nots in silken relief against the snowy background—a lovely white monument for the grave of a dead hope, with flowers for remembrance.

With much fumbling of paper and dropping of string the little dressmaker did up the two dresses, the blue one and the white one and the long mousquetaire sleeves of the white which had not been sewed in.

When Ellen took the money out of her purse, the woman said sympathetically: "Just for the blue, Miss Bishop. I wouldn't like to . . . take anything for the other . . . unfinished that way and . . . not to be used just now."

"Thank you—but I pay my obligations," Ella said firmly. And left with the finished blue dress and the unfinished white one which was not to be used just then—or ever.

CHAPTER XIV

AFTER supper Sam came across the street, stepping gingerly around through the young hollyhocks to the back door. When Ella met him at the entrance to the little porch, he stood in embarrassment, his thin throat with its prominent Adam's apple working convulsively.

"I know all about it, Ella."

"Please—Sam—don't talk of it."

"I won't, Ella—now or ever. But I have to tell you one or two things,—it's necessary. I thought if I came right now and got it over, I wouldn't have to bother you any more. Delbert severed his connections with father . . . and left town. You won't . . . won't have to be seeing him. And Chet's gone away."

"Gone . . . where?"

"St. Louis. Father owns a little property there. Chet went to transact some business in connection with it. He just didn't want to stay here longer. He was"—Sam looked up in embarrassment—"quite madly in love with Amy."

"Yes. And Irene?"

"He doesn't care anything for her."

"No—he doesn't. Poor Irene."

For a little while they stood at the back stoop, saying nothing—both in frozen misery.

Sam broke the stony silence then with: "I'd give anything in the world, Ella, to have you happy again."

"I know, Sam. And I'm grateful to you."

"That's one thing I came to say. If ever . . . if you need me, I'll always be there . . . right across the street."

"Thank you, Sam."

"You may seem pretty strong and self-reliant, Ella, but maybe there are times you'd need to . . . sort of lean on some one . . ."

It broke Ella. She, who had held her head high all day, suddenly burst into wild tears. Great wrenching sobs shook her,—and when she was spent with the rocking torture of them, Sam, with untold misery in his eyes, was saying: "That's good for you, Ella—a kind of outlet. God knows, I wish it was the last tear you'd ever have to shed in your life."

So Chester Peters had left town for awhile in the despondency of a weak and hopeless infatuation for Amy. The trail of wreckage left behind her coming was quite complete.

On Tuesday, Ella asked to see President Corcoran after school alone in his office. With no preliminaries she asked if her position had been filled, and when told that it had not been as yet, without evasive excuses she inquired whether or not she could retain it.

President Corcoran's bright black eyes looked at her quizzically through the steel-bowed glasses above the Spanish moss of his beard.

"But your other plans, Miss Ella? I ask only with kindest motives."

"I understand, President Corcoran. I've changed my mind. Am not . . . getting married . . ." If her voice faltered, it was only for a moment. "Probably I never shall."

"I see."

The president sat quietly looking out on the raw new campus with the barrel-staves around the bases of the young elms and maples.

"You are a fine young woman, Miss Ella," he said in a moment. "You would make the young man a splendid wife. If there is any uncertainty . . . yet . . . in your mind?" It was half question, half fatherly advice.

Ella, holding her lips together in a quivering line, shook her head.

"I see."

He waited another moment, thoughtfully, then reached to a pigeon-hole of his desk and withdrew a handful of letters,—apparently a dozen or fifteen,—and dropped them into the cavernous wastebasket at his side.

"Applications," he remarked casually, and held

out his hand. "It will be all right with the board, I know."

Ella took the hand which pressed her own in paternal sympathy, but she could not trust herself to speak.

In a moment he asked: "You will devote your fine young energies to the students of this school?"

Something suddenly ran through her body and heart and mind with the thought—some feeling of emotion, which was too deep for analysis.

"It's a wonderful work," the steady voice went on. "It's something like carrying a torch to light the paths for all the boys and girls with whom you come in contact. In dollars and cents it does not pay much—perhaps it never will. For myself—I know I might be able to make more money another way. I have just this spring had that very question to settle. My brother-in-law has wanted me to go into a new manufacturing business with him for which the financial prospects seem extremely good. I have had my struggle with myself and made my decision. I shall teach,—even when the school grows and I need no longer conduct any classes, the contacts will be the same."

When Ella did not speak he went on. "There is no way in the world, Miss Ella, to hold to one's youth. Time passes so quickly. To-day I'm forty. To-morrow I shall be sixty,—day after to-morrow, eighty. The only way I know to hold on to those fleeting years is to bind myself to youth. If in these swiftly moving years I can pass on a little of that living flame from the torch I carry . . . if I can help light the long steep paths for young people . . . the service I have rendered will be its own reward."

It touched Ella deeply. For days she had prayed for strength to take up her life—asked that something come into her mind and heart to help in blotting out the bitter thing she had experienced. This was it. Quite unexpectedly President Corcoran was helping make it possible to think of something else, to turn from the anguish that held her prisoner day and night.

She, whose life had been clean, seemed to have touched in the last few days the unclean. Some smothering vapor of impurity had blown upon her with heavy sickening May-apple odor, and she wanted to get away from its noxious breath.

This was cleansing. This was purifying. *To pass on the living flame.* That would be her life work. It would take the place of—of this other thing that had besmirched her. She would dedicate her life to it,—throw herself into the work zealously as one might go to a mission field.

Standing there in the plain, half-furnished executive office of the six-year-old struggling college,—with the sincere words of its earnest president still in her ears, Ella Bishop took a vow.

"I will, too," she said solemnly to her inner self. "I, too, will carry on the living flame. I dedicate my life to it—to the students of *this* college. I will stay young with them, help them, serve them. My whole life is theirs. The fleeting years! The torch! The living flame!"

For the first time in agonizing days a faint semblance of calmness enveloped her being—almost a feeling of exaltation uplifted her soul. It was as though, stripped of all earthly longings, she stood before an altar—as though, turning aside from desires of the flesh, she took the veil.

CHAPTER XV

BUT one may not stay on the heights for any length of time. It is not given to humans to breathe the rarefied atmosphere of Olympus continuously. So while Ella Bishop never forgot those moments of priestess-like exaltation, she was to experience them only occasionally, recapture their dignity and glory only at rare intervals in her life.

For the most part, the summer was one continuous battle against her constantly rising emotions,—one long period of bitter days and wide-eyed nights. Strangely enough, her greatest comfort was digging in the garden. She who had never cared for the raising of flowers as her mother did, whose love for books had been her hobby, now cared little for the printed word. Books? They were cold—only the ground was warm. Stories? They were lifeless—only the good earth had vitality. Fiction characters? They were puppets,—only the sturdy blossoms were real. Poems? They were pallid,—only the green grass in the wind knew the rhythm of song.

All that summer she spent every hour which could be spared from the house, working among the flowers. With spade and trowel, seeds and slips, she dug and planted, reset and watered. Prone on the ground with the warm brown earth running through her fingers, she came nearer to respite from the constant aching of her bruised self than at any other time.

"There is something elemental about us all," she thought, "something soothing about contacting our own dust with the life-giving dust of the earth."

Strangely enough, she never spoke of her tragedy to her mother, and her mother, less strong-minded than Ella, took the cue from her daughter's silence and never mentioned it either. But stranger still was the fact that the one person to whom she could speak of it in its bald entirety was Sam Peters.

And then on a warm July morning when Ella was weeding poppies, Sam came across the street. As soon as she saw his pale drawn face and the convulsive working of his thin mouth and chin, she knew he came with trouble.

"Why, Sam, what is it?" She got up from the red-blossomed bed and met him at the edge of the garden.

"It's Chet. He's . . . drowned."

"Drowned?" The dull word sounded like a hollow bell tolled in the distance.

"Yes. He . . . He was on a Mississippi

river-boat. The telegram says he just . . . disappeared from the boat. Father's going . . . to St. Louis . . . to find out. I'm to stay with Mother. My God, Ella . . ." The thin little man sank down on the garden seat. "Why couldn't it have been me?"

"Don't say that, Sam."

"But it ought to have . . . what do I amount to? But Chet . . . Chet's brilliant. And Father. . . ." His thin body shook with boyish sobs.

Here was grief again—grief, too, that went back to Amy's coming. For if Chet had not been infatuated with Amy, he would not have gone away—would not have been on a river-boat. Suddenly, with surprising clarity, Ella questioned in her own mind whether the death had been accidental.

It was only a few weeks later—after Judge Peters had returned from his investigation, crushed and bowed, with all the pompous jauntiness out of his walk, that Irene went east to visit relatives. The day before she left, Ella made herself go over to see her, dreading the interview as one dreads any disagreeable task.

But Irene was much calmer than Ella had expected to find her. "I've gone over everything in my mind a thousand times," she said, her thin face wistful. "And I guess there's something about

the whole thing that we can't any of us see—
something that just had to be for the good of us
all—something we may never know—fate maybe
—or destiny."

Ella was thankful beyond words when September came,—and work. It is life's most potent
medicine for grief. She threw herself into it with
mental and physical abandon. And when her heart
did not follow, she chided it for sitting on the
sidelines and watching her mind and body labor.
"Lazy!" she figuratively called to it. "Numb-
skull!" She used some of her ready sarcasm on it.
"You think you're crushed and ruined for life,
don't you? Well, you're not. Even yet a real
man may come riding by. Then you'll be the
thing for which you were intended—the heart of
a wife and mother."

To ease her pain she tried to picture again
some man she might one day love, attempted to
conjure up an attractive new face and features.
But all she could see was Delbert smiling down at
her with fresh young lips, as he looked before—
She would throw herself across her bed and moan
aloud in the depths of her unconquered despair.

All winter she held herself with ferocious
tenacity to her work. She managed freshman social events, was head of the college young people's
inter-church society, was on the Minerva board

advisory group, and chairman of the refreshment committee for the Faculty Family Circle.

"I know a lovely new way to serve potatoes to the Circle members," Professor Cunningham's very domestic wife would say. "First, you mash them . . ."

"The faculty members?" Ella would say languidly.

"Oh, you go on, Ella Bishop," laughingly, "and then you put them on the plate with an ice-cream mold and there they stand up just as cunning, like little pyramids with a clove at the top."

"A clove? Why a clove? Why not a clothespin or a prune?" Ella's apparently unquenchable spirits would rise. "I've always wondered if there could be a clove on top of any of the pyramids."

Every one would laugh.

"Thank goodness, I'll always be like that," she would say to herself. And then, as though she had just made a discovery, "I believe on the outside I'll always be gay and lively."

CHAPTER XVI

THE winter was long, cold, snowy. January was one succession of stormy weeks after another with snow heaped over the campus and piled high on the roof of Central Hall. Chris Jensen, shoveling the wooden sidewalk all day, his strong arms throwing out the white drifts, would turn around only to see those paths refilled by the wind-gods.

February was no better. The tips of the young trees on the campus looked thin and black against the opaque sky, with the wind whipping the brittle branches into a rattling fury.

On the third of the month, school was dismissed for a few days on account of a coal shortage. Ella dreaded the enforced intermission, knowing that the very inactivity of it would depress her.

On the afternoon of the first day of the recess a strange man drove up in a bob-sled and hitched his team to the post by the horse-block. Ella, watching him from the window, had a queer feeling that the stranger's coming was portentous. She could not have told why, but she suddenly felt herself grow nervously expectant. He came on up the walk between the drifts, swinging his arms together to bring warmth to them. His long drooping mustache was frozen white, an icy horseshoe above the muffler he wore.

Always afterward Ella wondered what peculiar phenomenon it was whereby she sensed that he came bearing strange tidings.

Her heart pounding queerly, she opened the door.

"Be you Miss Ella Bishop?"

"Yes."

"If I could come in . . . I got a letter here . . ."

"Oh yes, yes, come in."

Something made her walk over to the kitchen door and protectingly close it upon her mother making mince pies to be frozen for the month's use.

A letter! Letters were strange things. They brought happiness and comfort and companionship, but,—she caught her breath,—sometimes they brought black grief.

The man was having difficulty in producing it, what with two woolen jackets and an overcoat to search.

When he had produced and given it to her, Ella's fingers trembled at the tearing. It was from Delbert Thompson—a pale, sprawling letter of stark appeal.

Ella, I am sick—on my last bed. If you have a heart in you—and oh, Ella, I know you have— come back with the man who brings this. It's the last thing I'll ever ask you . . . for the time is short. Hurry. Please.

Wild thoughts sprang to Ella's mind,—mad thoughts that leaped and chased each other through her hot brain. No. She was through with him,—done forever with him and his little—

If you have a heart in you. That was good, that was! Who but Delbert Thompson knew whether or not she had one?

The man, standing with his arms around the sheet-iron wood-burner, shuffled and stepped about restlessly, soft chunks of snow melting from his high boots.

"Pretty bad, I guess," he volunteered. "Can't last long. Wife poorly, too."

"Where are they living?" Ella heard herself asking in a voice that seemed to come from the far end of the room, like a ventriloquist's.

"Maynard. Next door to me. I run a livery stable. But I come for nothin'. I said I ain't one to charge a dyin' man for an errand I can do."

Ella stood, tense and white, and stared at the man with his thawing horseshoe mustache and his big boots that smelled of his calling.

"I'll be ready in a few minutes," she said.

Her mother was upset. "Oh, Ella . . . a man who . . . who . . ." She had meant to say "jilted you," but something in Ella's stern face kept her from it. She darted about here and there excitedly, her small dainty hands still white from the flour board.

All the time Ella was throwing a few things together, she was saying to herself, "I'm like this. I'll always be like this. People can beat me and lash me, and I'll turn around and lick their hands if they need me. Weak! Emotionally weak as water."

She bundled up in two coats and woolen tights, leggins and four-buckled overshoes, put on earlaps and tied a woolen fascinator around her hat. Her mother had warmed the soapstone in the oven and wrapped it in a flannel shawl. A fifteen-mile winter ride in an open sleigh on a prairie road in the eighties was a thing with which to reckon.

The ride seemed interminable. Sometimes the two went miles without conversation, for when they opened their mouths to speak, the cold damp air rushed in to fill their lungs, which seemed to collapse like bellows.

On the last part of the trip the cold penetrated the buffalo robes so that Ella's tumbling thoughts even ceased their eternal questioning, her emotions were calm,—the benumbed physical holding complete sway over the turbulent mental.

It was nearly dark when the man drove up to a square house on the outskirts of the town. Ella could see a woman pulling down and lighting a hanging-lamp, a child pressing its face against a window.

"Here we be," he commented, and added, "Thank the Lord. My woman said to bring you into our house first to thaw out. She's been over a lot to the Thompsons'. Guess she's home now, though."

Ella went in, her limbs so stiff with cold that she staggered as she walked. She removed her wraps and sat down by a red-hot sheet-iron wood stove, but the sudden change from the intense cold to the closeness of the room made her feel a little giddy.

The woman flew about noisily, dishing up the supper, chattering, clucking her sympathy: "Poor little thing . . . tsk . . . tsk . . . ," stopping to whisper something to Ella that the child might not hear.

Ella ate a little, without tasting what she consumed. Her body craved sustenance, but under the nervous strain of the ordeal, rebelled at food.

The woman was curious, distressingly loquacious:

"Let's see . . . you're Mis' Thompson's cousin?"

"Yes."

"Let's see, now. . . how long have they been married?"

"I think it was sometime in April or May."

"Tsk . . . tsk . . . the very first thing," whispering a comment.

And when Ella was disappointingly silent: "Did you know Mr. Thompson, too?"

"Yes."

After supper she went over, stepping high through the snowdrifts in her four-buckled over-shoes. At the porch of the little shoe-box of a cottage she paused: "Stay with me," she said to some unseen source of strength.

There was a single light in the main room. On hearing the door open Amy came from the dim bedroom. At the sight of Ella she began to cry, weak tears that distorted her pretty, swollen face and shook her misshapen body.

"She's here," she whispered back to the gloom of the bedroom, and apparently with no rancor at Ella's meeting alone with the sick man, crossed over to the far side of the living-room and sat down heavily.

Ella went alone into the chamber of death.

Yes, he was dying. She could see that. This was Delbert dying, she told herself coolly. She would not let herself feel emotion; made of her heart and mind cold and callous things. For a moment she stood by the side of the bed with no word. The dying man only looked at her, searching her face for the answer to some question—perhaps the queer question of why everything came to be as it was.

"Ella!" He touched her hand feebly with a clammy finger.

She drew the member back, shocked at her repulsion to the contact.

"It was all wrong, Ella. Nothing was right . . . but it's too late now . . . God, I've suffered." It was agony for him to talk. "There's no time to waste in going over it."

And when she made no comment, he went on:

"I wanted you to come . . . I had to . . . to look you in the eyes once, Ella . . . your clear, clean eyes . . . and say it was all wrong . . . and tell you . . . I love you . . ." He paused for a renewal of strength, and then went on: "Tell me, Ella . . . will you take her home with you a little while? Just 'til afterward? She's no place to turn. Promise me, Ella. I can't go like this— thinking she's nowhere to go. Poor child! Poor little . . . kitten."

Ella stiffened. "You're asking a hard thing." Her voice, breaking its silence for the first time, sounded as harsh and rasping as a buzz-saw in the still room.

"Yes, I know. It seems terrible . . . but more terrible not to. You can . . . ask strange things . . . when you're dying. Please, Ella . . . just through her hard time. After that, I can't see ahead. Something—God knows what—will solve it . . . maybe. But this very month . . . it's so near. Home to your place—with you and your mother. Just this one thing, Ella. My responsibility to her . . . to the end. It'll make the going less hard . . ."

Ella broke. Like a dammed-up stream from which the bulwark was washed away, all her emotions came surging suddenly. Standing there at the side of the bed she pressed her fingers into the flesh of her face,—into her eye-sockets,—to keep from the wild hysteria of sobbing. Like the rushing of the water through breaking ice on Oak River in the spring of the year, her grief now came surging through her bitterness. For the first time her suffering was for all three,—for Amy crying out her spineless, superficial sorrow—for Delbert going down alone into the strange darkness—for herself, the scorned one, whose agony had been greatest of all.

"Promise, Ella."

"Oh, why is life such a drear stark thing,

Delbert? Life was meant to be joyous and lovely."

"You will always have joy and loveliness in you, Ella."

"It should have something besides loneliness and despair."

"You will have neither one, Ella."

"I've suffered so . . ."

"So have I . . . God, how I've . . . suffered."

"How can I go on?"

"Promise you'll . . . look after her . . . through it."

"But what about me? Is my life to be nothing but duty and obligations and service to others?"

"You are so strong . . . and clean. Hold my hand . . . things are . . . are slipping . . . quick,—promise, Ella."

"I promise."

CHAPTER XVII

ELLA stayed through everything—death, and the many little tasks to do for the dead. Amy had no decision, wanted only to escape the distasteful experience. She wept, and wondered if people thought she looked terrible,—moaned out her sorrow, and was disappointed that her long black veil was not lace-edged.

On the fourth day, the livery-stable owner took them home,—protesting against pay with: "I'm just a neighbor in this case."

The sun was out for the first time since the last heavy snows. Everywhere the drifts were hard, high, and sparkling, but the cold had abated a little.

Arriving at the house, Amy could scarcely move from bodily weariness. It took the combined efforts of the driver and Ella to assist her from the low seat of the sleigh. In the warm sitting-room, she stood with her back to the door a moment waiting to see what her aunt's greeting would be.

Ella's mother was upset. She scarcely knew what to do with the peculiar situation. The natural warmth of her hospitable nature fought with the cruel circumstances so that she looked to Ella for her cue.

Ella was matter-of-fact. Mrs. Bishop decided that if her daughter was not her natural humorous self, at least she was not uncompromisingly stern. So she immediately became equally matter-of-fact, but without austerity. She shook hands with Amy, but she did not kiss her. She told her she was sorry for her that she had lost her husband, but she said no more about it.

Amy began to cry—weak childish tears, her soft little lips puckered into tremulous sorrow. Ella stalked out of the room and made preparations for supper.

Two days later the enforced vacation was over, and she went back to pick up the loose ends of her work. Sam Peters came over to tell her that if she ever needed him—in the night for errands or anything—he'd be right there across the street. Irene Van Ness came for two reasons—to tell her she was engaged to a Robert Hunt in Ohio, and that she thought Ella was the noblest-souled girl that ever walked on the top of the green earth. And about the first, Ella was sincerely happy. But about the other, she said acridly: "Oh, no, I'm not. I have a special brand of selfishness, all my own. When I give up and do something for some one, the more sacrifice it takes on my part, the more of an exalted feeling of happiness

it gives me. I like the abnormal thrill of the self-righteousness. And if you call that nobility of soul, I'll bet the Lord is grinning about it."

"Oh, Ella, you do say the queerest things," Irene had to laugh.

Amy was taken sick on the twenty-fourth of February. There was a wild wind in the night which blew out the street lamps, and Ella, hurrying down the street for Chris' wife, was buffeted about by it. After she had aroused Hannah, she went on to the doctor's, and even though he took her home among the warm buffalo robes of his cutter, she shook with the cold and nervousness.

The wind howled its coyote-like fury around the house. The street lamps went unlighted so that to look out was to look onto the blackness of nothing. Mrs. Bishop could not stand the nervous strain and locked herself in her room. Hannah waited on the doctor and Ella waited on Hannah.

The wind wailed like the crying of a child, and the night wore on. Then a child wailed like the crying of the wind, and the night was over.

When the first gray light came into the sullen eastern sky, Hannah carried the baby into the kitchen. It was a girl—plump, healthy, well-formed.

Without a wink of sleep, Ella set out a breakfast for the doctor and was preparing to leave for school. But he said there was no time to eat and he asked her not to go.

As the day wore on, Amy, coming out from a semi-coma, did not appear to be greatly interested in the dark-haired mite Hannah showed her. She slept, roused to tell the doctor she must look a fright, slept, grew weaker, fluttered white lids over glazing china-blue eyes,—died.

For the second time that month, Ella looked at Death as he came for his prey. And for the second time, it was she who had to make all the necessary arrangements, so trivial to the gaunt-eyed specter, so necessary to civilized humans.

The day they buried her was foggy, moist, raw. The pines in the cemetery dripped clammily on the people standing around the pile of yellow clay. The new bronze Civil War soldier on the cenotaph held pools of water in his cap and knapsack. An early bluebird, the color of the dead girl's eyes, fluttered outstretched pointed wings in the hollow bath-tub of the bronze cap. Irene Van Ness came over and slipped her arm through Ella's. The minister intoned the service for the dead in a drawling, nasal voice, and then: ". . . we give back to the God who gave her— this lovely young woman—to join her earthly lover in Paradise."

Sam Peters stood a few feet back of Ella, his thin face drawn with sympathy.

When Ella and her mother arrived home from the cemetery, Hannah, walking about with the baby in her arms, said in her broken English she would have to get back now to her own little boy.

The doctor came in to talk with Ella and her mother about the child and give directions for its food. A neighbor handed in a loaf of fresh bread at the back door.

When they had all gone, Ella took the baby in her arms and sat down in a rocking-chair by the western window of the sitting-room where the cold February sun had broken through the fog and was slanting feebly across the floor.

Mother and daughter sat silently for a time and then Mrs. Bishop ventured: "What are we going . . . what to do . . . what about the little thing?"

Ella rocked the soft warm mite pressed to her sturdy body. Under the blanket it stirred and made peeping noises like a chicken.

Oh, why was life so hard, so complicated? Nothing was as it should be.

You will have neither loneliness nor despair.

"Keep it," she said finally.

"Oh, Ella, the child of a man you had expected to marry?" Some unusual temerity gave Mrs. Bishop the courage to complete her thought in words, swiftly, and with no vagueness.

Ella's lips were pressed together in an aching line. The baby stirred and stretched.

"Maybe I'm starting something new," Ella said grimly, "something biologically new. A youngster with three parents."

CHAPTER XVIII

LIFE does not appear to arrange itself into definite periods at the time one is living those years. It is only when a woman looks back upon it from the hilltop of maturity that she is able to say, "That was the period of my darkest sorrow," or, "Those were the years of my uncertainty."

And though she could not perceive it just then, this was the time that definitely ended Ella Bishop's girlhood and became the period of her vicarious motherhood.

There had been no relatives of Amy but Mrs. Bishop and Ella. Delbert Thompson's sister wrote that if there was any possibility of another than herself taking the child for awhile, it must be done. Her own three children were still babies and she could not add the newcomer to the group for a year or two at least.

So because there was no other place for it, the baby was to stay for a time. And life became very full for Ella Bishop,—this double life, which was both that of teacher and of mother. And if one thinks as the years went on, she neglected one for the other he does not know the infinite capacity

for work and love and understanding in the body
and heart and mind of an Ella Bishop.

As for help in caring for the child, the answer
came from the Jensens. A sister of Hannah Jensen came from the old country to join them and
Ella wanted to know at once about the girl working for her, so Hannah brought her over as soon
as she arrived. She wanted to explain something
about her sister—tried so hard to make Ella understand, had almost given up to wait for Chris to
come and tell it, when Ella suddenly began to comprehend.

"Oh, I see, Hannah. You mean she lost her
lover."

"Ya-ya." Hannah glowed at the result of her
effort. "S'e luffer . . . s'e los'. . . ." And
added with naïve honesty and sadness: "S'e baby
. . . s'e los', too."

The girl sat stoically, not understanding. Ella
looked at her—healthy, buxom, clean, honest looking. Dear, dear, what a queer thing life was.
She hesitated, remembered the child upstairs in
her crib. Life was teaching Ella Bishop many
things.

"Yes, I'll take her, Hannah, for awhile, until
we see how we get along."

So Stena Jensen brought over to Ella's home
the various bundles that had come with her in the
steerage, expecting to stay a short time—and

stayed fifty-one years. Ella gave her the room that had been Amy's, and there Stena unpacked her other two dresses and countless white aprons of deep hardanger work, put her own spread with its wide crocheted trimming on the bed, set up mementos of numerous Jensens left behind in the old country and a pale tintype of a young man, under which she kept for a half-century a pink tissue-paper rosebud, changing it for a fresh one at house-cleaning time from year to year. Sometimes Ella, hearing the girl singing a guttural-sounding Danish song in the kitchen, would stop at the bedroom door and look in at the neatly arranged keepsakes—and gaze for a moment at the photo of the phlegmatic "luffer" with the little artificial rosebud underneath it, placed there no doubt for s'e baby s'e los', too.

Amy's child thrived and grew strong. She was a good little thing after the first part of a year, sleeping usually the whole night through. Ella seemed to have a natural flair for knowing what to do for her. But Stena also assumed much of the care of her and so relieved Mrs. Bishop of any responsibility about the house that Ella sometimes wondered which required the more waiting upon—her mother or the baby.

"Stena spoils you, Mother," Ella would sometimes say jokingly. At which her mother's eyes would fill, and she would say, "Ella, . . . you're

not . . . Mamma's sorrow . . . you don't be-
grudge . . . ?"

Ella would put tender arms around her frail
little mother and laugh away her hurt. But she
would also say to Stena: "Don't do everything for
her, Stena. Just purposely leave her a few tasks.
It's better for every one to have something to do."

For months the baby had no name,—then quite
suddenly Ella began calling her Hope. For no
reason at all, it satisfied something in her—young
Ella Bishop, who was not to know the full fruition
of any hope.

She had so much to oversee now, her days were
so filled with tasks, that she had little time to
brood over her troubles. No student ever came
to Ella's door to find her too busy to give him attention. If necessary, she stayed at school until
shadows fell across the floor of the classroom in
Central Hall. If some one needed her, she arrived at her desk soon after the morning dusk
had cleared from the sky. She assisted them all,
—boys and girls alike. She helped them about
participles and finances, adverbial phrases and
clothes, split infinitives and bodily ailments, clauses
and morals.

Sometimes she scolded about it just to relieve
her mind. Ella's tongue could be sharp. She was
no soft sentimental teacher. "That Cowan girl,"
she would say, "thinks conjunctions grow on

bushes along Oak River. And she doesn't know a preposition from a thousand-legged worm. I vow I'll never waste another moment with her." But the next morning she would be at her desk an hour earlier than usual to help that Cowan girl.

For a year and a half, then, Ella and Stena looked after little Hope, bathing her, feeding her, exclaiming over her first tooth and watching over her first steps—and one could not have told which was more interested in her development. If they disagreed about her at all it was because Stena thought Ella kept her up too late in the evening —and Ella had to use all her tact to keep Stena from overloading the little dresses with crocheted lace and hardanger trimming.

"Start making lace trimming for her wedding trousseau, Stena," Ella would laugh, "instead of putting so much on her now."

It was the evening of Hope's second birthday, when two of Stena's home-made candles had burned brightly on a huge frosted cake, that the letter came from Delbert's sister. She wrote that she had help now—the youngest child was four, and she thought they could relieve Ella for a time from the care of brother Delbert's child.

As she read, Ella was frightened at the way her heart contracted and her whole body grew cold. If she harbored any idea that her own care of the baby up to this time had been from a sense of duty alone, that letter expelled the last vestige of it. No one could take Hope from her,—no one. If she were served with a law summons even,—she would fight it. Hope was hers. Hope was her baby. She grew almost hysterical in her imaginings—she who was usually so strong and placid, —caught Hope up to her, buried her face in the fat baby neck, drank in the clean sweet-smelling odor of the little body, kissed the palms of the pink hands.

Hope laughed and kicked her little kid shoes together in exuberance that Aunt Ella was so excited over some unknown cause.

Ella wrote the woman a half-dozen letters before she was satisfied with the one she mailed— that the child was well, and as long as she had such good help in a capable Danish girl, she would be glad to absolve the relative from any responsibility for the child. But she could not relax from worry until the answer arrived which plainly signified the woman's relief.

Now she could give her time whole-heartedly to her students, and then hurry down through the campus and past the intervening blocks to the modest home on Adams Street knowing that Hope, her little nose flattened against the pane, would be waiting for "Aunt Ella."

In that summer of 1885 Ella made some

changes in the home,—had a new downstairs' bedroom built for her mother and a wide porch across
the front and one side of the house after the style
of the day. It necessitated digging up the big
roots of the trumpet-vine which she always associated with Delbert.

Chris, bringing a spade to do this for her after
his working hours at the college, shook a shaggy
head over the destruction of the nice shade at the
old porch.

"You may have it, Chris, if you can get it reset."

"Py chingo, I take him qvick. But you sure
you not voolish to pull him up?"

"No, I don't want it. I just don't care about
having it around the place."

So it was with other mementos—Ella carefully
removed anything that reminded her of Delbert,
as though she would throw open the rooms of her
heart to the sunshine and clean that battered and
shaken house of all remembrance. She worked
faithfully at the task, took out this and that article, hung out all the tender moments to air, shook
vigorously all the loved plans, burned every vestige
of sentiment. But what did it avail? For every
day Hope looked at her with Delbert's eyes and
laughed roguishly up at her with Delbert's lips.
Even the trumpet-vine, having dropped its seeds,
sprang up anew the following spring. You could
not destroy that which had so vitally lived. So

she gave up the futile task of forgetting and moved all the memories back into the house of her heart.

Because of these, and because Hope grew to look more and more like her father, it came in time to seem to Ella that Hope was her own, and had been born of her love for Delbert before any tragedy entered in. She came to feel that she had given birth to Hope in a travail of physical agony, just as she had borne grief in a travail of mental agony. As time went by, and a measure of surcease came, there grew in the inner court of her heart a little garden of fragrance from which the rank growth of noxious weeds had been miraculously removed. With the child's hand in hers and the child's sweet face upturned to her, by some gracious gift of heaven she was able to walk unmolested in that garden of memories. She confided in no one, could not have put it into words if she had so desired,—but in time she came to know vaguely that to the groveling cry of her prayers had come from Somewhere through the child—a comforting benediction.

CHAPTER XIX

AND now changes came to the young college. For a year or so, Central Hall had taken on a crowded condition. Instructors had been changing rooms at the end of certain periods, in order that some of the growing classes might have places large enough to hold recitations. It had been a common sight to see one of the dignitaries gathering together his paraphernalia in pompous haste and removing himself with reluctance from the room he chose to look upon as his own. Professor Carter with his arms figuratively full of English authors, or Professor Wick clutching a wheel and axle, marching a little grumpily down the hall had been every-day occurrences.

But now all this was changed. A new building had gone up on the campus—a three-story brick with stately white pillars across the front. Administration Hall it was called, and it made Central look a little pale and colorless, although the older building still retained the dignity of possessing the bell which tapped out the periods.

The Minerva Society had rivals—three of them—Greek and Roman goddesses having been named their patron saints, with a fine disregard on the part of their girl followers for the rumored behavior of those early guardians. Two literary societies for the young men also made Saturday night at the college one long period of forensic frenzy.

In 1888, President Corcoran left for another state and President Watts came. Ella dreaded the change. She had gone to school four years while the former was president and taught with him eight more. Twelve years! And he had been a good friend to her. For a few weeks that fall it seemed as though there had been a death on the campus.

President Watts at first acquaintance appeared rather hard and cold. He was an extremely tall man, dark-visaged, as bearded as the men of Biblical times, his hair unruly and his clothes loose fitting. He was only thirty-six and looked much older. Partly because of his height, he gave the impression of being loose jointed—his arms swung awkwardly, his legs seemed more insecurely connected with his body than other men's legs. Ella grew in time to know his step down the hall outside her door—the quick shuffling gait of those long limbs. President Watts did not teach a class as President Corcoran had done. The school was large enough so that the executive must give his entire time to administrative work.

It was not long before his strong personality began to penetrate every classroom, sweep the campus with ever-growing vitality. Student enrollment began to increase. New courses were planned. And already there were blueprints on exhibition for a third building. Something about the man was dynamic. Apparently every one responded to the vigor of the new administrative head.

The older professors, who had been connected with the school for all twelve years, might not have shown any outward manifestations of agility. Professor Wick trudged up the board walk of the campus as heavily as ever, the vague suggestion of his last lunch somewhere on his vest. Professor Carter never forsook the dignified calm of his New England upbringing. But even so, they felt a new impetus to work,—the injection of something forceful into the school, and responded loyally. Even Chris Jensen swung his scythe or fed the furnaces with a little more nimbleness.

Classes were rearranged. The hour of convocation was changed. Long-winded senior orations at the chapel hour were dropped, thus rather summarily dispensing with Professor Wick's daily nap. Out of the shuffling of old customs and the side-stepping of an old routine came plans for a larger and more comprehensive educational system.

As much as Ella had thought of President Corcoran, she could see now where his vision for progress had not been so keen as that of President Watts. The former had been an instructor —the latter had the viewpoint of the teacher but also the ability of an executive. The combination was irresistible.

By 1890, music in the college became something besides the spontaneous combustion of youthful voices. The word athletics was rolling glibly off masculine tongues. New teachers were added. A librarian came to sort and list the now-growing collection of books, deftly separating the Emerson *Essays* from the seed catalogues, the popular new *Locksley Hall* from the bundle of Dr. Miles' *Almanacs*.

A Professor O'Neil, representing Messrs. Cæsar, Ovid and Livy, taught for a single year, as his radical views on the origin of the human race, which he so often found occasion to wedge in between the Aquitanians and the Belgæ, proved his undoing and he was summarily dismissed.

Little Albert Fonda, of Ella's class, fresh from post-graduate work abroad, came now as instructor in astronomy, his dark eyes filled with the recent vision of heavenly bodies,—his dark face alight when he spoke intimately of the sun and the moon and the stars.

Nor was Professor Fonda the only member of Ella's class added to the teaching force. In another year came big George Schroeder, back from Heidelberg, for German classes.

Ella met him on the campus just before the first faculty meeting of the new year. They stopped to greet each other under the big elms and maples from which the barrel-staves had long been removed, and in which the purple grackles, having matriculated in their own Midwestern, now gathered to give their harsh college yell of "tchacktchack."

Although the two had been classmates, Ella called him "Professor Schroeder" when she met him. And he responded with "Miss Bishop." It seemed the better way.

They talked there under the elms of the big new college this was to be. George Schroeder was enthusiastic, filled with a great desire to teach these Midwestern young men and women all he could of the artistic and intellectual life of the universities of the old world. His big voice boomed, his big hands gesticulated, his big shoulders shrugged expressively, as he attempted to convey to Ella all that he hoped to do for the school that had started him toward the goal of his ambitions. Although he spoke perfect English, his voice carried the accent of a fatherland as unmistakable to place as was the throaty "tchack-tchack" of the purple grackles above his head.

Standing there under the elms and maples, he unfolded his plans to Ella, his old classmate,—a desire to make his department at Midwestern in time second to none, to gather about him an excellent corps of instructors, to set a high standard of scholarship, to give courses on Goethe and Schiller that every student of Germanic languages would want to take.

He swung into a fiery German quotation, but Ella laughed and stopped him: "No, no," she admonished, "I can sense the fire and drama of it, but you'll have to give it in my mother tongue if you want me to understand it fully."

"Ach," he gave a shrug of the massive shoulders. "It loses some of its beauty,—my Goethe's *Faust.* I distort the meaning of course when I use it here. And I should not do that. It is disloyal to the master. But I apply it to my new work,—to the buoyancy I feel in the new field.

"A fiery chariot, borne on buoyant pinions,
Sweeps near me now! I soon shall ready be
To pierce the ether's high, unknown dominions,
To reach new spheres of pure activity."

His dark eyes glowed. "I see some day here on the fertile prairie a new Heidelberg, a new University of Leipzig. Can you not see it, too?"

His great arm swung out in the direction of the two brick buildings, and Ella, under the influence of his forceful personality, said: "Yes, . . . oh, yes . . . I see it, too."

When she left him, she had contracted his enthusiasm. She, too, saw a great school on the fertile prairie. "If in these swiftly moving years I can pass on a little of that living flame from the torch I carry . . . if I can help light the long steep path for boys and girls . . ."

She walked swiftly to the faculty meeting in a glow of eagerness for the year's work that seemed almost of divine inspiration. She felt a great uplift of the spirit,—a warmth of heart toward all the newcomers. This year she would teach as the Great Teacher taught, with fervor and humility.

CHAPTER XX

QUITE as though her own world were divided also into two hemispheres, Ella's interests these years were in two distinct parts—school and home. As to the former, it was becoming more apparent that the childish days of Midwestern were over, that the school had been but a glorified academy under President Corcoran. Some of the new teachers these days had degrees from eastern schools which Ella imagined they wore like halos. And now came a man named Wittingly—Dr. Wittingly because of a Ph.D.—to be professor of Pedagogy (which was a stylish new title for Professor Cunningham's old classes in Didactics) and whose flag Professor Cunningham was rather forced to kiss.

It grew popular to obtain a leave of absence and go east for a year. And to say that a teacher had just come from Columbia University was to say that he had just held communion with the gods on Olympus. Ella knew she ought to work for another degree sometime if she were to compete with people from the east.

"But after all," she said to President Watts, "a noun is one of the few things that won't change in a century, and a verb, as full of action as it pretends to be, is still a rather stable thing."

President Watts laughed. He had grown to like this frank and energetic Miss Bishop. "But," he added seriously, "I really think you ought to plan to go."

Ella did not see how she could manage. Her salary had to cover all the household expenses. Her mother, little Hope, Stena, the house, all these depended upon her alone. And then to leave for so long,—she had so many responsibilities here.

Hope was growing like a little milkweed. First there had been messy bits of colored papers or crooked little drawings to show Aunt Ella every night, later a wavering seam made with a huge darning-needle, then as time went on, genuine school work, a real number lesson, the word "Hope" written laboriously with plump fingers assisted by the sympathetic wiggling of a pink tongue protruding from pursed lips. For Hope was in school over in the Washington Building of Oak River—the town grown now to over five thousand.

Houses had sprung up around the campus— professors' homes, boarding houses, even a book store and a lunch room. The old narrow board walk had given way to wide black cinder paths and the curving campus drives were hard packed, too, with cinders. A cow on the campus now would have been too embarrassed to remain.

Besides Didactics giving way to Pedagogy, Mental Philosophy was now flaunting itself as Psychology, Moral Philosophy had become Ethics, and proof was substantiated that the odors of gases in the old Natural Philosophy classroom by the new name of Physics would smell as sweet.

There were more new teachers, a Professor Crooks now was a popular addition to the history department. He talked a great deal about a new freedom of thought and of action, and, though rather permanently married, put his theories into practice by pointed attention to a dashing new Miss Zimmerman of the piano department.

Each year Ella thought the time had come for her break to go east. To study a year at Columbia became almost a necessity toward furthering her teaching career. With President Watts's advice approaching the utterance of a command, she grew more and more sensitive about the delay. But her mother's health was delicate—and she herself was like a mother to Hope. How could she go and leave the child now in these formative years? Under Stena's watchful care, Hope would be clean and well-fed, but also she would be ready to qualify as a citizen of Denmark when the year would be over.

It was 1893 when she went, with Hope ten and

Mrs. Bishop at fifty-seven, an old lady, as indeed she had been for a dozen years. Her plan was to stop at the World's Fair in Chicago—which worried her mother almost into an illness, so fearful was she of disaster to her daughter.

"For goodness' sakes, Mother," Ella was moved to one of her infrequent moments of exasperation, "of what are you afraid? I'm thirty-three years old and ought to be capable of looking after myself."

But Mrs. Bishop's anxiety would not allow her to relax until the unknown perils of the Fair and the long journey were over and word had come back that her daughter was safely housed.

The year was a wonderful experience for Ella —with a new viewpoint, a freedom from home responsibilities, a realization that at thirty-three she was still young and full of buoyant spirits in spite of those early tragic events. The whole thing, passed as it had into the shadows of memory, became on that year of freedom a bad dream which was all but forgotten. Only the scar remained—only a sensitive hurt—that made her feel she was not like other young women to whom life gives love and romance.

On her way home she stopped in Ohio to visit Mrs. Robert Hunt—Irene Van Ness. She found Irene happily married, the mother of three little girls, and ready to admit in a moment of confidence a merry disgust of her former mooning over Chet Peters and his indifference to her. They talked of them all freely—the tragic deaths of Delbert and Chester—of Sam's devotion to his parents,—of all the classmates of thirteen years before. Ella went home happily, as though Irene by talking freely of those old days had helped her to bury them. Life was still all before her,—a thing of warmth and light, of friends and family, of work that was pleasant.

She found her mother looking more frail, with a multitude of minor complaints about Stena— she seldom brought the tea in hot enough and she changed the sheets too often,—and Stena looking more buxom, with a multitude of minor complaints about Mrs. Bishop—she didn't get out in the yard enough for her own good and she wasn't careful of her eating.

It was at the sight of Hope that her heart warmed. Hope had celebrated her eleventh birthday, and had shot up almost another half-head it seemed. She was in the sixth grade and her essay on "Why I Would Not Use Narcotics" had won the first place in the contest. She had a new dress that Stena had made her with tucks and crocheted trimming set in the yoke and even in the skirt—and a bead ring that Harry Jensen had given her—

Ella's heart contracted. A bead ring from

Chris's son! Boys! It was time she was home. But Hope's sweet face looked honest—her clear gray eyes gazed frankly into Ella's. Ella pulled her close in a swift embrace. "Aunt Ella is home now to stay. We'll have good times. I've lots of plans for you—for one thing, what do you think of this—to start music lessons?"

Hope was to have organ lessons—a piano as soon as Ella could manage—more books of her own—was to go to Midwestern— Everything from now on for Hope. No more dreams for Ella herself. All the air castles for Hope—*hope, which is eternal*.

CHAPTER XXI

IN the spring of 1897 pussy-willows over on Oak Creek had scarcely given place to leaves, until two bombs of gossip burst on the campus with such devastating force that students, meeting, could not decide which piece of news to start discussing first. Usually they gave priority of choice to the Crooks-Zimmerman scandal.

Professor Crooks had carried his freedom-of-thought, freedom-of-soul theory one step too far with the dashing and musical Miss Zimmerman—and now on a Monday morning in April the two were so conspicuous by their absence from their respective classrooms that the ensuing vacuum called for much conversation on the cinder paths under the elms. Wild stories flew about among the students, ranging from the detailed remarks which President Watts allegedly had made to the two in a certain music room, to the detailed actions of Mrs. Crooks upon the facial features of the smug Miss Zimmerman. No one knowing for a certainty just what had happened, there was ample room for the imagination to have full play—and imagination given full play on a campus makes a complete and devastating recreation of it.

Scarcely less exciting to collegians and towns-people alike was the news percolating from the girls' side of the gymnasium that a new game called basket ball had arrived at Midwestern and what was practically unbelievable, that it was to be played outdoors.

For weeks the daring souls who were to launch the new sport sewed on the costumes in which they were to appear, and when the news leaked out that the lower extremity of those costumes were to be *bloomers,* many and sundry were the meetings held behind closed doors by faculty, board, gymnasium instructors, parents, and students, in which the moral and ethical versus the convenient aspects of the garment were discussed.

And for those same weeks practice was conducted in the gymnasium where no prying masculine eye might see. And when the afternoon arrived on which the first outdoor game was to be held, dozens of horses and carriages were hitched at the long rows of posts outside the campus, countless bicycles leaned against the walls of Central and Administration Buildings and more pedestrians wended their way to the ball-grounds than during the previous Commencement.

The girls came out of the gymnasium at the scheduled hour walking sedately enough, eighteen of them, nine for each side, their long hair tied back in horse-tail formation. Their costumes proved to be of sober black flannel augmented by red and blue sashes tied at the side—and the most flagrant critic among the anti-bloomer onlookers could scarcely have found fault with those maligned nether garments, for each pair looked like nothing so much as a skirt, contained six yards of fifty-four-inch flannel, was built solidly below the knees, and when raised at the side would form a high fan-shaped mass of dry-goods to the shoulder with still no sign of parting between the limbs. That potential embarrassment disposed of by the citizenry, there still remained the shock of the partial sight of thirty-six legs, even though a mere one-third of each was exposed,—and when the audience left for home at dusk, after witnessing a long but gently feminine tussle for a ball, they were still as divided in their opinions as the bloomers, whether or not the innovation was right. But the advanced thinkers won, as always, and feminine athletic history was made that day.

Two more new buildings went up that year, Corcoran Hall and Teachers' Training, big brick structures with imposing entrances, and they made Central Hall look like Cinderella in the presence of the haughty sisters. The authorities were planning for the future,—the two new buildings forming the outer corners of a prospective huge quadrangle.

Transportation had gone forward a step. One rode in a jangling street car to the campus entrance now, and the old hack sat among the weeds of an alley in wheelless ignominy, while the little girls of the neighborhood, playing travel, soaked up red stain from the plush seats.

By fall a model training school had opened in one of the buildings with a Miss Sallie Withrow in charge. Miss Withrow was eastern, modern, and as revolutionary in methods as an original colonist. Whereas in Oak River schools, under the eagle eyes of staid midwestern teachers, children were dutifully obeying commands, marching in what approached goose-step formation, reciting when called upon, and raising hands for permission to breathe, Miss Sallie Withrow was allowing children freedom of speech, freedom of action, freedom of study. The bans were off,—and freedom-from-her-mountain-height swooped down upon the children of the model training school.

Ella used to look in upon them sometimes. And fairly often she and Miss Sallie Withrow clashed a little about methods.

"To teach them to look after themselves . . ." Miss Withrow was always explaining.

"Yes, I have a neighbor who does that," Ella would say. "She's just never at home and they always have to look after themselves. So why

149

wouldn't that be the very best instruction of all—
not even to be in here?"

They became good friends, but they argued
constantly.

"You're just an old-fashioned schoolma'am—
the kind that taught Paul Revere," Miss Withrow
would say in exasperation.

"But why should children be expected to get
through life without discipline—good old discipline outside of self?"

"You don't catch the point at all. They really
obey me but they don't realize they're doing it."

"But why shouldn't they realize it? They can't
go through life with their civic laws colored over
like Easter eggs."

Good-natured banter, but half seriously, shut-
tled back and forth.

Hope was in High School, dark glossy braids
wound round her head, a sweet girl, tractable and
appreciative of all that Ella did for her. Sometimes in her imaginings Ella removed the young
girl from her life, tried to think how it would have
been all these years without her upon which to
lavish affection, realized that Hope had given
her in return much of the joy of these years.
"You will always have joy," a dying man had
said.

And now another bomb burst, this time of far
more serious import than mere campus gossip.

Peace, which had seemed so unimportant in Oak River because it was ever present, now became a thing of vital importance because it had suddenly flown. Far away the *Maine* had been sunk in Havana's harbor and the wash of the waves caused by its sinking had rippled to a half-hundred homes in Oak River.

The company of guards was leaving for camp —and Harry Jensen, Chris's and Hannah's son, was to go.

Hope went all to pieces emotionally. Ella was amazed, and not quite sure what she should say to her—such a little young thing to be so upset about an older young man.

The two went down to the Armory to see the company leave.

It was a lovely April day in that year of 1898. The grass was beginning to come out, the elms along the streets were showing signs of bursting buds.

Hope was sad, almost hysterical. Ella felt out of patience with her. Just a child! What could she know of the depths of despair? "But I must stay by her," she thought. "She's unduly emotional about it but I must help her all I can."

All was excitement when they arrived. The sidewalks in front of the Armory were jammed with friends and relatives. The Civil War cannon in the park across the street was booming. The

G. A. R. band and drum corps stood outside ready to accompany the boys on their way to the train. Ella and Hope could scarcely get near enough to see. Then the crowds were pushed back, the band began to play and the boys were coming,—fifty of them. Ella caught a glimpse of Chris and Hannah Jensen and their two little girls in the crowd. The poor Jensens—with their boy going to—they knew not what.

Near the station the boys were halted and presented with a flag from the Oak River Literary Society. The crowd was so dense that the young captain could scarcely get back to his company after going inside the station for transportation. Children and women were crying. Hope was sobbing wildly at the thought of a young boy. Ella herself wanted to cry aloud—but for *all boys*.

They tried to get closer, but it was not a possible thing. Fathers, mothers, sisters, sweethearts, composed a highly charged emotional mass. The train came in. By some miracle all the fifty were pushed on board. The train left,—and the boys had gone bravely off to the Spanish-American War.

Ella and Hope walked back home slowly. "He is the nicest young man I shall ever know," Hope said in a tragic voice. But Ella's thoughts were with poor Chris and Hannah and the two young sisters. She glanced at Hope's swollen eyes and soft puckered lips. It was the only time Hope ever reminded her of Amy—when she cried. It was distressingly distasteful to Ella.

CHAPTER XXII

COMMENCEMENT again—eighteen of them now for Ella as a teacher. Summer again—thirty-eight of them now in Ella's life.

Soon after school was out Sam's mother died —slipping away with as little fuss as possible, humbly sorry that she was causing the Judge and Sam any extra trouble. The Judge seemed dazed, surprised that she could have done anything so radical without dictation from him. Sometimes that summer he tried to get back into his pompous stride, but his cane had lost its jaunty swing and there was no one to raise red geraniums for his buttonhole. His mother's death meant such deep grief for Sam that Ella tried to show her unspoken sympathy in every way she could.

And by September there was grief for Chris and Hannah, too, for word came that Harry Jensen had died in camp "in the line of duty." When Stena came back from her sister's, Ella hurried to the little white house across from the campus.

The two were sitting quietly, their usually busy hands idle. Ella wanted to say something helpful, do something for them in the agony of her sympathy. They appreciated it, they told her with drawn patient faces, but there was nothing to do. The two girls were up in their room and would see no one. The house was clean—in its cleanliness the little white house was always ready for death. Chris said he would sit with Mamma awhile and then he must get back to the sweeping. Their grief was their own. Hannah, staring into the nothingness of space, asked in her broken English what was the use of bringing a child into the world—for this? And no one could answer.

Ella left, her sympathetic heart torn with sorrow for the Jensens and for all who suffer.

At home she found Hope sobbing wildly in her bedroom. "Say it isn't true, Aunt Ella. Say it isn't true." She was inconsolable.

It took all of Ella's patience and tact to handle her. Coming from the parents with their deep grief to this superficial sorrow of the young girl, she wanted to shake her, to tell her that she did not know what grief was. "But it's all in the mind," Ella would tell herself. "If one *thinks* he is grief-stricken, why, then he *is*."

Harry Jensen was buried with military honors. The mayor, public officials, veterans of the Civil War, hundreds of citizens in all walks of life participated in paying last honors to the humble janitor's son. Flowers from President Watts and from other members of the faculty, from Banker Van Ness and Judge Peters—a procession of horses and carriages over a mile long—the college glee club singing "He Giveth His Beloved Sleep" —taps over the grave and an echo of taps from the far end of the cemetery. And Chris and Hannah Jensen had paid with their life's blood for a war that need not have been.

It was in the fall of that year also that Professor John Stevens came to Midwestern from the east as an instructor in English literature. He was slender and well set up, with a fine sensitive face. Probably forty, with a touch of gray at his temples, he was the first of the faculty members to be clean shaven. It was almost as though a new type of man had appeared among them, for he possessed more of the appearance of a well-dressed business man than any of the other masculine instructors had theretofore presented. He had a boyish, springy walk, a quick energetic air which set him apart from some of the other rather easy-going dignitaries of the faculty.

He had not been at Midwestern two months until there was a noticeable influence emanating from his well-groomed person to some of the other members. Professor Cunningham startled his classes one day by emerging from behind his fountain-like mustache which to their surprise had hidden a well-shaped mouth. President Watts had his own wild hirsute adornment trimmed down to a mild bun-like appendage on his chin.

Professor Carter appeared in a new well-tailored gray suit. Professor Wittingly followed in a dark blue one and a tie that made a genuine effort to blend with the rest of his outfit. Only fat Professor Wick remained impervious to the new influence and presented the same rumpled front with its faint suggestion of his last lunch somewhere on its vast expanse.

Ella found herself admiring the new instructor, his immaculate appearance and his quiet air of deference toward his coworkers. He and his wife took a house on the same block as the Bishop home, so Ella and her mother went over to call soon.

To her disappointment, she found Mrs. Stevens to be an odd little creature, sallow and unattractive, with an almost furtive expression, and so inferior intellectually to her husband that one wondered how she had ever attracted him. Harsh-voiced, querulous, a semi-invalid according to her own diagnosis, she apparently demanded everything and gave nothing. She complained of the change out to the midwest which evidently she held in contempt, and gave the impression that she would make no great effort to fit in with her new associates. Ella went home with the depressed feeling that life had played a shabby trick on that nice Professor Stevens.

The couple came over several times that fall.

While Ella and John Stevens talked of books, plays, or school affairs, Mrs. Stevens and Ella's mother discussed medicines, doctors, and a choice assortment of bodily ailments.

It did not take long for Ella and John Stevens to find that they possessed a half-dozen interests in common—James Matthew Barrie with his whimsical writings, Hamlin Garland's new works, and a strikingly original writer by the name of Elbert Hubbard. When Mrs. Stevens, listening in for a moment, remarked that most of what her husband discussed was Greek to her, Ella felt an unbearable embarrassment for him and admired the tact with which he half-smilingly met the statement.

Life took on an added interest now. The days that Professor Stevens walked with her to school were days that started out happily. They talked and found that their ideas on a hundred subjects were interesting to each other. They were silent and found that their silences were pregnant with unspoken thoughts.

He took to dropping into Ella's classroom every day with something humorous to tell her, or pathetic, or instructive. "I thought you'd enjoy this . . ." or "I thought of you right away when I ran across this . . ." would be his greeting.

He formed a little group for reading the new

books aloud,—he and his wife, Professor and Mrs. Schroeder, Doctor and Mrs. Wittingly, the Fondas, and Ella.

And when the others found what a splendid reader he was, they gave the unanimous decision that John Stevens should do all the reading. Garland, Kipling, Barrie, the *Little Journeys*—he read them aloud in his expressive way to this small and sympathetic group of listeners.

Ella's admiration for him grew with every contact. It came to be that she was conscious of his entry into a room even as she had been of Delbert in those long-gone days. A door opening behind her and she knew in some psychic way that John Stevens had entered. Always frank with herself, she tried to analyze this new emotion which was filling all her days—knew to an honest certainty that it was the same feeling she had once had for Delbert, augmented now by a maturity of heart, but held in check by a maturity of mind.

Sometimes in the privacy of her own room, with all subterfuge stripped away, she admitted to herself that it was almost as though she loved him. But that was ridiculous,—one of those things that just did not happen to people of her type. However, school herself as she might, the appearance of that tall figure with its springy step coming up the curving walk under the elms was the signal for a sudden acute interest in life. That the regard was mutual was so apparent as to be without question. Straight to her he continued to come with every new article that interested him, knowing that it would interest her, too,—with every new plan for his department, knowing that her approval or condemnation was worth considering.

"It's just friendship," Ella told herself repeatedly, "—a platonic friendship." But she said it so often to her *alter ego* that she grew conscious of her own attempt at deception.

It was true that one listening to their daily conversations could have found not the slightest cause for comment, but Ella Bishop knew in all honesty that something physically attractive held them together. "Is this the way people drift into affairs?" she asked herself more than once. Sometimes she thought of Professor Crooks and Miss Zimmerman, dismissed under a cloud of gossip, and shuddered at the memory. But this, this was different. Her liking for John Stevens was so sincere, so thoroughly decent. "Oh, that's what they all say," she broke off wearily, and put him out of her mind, only to find that she was thinking of him again at the earliest opportunity.

Just after the holidays, Sam Peters came across the street one evening to see her. He was nervous, disturbed, experienced a difficult time in getting started on something he wished to tell her.

"It's a little hard to speak about. You've never
. . . you've never known me to be gossipy, have
you, Ella?"

Suddenly she was frightened. Gossip, how she
hated it! Her heart contracted for a moment
with the horrible sensation that her very thoughts
had broken loose from the cage of her mind and
become known. How foolish—no one knew her
innermost feelings. Most certainly she had not
worn her admiration on her sleeve.

"It's about . . . Professor and Mrs. Stevens."

She felt the blood mounting to her forehead,
stooped to pick up a book to hide the tell-tale fear
in her eyes.

"She . . . she takes things from stores," Sam
brought it out with painful reluctance. "Klepto-
maniac, Ella. Isn't it awful?"

Oh—poor John Stevens! All the sympathy she
had half felt for him before this was now doubled.

"Oh, Sam. How terrible!"

"Yes . . . poor Professor Stevens,—I'm sorry
for him. Came to Williams and Witwars this
afternoon to pay for something she had taken,—
told them there was nothing to do but charge anything to him she might pick up. Only he put it
a nicer way, said anything his wife might buy and
forget to pay for, just charge to him. Went
out of the store with his head high, but looking as
though he had been hit."

To her secret admiration there was now added this new sympathy.

The reading group was to meet on the first Monday night in March at Ella's home. The day proved to be stormy. The wind blew from the north. The big trees on the campus strained against the force of it but gave up and bent with mad mutterings to the south. It was as though unseen monsters flew by, one behind the other— a long unending procession of madmen. They blew the snow from the roofs of the college buildings, threw down branches, tossed the tops of drifts into the air. They growled and groaned and hissed as they passed by,—all invisible, save their long white hair streaming out behind them.

No one came to the reading circle but John Stevens from a few doors away. When the time was quite past to look for any of the others, the two alone settled down for the reading. Ella asked her mother and Hope to come in, but the former said her head ached and she would rather not, and Hope had to study.

John Stevens had brought *The Little Minister.*

"Long ago . . . a minister of Thrums was to be married, but something happened and he remained a bachelor"—the low throaty voice of John Stevens made the words a melody. *"Then when he was old, he passed in our square the lady who*

162

was to have been his wife, and her hair was white but she too was still unmarried. The meeting had only one witness, a weaver, and he said solemnly afterwards, 'They didna speak, but they just gave one another a look, and I saw the love-light in their een.' No more is remembered of these two, no being now living ever saw them, but the poetry that was in the soul of a battered weaver makes them human to us forever."

The fire burned red in the big coal stove. The mad wind outside whirled down from the north. A deep peace enveloped the two.

"The life of every man is a diary in which he means to write one story and writes another."

Oh, this is what life should be, Ella was thinking. *This* is the way it should be *any* evening,— any time. He and I . . . he and I . . . ! Mad thoughts,—as mad as the unseen monsters passing by outside,—Tam-o'-shanters of the night,— both.

For a long time the voice went on in rhythmic cadence. *" 'I am glad of that,' said the gypsy. 'Mr. Dishart, I do believe you like me all the time. Can a man like a woman against his will?' "*

John Stevens closed the book with a snap. "It's much later than I thought," he said almost brusquely. He left hurriedly,—so hurriedly that Ella knew he too was harboring wild thoughts that passed by like those demons of the storm.

Upstairs in the haven of her room she sat down on the edge of the bed, trembling.

"Now let us look this thing in the face," she said to her reason and to her emotional self,—as though they were two individuals. "It looks to me as though the time had come to let your mind and heart have it out, Ella Bishop. Close the door on the outside world. Speak freely, both of you. No one need ever know. What have *you* to say, poor thing? Out with it!" She pretended to speak to her heart.

"I want this man for my own. I'd rather be near him than any other human I've ever known. I think he feels the same way about me. I *know* it. I can *feel his* feelings. I'm entitled to happiness. A girl took my lover away once. Why can't I do the same thing? He has no real wife. He's misunderstood, his life half ruined. I could give him everything,—love, companionship, happiness. I've only *one* life to live,—why can't it be completely happy?"

"Now, *you!*" She was as impartial as a judge. "What can you say to that?"

"I can say enough." Her clean honest mind took the chair. "In the first place, every one *isn't* entitled to happiness, not at the expense of some one else. Happiness gained that way ceases to *be* happiness. Have you ever heard that two wrongs don't make a right? And just why do you drag into this that weak young Amy? You, with your years and your education and your so-called poise and judgment! 'Misunderstood!' Where have you heard that feeble little excuse before?"

"But I want him."

"Perhaps you'd like the moon, too."

"If I gave him the least bit of encouragement . . ."

"You *weakling!*" The judge turned on them both in fury. "You carry a torch, do you? So you're a teacher, are you, carrying a torch to light the way for boys and girls up the long rugged hill they all must climb? That's what you've pretended to be doing all these years, is it? Well, then . . . *carry* it, you *coward!*" She threw herself sobbing across the bed. "You little *fool* . . . *carry* it!"

CHAPTER XXIII

ELLA was thankful when Commencement arrived. John Stevens was to leave for the east for the summer months and with his going, she told herself with infinite sarcasm, she presumed she would regain her sanity.

Over and over she said to herself: "This thing has happened to other people, and I've scorned their idiocy, and now it is happening to me." With deepest contempt she used scourging methods on herself, enjoyed with ironic pleasures her own mental flagellations. By autumn time and school she was able to look at the world through crystal-clear eyes, until the day before matriculation when from her office window in the tower of Central she happened to see John Stevens coming up the walk under the elms, stepping along with that boy-ish springing walk. And then she knew the summer's battle had gone for naught.

She saw him stop to talk with big George Schroeder and in a fever of haste, hurried down to greet him while he was there with the German instructor. The three talked of their respective summers and of plans for the fall. Ella told a humorous anecdote about her vacation, walked down the long cinder path with Professor Schroeder when he started away, and went home highly pleased with the Ella Bishop who was her outer and civilized self.

This was Hope's senior High School year, and Ella made herself simulate such a deep interest in the young girl's dreams that she could have no time or thought for foolish dreams of her own.

In October, she was to go to Maple City, a two hours' ride by train, to address a teachers' meeting. She had no special knowledge of what other members of the faculty had been asked to speak, but assumed that there would be others, for it was a very common custom for several to go each fall.

On the day of the meeting she rose early, dressed with care, and was at the station in time for the eight o'clock train. Miss Sallie Withrow, the primary supervisor, was there,—"primed, I suppose, to expound to all the waiting pedagogues your ideas on complete freedom for the child," Ella joked her.

Just before the train came in, John Stevens arrived. Ella felt that old unwonted happiness surge over her at his presence. As he swung into the station now with his light firm tread, she was thinking again how he was everything any woman could desire,—intellect, manners, appearance,— everything. Far from handsome as to features,

167

that art of dressing well, businesslike air, and general manner set him in appearance far apart from the George Schroeders and the Professor Cunninghams of the faculty.

To-day she felt so pleased that he was to go to the meeting that she set a stern watch upon herself for fear she might put that emotion into her expression. If her feeling for him had progressed beyond the pale of recall, it was at least unknown to any mortal, she told herself, John Stevens included. She was glad that she looked nice, with feminine pride gloried a little in the fact that her new fall outfit was so becoming. She had a blue camel's-hair dress the exact shade of her eyes, with long blue corduroy velvet wrap and velvet toque made from the same material, a gray pointed sea-gull wing on each side fitting over the puffs of her hair and outlining the curve of her face.

If she kept her interest in this man thoroughly concealed, she was not unaware that his face lighted noticeably at the sight of her. Immediately he was merely the courteous fellow-worker of them both, addressing himself rather pointedly to Miss Sallie Withrow.

The three sat together on the train, talking about many things after the manner of those who have much in common. It came out that John Stevens' program was a morning talk and the evening lecture, Miss Sallie Withrow's morning and afternoon talks, Ella's the same. The return trip would have to be made on the evening ten-thirty train.

"But I'm staying over Sunday," Miss Withrow was saying, ". . . a second cousin of my mother's whom I have never seen lives there, and it's my best opportunity to make her a visit."

A silence settled upon the other two. It might have been only a natural one, and it might have been pregnant with thoughts unspoken.

Maple City was several times larger than Oak River, a midwestern city of factories and hotels, schools and churches. Built on a high bluff it overlooked the river making its lazy way to the sea.

The meetings were held in a rather fine new high-school building. During her morning talk, Ella was all teacher, gave her best to these people of her own chosen vocation, but constantly, and without her volition, through all her professional speech ran a minor pleasurable thought like the far-off sound of a silver bell that she was to be thrown in the company of John Stevens for one whole day by no act of her own. No conscious effort on the part of either had thrown them together. Just fate. Sometimes fate was cruel, and sometimes she was very, very kind.

At the close of the afternoon session, she saw Miss Sallie Withrow leave the high-school build-

ing with the cousin, stayed a few minutes longer
to answer questions, and went down the long stairway to find John Stevens waiting for her in the
hall. The far-off sound of the silver bell became
suddenly the chimes of a cathedral.

"Shall we walk?" he said, as casually as though
he had asked her to meet him here.

"Yes," Ella said, as though she had told him
that she would.

They followed a long wooden walk to the end
of a street, then took a path that led along the
river road to the top of a bluff. It was then but
the beginning of a park which was to be a beauty-
spot in later years. Great trees which had clung
to the river's bank for a century crowded the hill.
Open spaces between the heavier growth showed
the burned-out embers of old Indian camp fires.
Wooden seats had been placed along the edge of
nature's parapet to which an iron fence gave protection from the abrupt fall of the bluff.

Here they sat down and looked over the rich
farming valley. October's sunshine slanted
through the huge oaks and maples,—October's
bright blue sky formed a dome over the scarlet
and green and gold of the valley,—and the river
ran its lazy way to the sea.

"It's ideal, isn't it?"

"Oh, why can't it always be this lovely?"

They were ordinary words. Any one might

have said them,—any one heard them. But they were weighted with much more import. It was as though he said: "Because you are here with me it is ideal," and she, "Oh, why can't we always be together?" But the words remained unspoken, though the two talked of many intimate things.

He told her of his parents, his schooldays, his early engagement to a neighbor girl before he had finished his course, and the struggle to get his extra degrees after this boyish marriage. Down in her heart Ella was glad that at no time did he speak disparagingly of the peculiar woman who must have been a cruel hindrance rather than a helpmate. Only once he said: "When you are young, you go through a forest blindly, seeing nothing very clearly. At middle-age you see both ways, forward and back. I suppose Old Age, looking backward, can see and understand it all."

In turn Ella simply and naturally told him of her girlhood. When she came to the part Amy had played in her life, he put his hand over hers, and they sat so until the shadows lengthened.

Everything had been said, everything but the thing they could not say.

It did not seem wrong. Anything so natural and so mutually lovely could not contain evil, Ella was thinking. If she gave any thought now to her early love affair, it was merely to think of it as a song that had been sung and forgotten.

Sitting there in the warmth of the October sunshine she had a feeling that she would carry the
memory of this day with her always, for common
sense told her it could never be repeated,—that
it would be the golden leaf of all the pages in the
book.

When the dusk suggested itself they rose and
retraced their steps down the river road. They
had dinner in an obscure little café where no prying eyes might see them and misinterpret. And
then Ella went over to the lecture hall with him,
slipping into a rear seat while he went to the
front with the committee in charge.

Sitting there in the back seat, hearing the voice
of the man with whom she had spent a precious
day and with whom she wished out of the entire
world she might spend all days, she gave herself
wholly to the emotion of his unspoken love for her,
let it play about her body as a swimmer revels in
the waves. To-morrow she would go back to face
the problem of what to do with this friendship
which had become something stronger than friendship. Only this evening she would hold it to her
heart, would pretend that it was her own, paying
no attention to the sober fact that it was but a
wistful dream.

The lecture was over. In three-quarters of an
hour they would be on the train bound for home.
He was speaking to a few people, then hurrying

through the crowd to her,—just as it ought always to be. When they had gone out of a side door, and turned to go up the street, there was a far distant flash of lightning and a reverberating roll of thunder. They spoke of the queerness of it so late in the season, but the day had been hot and the storm not unexpected. Another far-away flash and its resultant crash of cymbals!

And now, a few great thudding raindrops hit the sidewalk with noisy clatter so that he drew Ella into a darkened stairway entrance for momentary shelter. Together they stood in the narrow archway while the heavy drops became a pelting shower only a few feet away. Suddenly John Stevens' arms went around Ella and he drew her close.

"Well . . . ?" he asked huskily. "What shall we do with this thing that confronts us? Shall we . . . go home?" His face was bending close to hers. "Or stay?"

Or stay? Ella caught her breath in a gasp of understanding. The lights of the dark city were all about them like jewels on an enveloping mantle. Strangers passed back and forth through the summer shower. A dozen hotels sent out their welcoming gleams from a hundred windows. Go home . . . *or stay?* The lovely day had been theirs. And *now?*

A streak of lightning shot across the sky in sprawling fashion, like the rivers of a map.

"Is it . . . is it I, alone, who must make the decision?" Her voice sounded as strange as though it were not her own.

"You are the woman."

You are the woman. She had a wild confused notion that two worlds suddenly stood still in their orbits waiting for that woman's answer,— two worlds, into one of which she must step forever. There could be no half-way measures. She must live either in the one or the other, for entering into one, she must forever turn her back upon the other. Go home! *Or stay!* There were those who broke marriage vows lightly, who shattered the moral code with little compunction. The arms of the man she loved were about her, the face of the man she loved above her, waiting for her in the world of love and desire. In the other waited her mother, Hope, friends, students. . . .

A great flash rent the skies with such blinding light—became for a moment so like a living flame —that it looked to be a flaming torch high above the city streets. *A flaming torch?* Why,—*a flaming torch was meant to light the paths of boys and girls along the rugged way!*

Suddenly she felt sane and strong. Putting the unspoken feeling into words had brought back all her sanity and her strength. There was only one answer. There could never be another.

She put her hands on his shoulders, not in a gesture of love, but rather in one of sadness and pity, that in a world of unhappiness they must forever renounce this exquisite thing.

"Go home," she said.

He drew her close for one disturbing moment as though he could not accept the verdict. Then, "Of course," he said. "You are right."

He slipped her arm into his and they went out of the sheltering stairway onto the moist street and down to the station.

Old Judge Peters was there to take the train. He greeted them affably with long-winded ponderous explanations and the three sat together and talked all the way home.

Sam was at the station with the carriage to meet his father and so took them all up to the Adams Street neighborhood.

"Good night, Judge Peters," Ella said gayly. "Thank you, Sam, and good night." And, as though it were not the end of everything, "Good night, Professor Stevens."

"Good night, Miss Bishop."

CHAPTER XXIV

SCHOOL went on. Classes met and recited. Students passed and flunked. The blackbirds shrilled their "tchack-tchack" in the big trees. The reading circle members came together and listened to John Stevens' attractive interpretations of the modern writers. Ella had her fortieth birthday. Everything was just as it had been, everything but one. Ella Bishop had found a certain peace of soul in the situation.

If John Stevens had been free, she would have given up everything for him. John Stevens was not free. Therefore, she could not continue to think of him in any way but as a friend and co-worker. Q.E.D. To Ella Bishop's uncomplicated code of life the problem was as simple as that.

"That's one thing about me," she said to the image in the mirror on that anniversary of her fourth decade. "I can always get the better of my emotions in time. I may fight windmills, but after awhile I have them too scared even to turn in the wind."

She stared for a moment at the face in the glass, admitting with accustomed candor that she

did not look the years with her well-kept skin, her
dark hair, deep blue eyes with humorous crinkles
at their outer edges, red-lipped, generous mouth.
For some little time she looked at the woman
in the mirror who stared unabashedly back.
"Forty," she said aloud to herself. "Well," she
shrugged her shoulder and grinned to the appari-
tion who grinned cheerfully back, "abandon hope
all ye who enter here."

It was noised about on the campus in the spring
that Professor Stevens was leaving. Ella heard it
first from Miss Hunter of the training school.
For a moment the solidity of the trees and bushes
and the green sloping lawn seemed wavering in a
liquid mist. The college without John Stevens
dropping into her classroom, without his springy
boyish step down the corridors, without his voice
at the reading circle—! All the weeks without
John Stevens! Beyond the day of his going lay
the bleakness of nothing,—all the to-morrows
would be gray. Then she was herself,—calm,
poised, unshaken by the news. It was better so.
No more watching herself for any betrayal of her
feelings. Life would be easier and more simple.

Just before Commencement he came into her
office in the tower room to say good-by.

She was bending over a low drawer of supplies
when, startled, she grew aware that some one was
behind her. She stood up hurriedly and for a

long moment they stood facing each other. Then he put out his hand.

"Everything to make you happy and successful," he was making an attempt at gayety.

"Thank you. And to you."

He held her hand a moment, looked at it as though not quite sure of its identity, dropped it and walked out of the office.

The bell overhead tapped and the pigeons with a great whirl of wings brushed past her window.

She was standing just as she had been, when suddenly he stepped back in. His face was drawn and he was biting nervously at his lip.

"If it's ever . . . if it's possible for me to return . . . some day . . ."

"Don't say it," Ella said a little breathlessly. "Don't."

He stood for a moment. Then,—"No," he said, "I won't. Good-by."

He was gone. And all the to-morrows had begun.

Luckily Commencement held double duty for Ella. Hope was finishing her High School course, and the importance of the occasion gave the little home on Adams Street a festive air. There was a fluffy white dress with embroidery ruffles for her made by old Mrs. Finch who was still holding her own with the other dressmakers of the town. It had taken tears and tact to get the sewing out of Stena's hands,—tears on Hope's part and tact on Ella's, for Stena had wanted to make yards of wide crocheted insertion for the gown, —and as Ella said: "Hope, she just doesn't realize that:

> *"Crochet*
> *Is passé."*

Which had the effect of turning Hope's tears to laughter—Aunt Ella was always so funny and understanding.

And so in the excitement of the High School graduating exercises with their attendant festivities, Ella's inner emotional life was set aside like an old worn-out shoe.

"Before I forget all these emotions, I ought to write a book," she said ironically to that other self with whom she always held gay converse. *"The Love Life of an Old Maid*—and wouldn't it contain a gay set of lovers—a man who had married another girl *before* he met me, and a man who married another girl *after* he met me? And Sam," she added to herself, "don't forget poor old Sam."

And Ella had occasion not to forget Sam that summer.

It was on an evening in August that some one tapped on the screen door and she went downstairs to find Sam standing there, his slim bony face looking white and drawn. He was breathing hard, partly from hurrying and partly from agitation.

"Can you come over to our house, Ella?" he wanted to know. His voice sank to a whisper. Evidently he was laboring under great stress. "I'm in trouble, and I've got to have somebody to talk to. You're always so . . . so . . ." He did not finish.

Hatless, Ella stepped out on the porch and closed the door behind her. "Is it your father, Sam?"

"No, Father's well. He's gone to Maynard to look after his place there and collect the rent. He won't be home until to-morrow."

"What is it, then?" She felt impatient with this mild Sam who could keep her in suspense over a mere trifle.

"Wait until we get over home. You'll come, won't you?" She saw he was trembling.

Ella crossed the street with him to the fussy old house. As they stepped up on the porch it occurred to her that in the two years since his mother's death, she had not been beyond the doorway. She had talked to Sam and his father in the yard, taken neighborly gifts of food across the way many times, but had not gone in.

It was neat inside. She had a swift impression that everything was just as it had always been,—
180

the pink flowered vase on the table, the black crocheted afghan on the couch, the plaster cast of "The Milk Maid." But there was a musty odor as of slack housekeeping.

Sam closed the wide hall door and put his hand heavily on Ella's arm. "I've a sick man here in Father's bedroom. He's very low. The doctor just left, but he's coming back."

He turned and beckoned, and Ella followed him through the old sitting-room with the wide bay-window to the door of the downstairs bedroom. She could hear labored breathing even before Sam held back a faded brown chenille portière and motioned to the humped bulky form of some one under the patch-work quilt.

For only a moment he held it back, then dropped it nervously and came back on tiptoe. He raised miserable eyes to Ella.

"It's Chester," he said simply.

Ella, startled beyond coherent thought, could only stare.

"He wasn't drowned," Sam said quietly. "He came back to-night."

CHAPTER XXV

ELLA, standing there and staring at Sam, could find no word to say.

"It was about seven when he came," Sam said nervously. "Father was over to Wittingly's. Some one came up the side door and tapped. I went to the door and this man . . ." Sam was still having hard work to believe the incredible. "Chet stood there and laughed kind of silly. My first thought was that he had escaped from somewhere. . . . Then he said with that foolish laugh: 'I guess you don't know me. I know you though, Sam. It's Chet.'

"It was horrible. I was terribly frightened. It was like a nightmare. I wanted to call somebody and couldn't speak. I wanted to go and get somebody and I couldn't move."

"Oh, Sam!" Ella's heart went out to the thin little man standing there, locking and unlocking nervous fingers.

"We both stood there, and then he said, 'I guess you thought I got my everlasting by drowning. Well, I didn't. I was mad about . . . Amy . . . and just slipped out to see the world a bit.' Then he stopped and that foolish grin left him and a sober look came over his face, sane, but bitter and terrible, and he said, 'Well, I've seen it, all right.' My God, Ella!" Sam burst forth, "he *has* seen it—the *under* side."

For a few moments the muscles of Sam's thin throat worked convulsively, and then he went on quietly: "Chet stood still there outside the door, and I not moving either. Then he said, 'I meant to come back in a little while . . . after I got over . . . about Amy.'"

Into Ella's numbed mind came a sudden rush of realization, a fleeting thought of all the misery Amy's coming to town had left in its wake. But Sam was still repeating Chet's words:

" 'I got passage for Hong Kong on a freighter, and then when I got there . . .' He mumbled something about a Chinese girl, and some more that I didn't catch. I hadn't said a word yet. All I could do was stare at him. And then he asked: 'Are Father and Mother . . . ?'

"Then he sort of put both hands out on the door jamb and crumpled down. It was terrible, getting him in. He's huge, a big bloated unhealthy size. I pulled him into the sitting-room and tried to get him up on the couch. I could see he wasn't dead, just unconscious. I kept thinking how Father would come home in a few minutes, over and over in my mind kept going the thought of Father's pride in Chet.

"There wasn't any time left to hesitate. And quick—like that—" Sam gave his thin fingers a snap—"I decided to lie to Father. Lies don't come easy, if you aren't used to them, Ella." He said it as naïvely as a child. "But I knew I'd have to lie or else kill Father. And I owed it to Father. He—Chet—looked pretty near gone. I ran to the telephone and called young Doc Lawrence . . . these new telephones are wonderful, Ella. . . . I thought being a newcomer there was no risk of his recognizing Chet. I figured that I'd say it was just a . . . tramp. If he came to and talked, and Father *had* to know . . . I'd just pretend it was news to me too. But he hasn't been conscious. He's talked some but it's disconnected things—just rambling. Sometimes he thinks he's in Shanghai. Oh, you wouldn't want to hear him, Ella. But sometimes . . ." Sam's voice broke, "sometimes he thinks he's a kid . . . coasting down College Hill."

Ella wondered whether she had ever before felt such deep emotion, known such moving pathos. She wanted to do something for Sam, take over the burden for him. In that one poignant moment she had a fleeting vision of herself living here as Sam had always wanted, helping him. But almost before its inception, she thrust it from her.

Sam fumbled for a minute with the old blue

vase on the table and then he spoke again: "I couldn't think of getting him upstairs, so I had to put him in Father's bedroom. Young Doc Lawrence and I got him in there finally. Father came home," his low voice went on. "He was annoyed by it,—scolded some for putting a tramp in his bed. Said I'd have him dead on my hands, and that if I'd had any backbone I'd have called the authorities first thing. I've always been honest with Father and it took all my strength of will to carry the lie through. When he said he'd have gone to Maynard if it hadn't been for the sick man here, I told him to go ahead, that Doc Lawrence and I would look after him. I felt relieved and thankful. When he wavered about going, I could hardly stand it. But he went."

"Oh, Sam." Ella's heart went out to the quiet little man.

"He won't live through the night, Doctor says. It's like having him die twice, you see, to have Father know. I'm praying that he won't regain consciousness. To have him come to and tell! Think how it would kill Father's dream of him —all his old pride in him!"

When Ella could only nod in affirmation, he went on: "When he passes away I've got to carry the thing through. He can't be buried in our lot. Mother would have wanted him by her, but then, there's Father to think about?" He put it as

185

a question but his decision was his own. "No, I've thought it all out. He's got to stay just a stray bum that asked for his supper . . . name unknown . . . until after Father passes away. Then if I outlive Father, I could have him moved —and tell folks."

Ella found her voice: "You're doing a big thing, Sam,—a mighty big thing. Your father hasn't always . . ." Then she stopped, annoyed that she had said it.

Keen, sensitive, Sam looked up. "Yes, I know. He hasn't thought I've amounted to anything— handling eggs and sugar and keeping books. Well, I guess I haven't. You'll have to admit yourself, Ella, that Chet would have been . . ." The old familiar phrase died away on his lips, and he changed it apologetically: "If he'd gone straight, Chet would have been a great man."

They stood for a few moments while the labored breathing rattled hoarsely in the room beyond.

Dr. Lawrence came in quietly then. Her heart filled with sympathy for Sam, Ella offered to stay, —to go home and get Stena and come back.

"No," Sam said, "I don't want you to have to be here, Ella. I want to think of you over home, away from it."

"I'm not afraid of death, Sam. I've been . . . I've seen death."

"Yes, I know. But you go on. Come over in the morning if you feel you can."

Stena went over with Ella in the morning. Death had been there and gone. The body had been taken down to the undertaker's when Judge Peters arrived home from his trip.

Sam, pale but steady, met his father at the door. Only his lips trembled. "Father . . . the man . . . the man is dead."

The old judge was pompous, fussy, a little sorry that he had scolded about Sam bringing the sick man into the house. "Well! Well! We all come to it. The stream of humanity flows ever on-ward to eternity. Poor wayfarer! Somebody thought a great deal of him once."

Ella's eyes met the hunted eyes of Sam and would have dropped their tears if she had not used all her will power to stay them.

There were formalities to attend to, a law or two to be obeyed, and later a simple burying.

Sam said he thought there ought to be some-thing read at the grave and a song, no matter—no matter who the man might be. He went to the members of one of the church choirs but the tenor was too busy and the soprano had a cold, so there was no music.

Ella and Stena went out with Sam to the short service held on the side of the fence where the sleepers have left no funds for the upkeep of their narrow houses. The tall dry grass rubbed brittle stems together in the wind. Grasshoppers thumped heavily on the plain black box. The minister prayed solemnly for the soul of the dead. But Ella prayed for the living.

By pressing his thin lips tightly together Sam got through the ordeal bravely enough. He held his thin body erect and looked steadily over the nearby field of corn. It was only when they were leaving that he broke for a moment.

When he held the gate open for Ella, he whispered: "My God, Ella, we used to go fishing together down on Oak Creek . . . and we had a menagerie rigged up in the old carriage house. . . ."

Ella held herself rigidly against all emotion until she arrived at the dark haven of her room. Then she threw herself across her bed and cried because life was such a tragic thing.

CHAPTER XXVI

AND now Hope matriculated at Midwestern, the baby who only yesterday had stood with flattened nose against the window waiting for Aunt Ella's return. How the years had slipped silently by. Hope was a freshman and a Minerva sister and a student of primary work in the big new training school.

Miss Sallie Withrow and freedom were gone now, but Miss Hester Jones and bondage were there. And Hope, taking training under the critical, severe, and all-seeing eye of Miss Jones, lived in such a changeable condition of atmospheric pressure, low for criticism and high for commendation, that the little house on Adams Street became the center of all cyclonic disturbances. Ella sometimes thought she had double duty—her own work and Hope's. For Aunt Ella was the port in all storms. One never knew how Hope would arrive at night,—up in the clouds or down in the depths.

"She said,"—to Hope there was only one *She* in the whole college—Miss Jones—"she said I did very nicely with the games," Hope would be all smiles. Or, tearfully, "She said I taught the number-work class as though I didn't understand it myself."

"Well, *who would?*" Ella might be moved to sputter. "The ratio method. Everything ratio —just as though you could go through life settling all problems by comparing a little block with a big block. I'm going to talk to Miss Jones myself."

But it was largely braggadocio, and Ella knew it. For one did not talk critically to Miss Jones. Looking at her large, solid physique, her firm mouth, and her cold gray eyes, one who had come to express himself forcibly merely mentioned that it was a nice day and fled, leaving some one else to render any unfavorable judgment of her department.

And in truth, Ella had enough to oversee in her own department without dipping into another.

For some time the school had been of such size that freshman English was all she taught. But to say that Miss Bishop taught merely freshman English was to utter a half-truth. In reality she taught social science, business administration, morals, manners, religion, literature. Freshman English was but a cloak to hide her interest in humanity, a smoke-screen in front of her general helpfulness. Not that she was weak in her subject. No one could pass on to Sophomore English who did not meet the course's stiff requirements. To timorous and bold students alike she seemed to stand at the end of a long corridor of time, a semester's length away, like some avenging angel with up-thrust sword.

And she gave unstintingly of her time and energy. No student ever turned up the gravel path between the rows of evergreen hedge at the little house on Adams Street without confidence that he would see Miss Bishop if she were at home.

"They've seen me in so many and such varying degrees of dress, that I don't know how they can respect me. I've had on cold cream and kitchen dresses—loose house slippers and curl papers. But when a student comes to my house it usually means he has something spontaneous on his mind that, withheld for a while, would gradually curdle, and he would decide not to talk. So I never keep them waiting."

Being human, she often scolded about her tasks outside the schoolroom. "If I were only paid in proportion to what I do," she might sputter. "Look at the people who walk away from their jobs and have some time to themselves. Do I? Never. Papers, plans, picnics, parties. I do everything around that school but help Chris with the mowing and I'd not be surprised to have to take a hand in that some day."

All of which scolding is hard to reconcile with

the fact that when the school grew to such size that one or two of the freshman English classes were to be taken over by some one else, she began to make excuses.

"Oh, I can still handle them all, I think. By putting in two extra sections of recitation seats the room will hold twelve more, easily."

And when she was home, scolded furiously about herself. "Now, why did I do that senseless thing—deliberately assume more work than I needed to have done?"

She knew the secret of it was a sort of motherly jealousy for all freshmen. She wanted none to pass her by. "The minute they do that, I shall begin to lose connection with a certain percentage of them—never know them at all."

A queer mortal—Ella Bishop.

Each spring she took a special interest in freshmen students who were not able to go on with their courses, those who had to stop in order to earn money for another year. She would not relinquish her hold on them until she had exacted promises from them to return as soon as they could. She helped many of them get country schools,—often driving her own horse miles to interview directors in their behalf.

Miss Hunter, of the training school, used to say: "I don't see why you do all that. Isn't a written recommendation enough? It seems to me a bit undignified to go charging around the country in behalf of a student."

"Undignified—your foot!" Ella would retort. "The main thing is that *Annie Simpson wants a school.*"

There were more changes on the campus. President Watts's far-seeing eye and executive management had made possible many improvements. From year to year the building progressed. Central Hall was now usually referred to as Old Central,—the ivy vines on its walls were dense mats of green through which the windows peered as from under shaggy eyebrows. Chris was no longer head janitor. There was a supervisor of grounds and buildings, a young man fully trained in architecture. Chris was merely a general repair man, stoker, grass cutter. The supervisor was of Swedish descent, and Chris in the jealousy of his coming confided to Ella that "a Swede ain't not'in', anyway, but a Dane wid his brains knocked out."

The music department had made a reputation for itself, "teaching every known instrument," Ella said, "but bagpipes and the Chinese gong." Sometimes she had to laugh to herself over the jealousies of the voice teachers, particularly those fomenting between Miss Boggs and Miss Honeycutt whose artistic temperaments were of such extreme sensitiveness that a particularly pleasing press notice concerning one usually sent the other to bed with a headache.

Professor George Schroeder's department had grown beyond his dreams. Every day he taught his beloved Goethe and Schiller with all the fire of his own admiration. And every day little Professor Fonda brought to his students some new astronomical knowledge, as though bringing them a bit of the light from his sun and his stars. The faculty was no longer a big family. There were no more faculty picnics or parties. The group was too large. Like a snowball grown too big it had disintegrated socially into small groups.

In 1904 Hope, finishing her intensive training under the all-seeing eye of Miss Jones, modestly felt that she knew all there was to know about primary training.

Sometimes she and Ella had little arguments about it.

"You'll get over some of those theories, Hope. As President Cleveland said, 'It's a condition and not a theory' that confronts you, and all the training in the world won't make a good teacher of you or any one else, just because you or that person had Miss Jones's military sort of training, unless you're a born teacher and can adapt yourself to any situation and still function wisely and well."

"But, Aunt Ella, I can step right into any

school now and just *reproduce* Miss Jones's model classwork."

"I'm glad you think so and it will help you immensely to have a high standard before you. But don't forget that you may teach where you will not have model training-school equipment."

"But Miss Jones says we should *demand* the best of materials."

Ella smiled: "You could demand it in some schools until the cows come home and not get it, —and anyway there is much more to teaching than the material aids that surround you."

"Just the same I do think it's *beneath* a graduate of Miss Jones's course even to accept a position in a place where the aids are not up to date."

To which Ella said crisply: "Two of the greatest teachers in the world, Hope, were not equipped with up-to-date material aids—Socrates 'who brought down philosophy from the heavens to earth'—and a Man who wrote with his finger in the sand."

She was as proud of Hope, though, as a mother peacock, and just as at High School graduation, planned to get soft white mull and yards of dainty embroidery for a dress. And when the class play parts were given out and Hope arrived home bearing the rôle of "Rosalind, daughter to the banished duke" for the June presentation of "As You Like It," Ella made no attempt to conceal her delight and straightway began to plan cheese-cloth costumes in the Shakespearian mode.

In the late spring, Hope was elected to a good primary position at Maple City, and Ella suddenly realized that her pleasure over it was tempered by the realization that the house without Hope would be almost, in truth, a house without hope.

Commencement, with Hope graduating, took on more of a glamour than any of the twenty-four others had assumed since her own.

Finding almost at the last minute that the auditorium which had been undergoing a siege of redecoration was not to be finished in time, a harassed committee made hasty arrangements for a Chautauqua tent to be pitched on the campus. And so there with the lush campus grass under their feet and the June sun's rays filtering through the rippling canvas, in a forest of Arden composed largely of underbrush from the banks of Oak Creek, trod the duke and Rosalind, Celia, and Orlando and the foolish Touchstone. And when Hope's low vibrant voice came gently, clearly, through the wide spaces of the tent: "*To you I give myself, for I am yours,*" Ella had to wipe away a sentimental tear as surreptitiously as one sitting on the front seat could accomplish.

In July, old Judge Peters died, suddenly, spectacularly, in front of the court-house, his cane dropping from his numbing fingers and his Panama hat rolling into the street.

Sam grieved for him. "Not many had a fine father like mine," he told every one. The Sunday after the burial he went out to the cemetery with flowers. He put some on his father's and mother's graves and then slipped through the barbed-wire and put some on that other one. For a long time he stood there pondering what to do. Responsibility sat heavily upon him.

"I couldn't bring myself to decide," he told Ella. "Mother would want Chet over close to her. But Father—you know how proud he was of Chet, and his pride seems still to live. Seems as though it would still hurt Father to have folks know."

"I'd let things be as they are, Sam," Ella advised. "After all, it doesn't make much difference where one sleeps, does it?"

The summer went away and Hope with it. And the house on Adams Street became a dreary place.

School opened, and more freshmen came— among them a son of Mina Gordon and twin daughters of Emily Teasdale, Ella's old classmates and Minerva sisters. "And if that doesn't make me realize I've passed youth somewhere down the line," she said, "I don't know what would."

But Ella was only forty-four—and looked ten

years younger. Professor Schroeder with the prerogative of an old classmate always joked her about it. Meeting her on the campus, if there were no student ears about, he usually greeted her with some such approach as: " 'Hail, blooming Youth.' Always you are the same as when we were students."

To-day, with the September sun warm on the campus, and the recently returned students breaking into a hundred fall activities, she saw him and little Professor Fonda coming down the walk together,—the Damon and Pythias of the college in the way of friendship,—David and Goliath in the matter of physique.

Professor Schroeder greeted her with: " 'Hail, blooming Youth!' Fonda, she is like the verse from *Don Juan*.

> 'Her years
> *Were ripe, they might make six and twenty*
> *springs,*
> *But there are forms which Time to touch for-*
> *bears,*
> *And turns aside his scythe to vulgar things.'* "

Ella laughed and pointed out that if she had passed but twenty-six springs she must, perforce, have graduated at the tender age of two. "And by the way," she told them, "we should plan to celebrate our twenty-fifth anniversary next Commencement."

198

"Twenty-fifth? Ach—the time!—where does it go? If Fonda here would only stop his solar system awhile,—lock up his Milky Way and take a vacation . . ."

President Watts, bareheaded, was coming down the steps of Administration Hall, and toward them, his long loose-jointed legs moving rapidly. They turned expectantly to him as he came up.

"You remember Professor Stevens of several years ago?" he was asking.

The campus swam in a mist before Ella's eyes and she knew a sudden tenseness of nerves.

"I've just had word of his sudden death," he said. "In one of the new automobiles. They're really very dangerous affairs."

Both of the men were murmuring their surprise and sorrow. Only Ella stood transfixed and unspeaking.

"And perhaps a touch of sadness to our own college is added to the news," President Watts was saying, "by the fact that he was on his way to take the train to come out here."

CHAPTER XXVII

JOHN STEVENS was dead, killed in one of the new automobiles. ". . . On his way to take the train to come out here," President Watts had said.

All the way home in the hot September sun, with the zinnias and petunias still gay in the lingering summer weather, and with people calling out friendly greetings to her, Ella's mind kept repeating monotonously: *If it's possible for me to return some day* . . . Four years had gone by, and he had been returning.

She wanted to get home—to think out this bewildering thing—this new phase of her life—in the haven of her room away from all prying eyes —to remember him, to bring him before her in memory—his kind eyes and strong mouth and the backward sweep of his graying hair. She wanted to forget the bitter news of his death, to pretend for a brief quiet hour that the anticipated trip had been completed, to live in fancy the culmination of that journey. She wanted no one to see her, to talk to her, to mar this hour of memory and the bitter-sweet knowledge of what might have been.

But a student was waiting on the steps for her, and when she had finished with him, and had gone on into the house, Stena met her at the doorway with the information that Mrs. Bishop had one of her headaches and her heart was "acting up again." So Ella took off her hat and put on a big apron, gave her mother medicine and wrung out cold compresses until supper time. After supper there was a committee of Minerva girls coming for advice about celebrating the anniversary of the founding of the Society, so there was not even time to hold wistful memorial services in the secret places of her heart.

In the spring of that year of 1905, she tried to grow enthusiastic about reunion plans, fell to remembering all those first Minerva classmates whom, with the exception of Irene Van Ness, she had not seen for so many years, secured their addresses, wrote voluminously to each girl.

"Girls!" she laughed ironically about the word to Professor Cunningham's wife. "I guess women who have gone to school together continue to speak of each other as 'girls' on through a doddering senility."

She spent long moments thinking of them, calling the roll as it were. Irene Van Ness whom she had seen eleven years before, Mina Gordon, little and lithe and gypsy-like, Mary Crombie, frank and efficient, Janet McLaughlin, big-boned and homely and lovable—

Suddenly with something of a shock, it came to her that she was thinking of them as they had been—not as the years would have made them. With mental reservations she went on with the list: Emily Teasdale would be coming, and if not the lovely dashing beauty of the old days, at least spiritedly handsome in a mature way. Evelyn Hobbs—no, she suddenly remembered. Evelyn would not be there for she was dead.

It was a tender spot in her heart that this first old group held,—something akin to an inner chamber in which incense burned before a shrine of youthful friendship, and even as she received the answers to her invitation, she experienced a vague fear of disillusion and disappointment to see them as mature women. For much water had trickled under the little rustic bridge over Oak Creek since the seven had parted tearfully and with protestations of undying loyalty.

As Commencement drew near, she half regretted her urgent invitations—perhaps the old friends would seem like so many strangers in her home—half wished that she had kept the familiar memories of "the girls." How foolish, she told herself. After all, memory was but a pale moon which the bright sun of flesh-and-blood contact would throw into shadows.

Stena worked hard to get all the rooms in shape for the guests. The house looked nice. Prettily framed prints on the wall and soft rugs on polished floors showed Ella's improved taste. Her mother's first bedroom was now Ella's study, book-lined and containing her writing-desk and two or three fancy baskets concealing the ever-present English papers. The old enclosed stairway was now a wide open one with walnut railing. Some of the old furnishings of the living-room had been relegated to the barn—the stereoscopic views and the plaster boy who was still trying vainly in the dark of a stall to locate the thorn in his foot.

There were endless tasks for Ella, the house, looking after her mother whose frailty now at sixty-nine was marked, planning of the meals while "the girls" would be there, the final examination papers, assistance and advice to the present-day Minerva officers, the reunion dinner. "I wonder why I'm always adding something to my already full days," she said once to her image in the glass. "I just naturally soak up extra work."

At four in the afternoon of the day before Commencement, she drove to the station, holding her horse in steadily once or twice when one of the new automobiles came by. It was a typical Commencement homecoming, June sunshine, students to meet arriving parents, excitement when the train swung into view. There was nothing quite like it to quicken the blood if one were part of the scene, she thought.

When the train had stopped and the passengers crowded down the steps, she saw Irene immediately,—a strange fat woman in her wake. Irene, an old looking girl when she was young, looked scarcely older now than when Ella had last seen her. "Why," Ella thought, "they are not going to seem a bit different." She was elated. The magic of the reunion was beginning.

She and Irene clutched each other with abandon. "Irene," Ella was quite honest, "you don't look any older than . . ."

But Irene was trying to draw Ella's attention to the strange woman—some one to whom she was wanting to introduce her. "And here's Mina," she was saying gayly. And the huge woman was bearing down upon Ella, too. Mina! Mina Gordon, square of body, large spectacles, her face a full moon, two or three chins! Mina, who should have been little and lithe and gypsy-like. Oh, no! The magic was dissolving.

Irene had so many bags that they could scarcely get them in the back of the buggy. Evidently, clothes still played a large part in her life. The three drove up to Ella's home, Mina's share of the buggy seat by no means confined to her rightful one-third interest. There was much to be

said. Irene's oldest daughter was married now
—her name was Smith and she had a baby boy.
Irene was a grandmother. How queer! But
Irene laughed and shook her thin sallow face,
jangling her earrings merrily. Mina had four
boys and two girls. The family had been as poor
as Job's turkey, she said, but had always had the
most fun. Just this last year a bachelor uncle's
estate had suddenly descended on them like manna
and they scarcely knew how to act. Sometimes
she even wondered if they'd lost a little of their
family fun now that things were so easy.

Just before dinner, Janet McLaughlin surprisingly drove up in the station bus, having come
a day sooner than she expected. Janet was well-
groomed, her ensemble the last word in modish-
ness, her blue suit tight to the knees with its
stylish circular flare. She wore a modish blue
hat, close fitting at the back of her head but pro-
jecting far to the front with a long brim over
the high pompadour of her hair. Janet was a
teacher at a distant university, and having taught
English history so many years, as Mina puffingly
said, by this time she must have been on chummy
terms with Mary of the Scots and able to guess
every surreptitious thought of Queen Elizabeth's.

In the evening the four walked back to the station to meet Mary Crombie and Emily Teasdale.
When the train disgorged the two, the others

saw that the years had merely accentuated Mary's early characteristics. Domineering in her girlhood she had turned that quality clubward since clubs had become popular, and in the last few years had been local, county, district, and state Everything in the organization of her choice. A little thinner, a bit more wiry, far more efficient looking, she came elbowing her way briskly through the crowd just as they would have expected her to do. Across her flat chest were gold-mounted glasses on a long chain which she pulled out with a little zipping sound and adjusted in order to look the others over. Immediately Ella could visualize her in the Chair and hear her crisp: "The ayes have it."

Emily was trailing behind her, Emily Teasdale, the lovely spirited belle of their college days. But what had happened? Something or some one had taken all the starch out of Emily. Her dress was nondescript, her hat uninteresting, her face vacuous. She was a little wilted flower, a shadowy woman with no initiative left. Her conversation all the days they were together was one of alibis and excuses. Poor Emily, thought Ella many times, the embodiment of broken ideals, vanished illusions.

So there they all were, all but Evelyn who could not come because she was dead. The years,—what had they done to the six? Irene who had been unhappy over a love affair was now loved and happy. Ella, whose love affair had once been the envy of Irene, had not known the fruition of her hopes. Mary, who had once possessed a great deal of money, had lost it all. Mina, who never had a dollar ahead in her life, had come into a large heritage. Emily, who had been as lovely as a painting, was a faded pansy of a woman. Janet, who had been a homely, raw-boned girl, had developed into a striking woman of self-reliance and poise. All this had a quarter of a century done to a little group of schoolmates.

The four were quite unanimous in their decision that Ella and Janet had changed the least of all. The two seemed, the others said, to be the ones who had kept their youth. It was because teachers had no cares, they assured each other. For Ella and Janet they said there had been no tragedies, no business responsibilities, no hanging over sick beds in the hush of gray mornings, no dark graves. Teaching might be taxing, Mary admitted magnanimously, but it wasn't as though Ella had known the responsibility of trying to get votes for women, and Mina wheezily said that, after all, Janet simply couldn't have been heartbroken over Mary Queen of Scots or felt personally responsible for all of Queen Elizabeth's little escapades.

In the days that followed, the six, with Professors Schroeder and Fonda of their class, attended every activity on a very active campus,—a little group clinging together as though, from sheer result of the connection, they themselves might contact youth.

Emily Teasdale grew almost weepily sentimental over that first meeting with big Professor Schroeder whom she might have married; and Janet McLaughlin spent a large portion of her waking time thanking a kind Providence that she had not let the dashing drum-major in the first old college band hypnotize her into marriage, inasmuch as his career to date consisted largely in being head janitor at the gymnasium.

There were old students of other classes back, too,—successful, unknown, talented, ordinary, those who had accomplished much and those who had not known the fulfillment of any desire. At Commencements, more than on any other occasion, Time, the toll-keeper, says: "Halt. Who goes there? What have you done with the years?"

It was Ella, more than any of them, who bound the past to the present. Active, enthusiastic, apparently knowing all the students, she seemed no less a part of the young generation than of the old. But at best the others were standing at the outskirts of things looking on. Youth not only must be served, but it demands the center of the stage.

And so on the third afternoon they gave up attempting to enter into the Commencement activities and settled down in the study of Ella's home. A lowering sky with an occasional dash of rain and a grate fire added to the coziness of the mellow room where rows of books looked down upon them.

Emily Teasdale and Mary Crombie had brought pieces of needlework,—Emily making an occasional half-hearted attack upon hers, with Mary sitting up stiffly and working as though life depended upon it.

Reminiscences being as they are, the conversation could scarcely have been called enlightening or even interesting to the casual listener. It consisted largely of sentences beginning: "Do you remember . . . ?"

Mary recalled the purloining of grapes from Professor Carter's arbor, Emily a frustrated attempt to paint the brass band's mascot. Mina dragged out of its hiding place a gossipy campus skeleton that probably had not strayed from its closet to jangle its bones for two decades. With an uncanny aptitude for remembering all the foolish and forgetting much of the sensible, Ella and Janet found that they could repeat snatches of countless silly parodies they had once penned for

the Minerva society, not one of greater literary
value than:

> *"We were seated in assembly,*
> *Not a soul had room to stir.*
> *'Twas our annual debate day*
> *And a storm was in the air.*
> *And as thus we sat there silent,*
> *Not a maiden there would smile.*
> *'We are lost' the leader whispered*
> *As she staggered down the aisle."*

They all came back out of a carefree past,—
fatuous episodes, incautious escapades, scraps of
verse,—little half-memories. In the semi-gloom
of Ella's study one could almost smell the fragrant
pungent odor of rosemary, "for remembrance."

Their farewell dinner was a pleasant meal, with
Stena treading heavily in and out, anticipating
their every want. Mary and Emily and Janet
were going east on the evening train; Mina was
taking one to the north in the morning; Irene
was staying in town for a week. This, then, was
the end of the reunion.

Very soon after dinner they went upstairs while
Janet and Mary and Emily packed, all a little
sad at the parting. Something had drawn them
together again in the three days. The old friendships had been revived, and in addition, there
had emerged something more tender, a mature
appreciation of each other. Moving in six dif-

ferent orbits now, still the old attraction held them. The twenty-five years had thrown many barriers between them, distance, husbands, homes, children, businesses, social events, a thousand activities. But now that they had renewed the old acquaintance, it seemed as hard to part as on that long-gone time. To be sure, they were not shedding tears and pledging undying friendship, as then, but were promising to get together more often.

And the gathering had done other definite things to them, too: Emily had taken on a little stamina, expressing herself more freely, even wearing her hat with a bit of aplomb, Irene's life had sounded a merry new note. Mary's pronounced tendency to domineer all situations seemed a little less prominent, Janet's self-assured pertness mellowed. Even Mina, jealous of the others' relative slimness, was leaving for home with the solemn declaration that when next they saw her she would be of sylphidine proportions. As for Ella, she had resurrected the old feeling of friendship to such an extent that she felt she would cheerfully cross a continent to see them all.

Reunion! It was a pleasant thing.

CHAPTER XXVIII

MOST of the members of the faculty had been abroad at some time or were planning to go. Miss Hunter and Miss Jones of the training school, Professor and Mrs. Cunningham were going in the summer of 1906. "And I could go, too, if I would ever save my salary," Ella complained of herself. "I don't know what the trouble is. I don't seem to do anything worth while but it just goes."

But if she had taken a complete survey of her activities she would have realized that keeping up a home, paying wages to Stena, supporting a frail mother who often needed the services of a physician, caring for Hope and sending her to school all those years had made inroads on the teacher's modest salary.

The Cunningham group wanted her to join them, and Ella was tempted, but another duty faced her and she had no mind for the trip while the possibility of Hope teaching in the college confronted her. For two years now to the joy of Ella's prideful heart Hope had been very successful in her work at Maple City. And with the position for a primary critic teacher opening in the training school Ella played every possible card that she could to get the place for Hope. Honest and frank as nature itself, for the first time in her life she found herself playing up to people. "That's what mothers will do for their offspring," she thought. "I see now how parents will stoop to almost anything for their own."

She cultivated Miss Jones assiduously although they had not a great deal in common. She was especially solicitous to President Watts. She went out of her way to talk to the board members. "I'm ashamed of myself," she admitted. "But I do so want my girl home that I'm not quite level-headed about it. And it isn't as though she couldn't do the work well. My alibi is that I'm doing the school as well as myself a favor."

Ella's deep desire was granted. Hope was elected and took her place, as modest as it was, on the faculty, catalogued as assistant supervisor, in reality handmaiden to Miss Jones.

"Now this year," Ella thought, "I'll save every penny for the grand tour. The stage is all set. Hope home here with Mother, Stena so faithful. Next spring I shall be with the pilgrims myself." It gave her a warm feeling of joyful anticipation. She read travel books by the dozen, by day figuratively crossed the Bridge of Sighs and at night dreamed of wandering through the Louvre.

But she did not carry out those dreams.

For Fate, that old woman of the loom, stepped into the picture in the spring and directed that the time had now arrived for Hope herself to meet Romance. And like many of the tricks the old woman plays, the meeting took place in a most unlooked-for way and when least expected.

To be specific it happened at ten minutes past two on an April afternoon in Room Twenty-one of the primary training department. To be sure it was also ten minutes past two in other departments of the college; but in Room Twenty-one of the training school it seemed most specifically ten minutes past two—that lazy, languorous time of day.

The windows were open to the warm breeze. An unsanitary-looking fly buzzed in and out, daring the students to catch him. Out on the campus little new leaves were pushing their way hurriedly through the brown buds of the maples. Chris burned weeds by the tennis court.

Nineteen girls, who were taking the primary course, lined the walls of Room Twenty-one, notebooks in hand. Some of them were majoring in primary training and minoring in other subjects. Some of them were minoring in primary work and majoring in getting engaged. But on this Wednesday afternoon at ten minutes past two, there was no way of dividing the gayly frivolous from the deadly earnest by their appearance. Due to the spring weather, all alike looked sleepy, dull, uninterested. A pudgy girl with thick glasses over protruding eyes made objectless marks on her notebook. A homely blonde, whom no discriminating gentleman would have preferred, was frankly nodding.

Across the room, near one of the open windows, sat Hope.

It would have taken twenty guesses to have picked out Hope as the assistant supervisor, for having attained the mature age of twenty-four, she still looked as sweet and young as a wood sprite. Her warm brown hair was combed back from her calm forehead and rolled into neat buns just back of each ear after the fashion of the moment. She was dressed in leaf green which gave her the appearance of being one with the elms and maples just outside the window.

If one could not have picked her out of the group from point of age or appearance, neither could one have recognized her through any manifestation of unusual interest in the work going on in the center of the room, for she looked as uninterested and bored as any of the students.

The children in the circle were playing games under the direction of a short, olive-skinned student; and no one could have accused the children, themselves, of being bored. With that wide-eyed interest in life in which the mere matter of weather has no part. they were entering into the oft-repeated plays with as much ardor as though participating in them for the first time.

At that particular moment a very immaculate little girl, whom one knew at a glance to be a specimen of the perfect female child, spoke: "William is not standing correctly." She said it definitely, didactically and critically.

William immediately straightened his spindling, overall-clad legs, and the perfect child looked about her for further opportunity of correction.

"In years to come," said Hope—of course, to herself—"she will be president of a woman's club or chairman of some reform league."

A health game was now well under way. William, of the temporary slouchy attitude and the permanent overall legs, took the center of the circle.

"Will you have a dish of oatmeal and cream?" he asked, and pointed to one of the expectant group.

"Yes, thank you," said the honored one.

"Will you have some fried potatoes?" He pointed to another.

"No, thank you."

"Will you have a dish of stewed prunes?"

"Yes, please."

Any rank outsider could have sensed the point.

It was as apparent as the pointer, himself, or the pointee. There was on in educational circles the first of the great reforms in eating—all the edibles which did not point the way to health were scorned. All the dainty morsels which were over-rich received the "thumbs down" of these little Romans. Their attitude was that if you ate fried potatoes you would be relegated to some region of the lost. If you ate oatmeal you would enter some Valhalla of bliss.

"Will you have a piece of pie?" William's active if soiled index finger veered to the perfect female child.

The p.f.c. shook her yellow curls and assumed a horror-stricken air of dramatic proportions.

"Oh—no, thank you." She threw into the answer a world of repugnance. And then, further realizing her own nobility of soul, she turned to the student teacher: "Miss Anderson . . . my mamma had pie this noon . . . raspberry pie . . . a big piece sat right by my plate . . . and I never touched it."

"Why, you little halfwit!" said Hope. (Oh, certainly to herself.) From which unuttered exclamation one may gather how very far afield had gone her regard for her own teachings this warm afternoon.

Sitting there in the midst of her chosen life work, Hope was admitting to herself a waning interest in it. And simultaneously with her digression she was mentally flaying herself with a bludgeon of self-criticism. As mystified as chagrined at the way her attention was slipping, she realized that for some unknown reason she felt at odds with her profession. She had always been wrapped up in it,—just like Aunt Ella. She wondered what Aunt Ella would say if she knew how this third year of her teaching was beginning to pall.

Too often recently she had been picturing herself down a vista of years in a future of training schools and lectures, dividing the fried potatoes from the oatmeal, the pie from the prunes—and the perspective was not so satisfying as she had once thought. It was something she felt would hurt Aunt Ella deeply to know, and the thought made her disgusted with her own attitude.

In the midst of her self-chastisement, and near the close of the children's health game, the door opened and the Head appeared. Not a head, but *the* Head,—Miss Hester Jones. If one wanted to be facetious, one might say that there was a hat upon the Head, for Miss Jones was hatted and gloved in the correct tailored way that one would expect Miss Jones to be, and being large and imposing, she carried about her person all the dignity and age which Hope, the assistant, failed to possess

Quite suddenly the atmosphere in Room Twenty-one changed. It was as though, upon opening the door, Miss Jones had inserted the cord of an imaginary electrical charger into an invisible socket. The occupants of the room came to life. The blonde leaned forward with a deep and vital interest in the health game. The fat girl with the thick glasses began writing unimportant words vigorously in her notebook. The fly disappeared into an outer sun-flooded world, as though there were no use trying to fool with a personality like Miss Jones's. Hope, the good lieutenant that she was, almost saluted her superior.

The Head crossed to her now, said a few low words of explanation to her, looked complacently at the keenly interested girls flanking the walls, stopped to say good-by to the participants of the game circle, and vanished into the sun-flooded world herself, although not by way of the window.

The figurative electric cord having been withdrawn from the socket, the occupants of the room slumped into their former state of lethargy. The homely blonde closed her eyes. The fat girl tucked her pencil into her blouse pocket. Hope returned to her own analytical soliloquy.

The circle game was changing now. They were about to perpetrate the classic known as "Chicken Little."

"Heavens!" said Hope (oh, most assuredly to herself). "If I'm ever in a large brick building with bars at the windows it will be from an overdose of Chicken Little."

"The sky is falling," said Chicken Little, in the person of William the conquered. "I will run and tell Henny-Penny." And the orgy of gossiping was on.

In the midst of the wild rumors which seemed to obsess Chicken Little there was a knock on the door of Twenty-one—a loud and vigorous knock, almost immodestly so, for one usually approached the model training school with something of timidity, silence, and veneration.

"I heard it with my ears. I saw it with my eyes. A piece of it fell on my tail," declared the newsmonger in the circle.

The girls all straightened up, cheered with the pleasant anticipation of having the monotony relieved, although it would probably prove to be nothing more exciting than a student or a parent. Hope rose, crossed the room, and opened the door, preparatory to slipping out. But she did not slip. It was not a student. One had grave doubts about its being a parent. A very tall, very well-groomed young man stood on the threshold.

"I beg your pardon," his voice boomed hollowly from the empty hall.

"You'd better," thought Hope critically.

"May I speak to you for a moment?" His voice was still far from weak.

"I will run and tell Turkey-Lurkey," threatened the tattle-tale in the circle.

Hope had time to say acridly (yes, indeed to herself), "All right . . . go on and tell," as she stepped out and closed the door.

The man looked at Hope, standing there, cool and aloof and questioning. "I'm sorry to bother you." He had a most engaging smile. "My name is Jones—Richard Jones—of the firm of Blake, Bartholomew, and Jones of Chicago. And while I'm here between trains, I'm trying to form a rather belated acquaintance with a cousin of mine."

"Oh!" Hope smiled then also. And that made two engaging smiles turned loose in the hall. "You're Miss Jones's cousin." She became gracious and friendly. "Miss Jones is the head of our department. But she's not here. She has just gone . . . starting over to the Maynard High School to give her lecture. She's been gone such a little while—she was here a few minutes ago—that I'm sure you could catch her. She takes the yellow street-car at the northeast corner of the campus."

"Yes?" Miss Hester Jones's cousin looked at the cleft in Hope's chin, and repeated, with certain slight variations, "I see . . . the northeast street-car at the corner of the yellow campus."

"You can take a short-cut," the owner of the chin declivity suggested.

"Yes?" said Mr. Jones vaguely, and added more definitely, "Oh, yes."

"You go down these first steps and turn to the left. Then you follow the walk past the Administration Building . . . Do you know where the Administration Building is?"

"No," said Mr. Jones, almost in despair. "Oh, no."

"It's the first building to the north. Then you take the curved walk and you will find the street-car at the end of it."

And while the consensus of opinion among the other members of the firm was that Mr. Richard Jones was far from dull, he seemed to have acquired a sudden impenetrable density.

In the intensity of her desire to do the gracious thing for the head of the department, Hope further volunteered: "I'll walk out to the steps and point it out to you." Which all goes to prove that stupidity occasionally has its place in the scheme of things.

They went out on the training-school steps, where the elm leaves budded and the bees droned and the April sunshine lay in little golden pools.

"The campus is gorgeous, now, isn't it?" the man said affably.

"Lovely," the girl agreed. "Now, there . . . around that walk . . . over there."

"It's a perfect day, isn't it?"

"Quite perfect. You've only a few minutes."

"Thank you so much. I hope taking you away from your class like this hasn't queered you in any way with your teacher."

"I," said Hope, a little coldly, *"am* the teacher."

"You? Do you mean to stand there and say. . . . Well, can you beat . . . ?"

"You'll have to hurry," said the teacher with finality. "Good day." And she went into the building and closed the huge door impressively.

As she stepped back into Twenty-one, her head very high, nineteen girls watched her keenly, thirty-eight adult eyes looked at her curiously.

"They ran into Foxy-Loxy's den and they never came out," accused the gossiper of the circle.

Several girls grinned openly, not to say suspiciously. The homely blonde tittered and nudged the owl-eyed fat girl in her well-cushioned ribs.

"Just for that," said Hope (oh, absolutely to herself), "you will pay . . . and pay . . . and pay . . ." Aloud, and quite distinctly, she said: "Observation class dismissed. You will each hand in on Thursday a well-written nine-hundred-word paper on The Relation of Games to a Child's Health." And knew, with an unholy glee when something like a dull moan issued from the audience, that she had nipped in the bud more than one canoe ride and stroll on the campus.

At four o'clock, preparing to leave her office, she pushed back the calendar on her desk, weighted down a bunch of lesson plans with a plaster cast of *The Laughing Child,* straightened the sepia copy of *The Gleaners,* and closed the desk. When she turned around Richard Jones of Blake, Batholomew, and Jones stood in the doorway.

"I missed her," he grinned cheerfully.

"I'm so sorry," said Hope, and added (oh, exclusively to Hope), "Oh, no, you're not so grieved."

"And now I'm stranded here until ten o'clock, and you're the only one in town I know."

Know! The nerve!

"Well," she suggested pleasantly, "the college library doesn't close until nine."

He was thoughtful. "And I never *have* read Fox's *Book of Martyrs* or *Saints' Rest,*" he admitted.

At that, Hope laughed aloud. And Dick Jones laughed too. And the plaster cast laughed hardest of all—diabolically—but behind their backs.

All of which is the long and circuitous sequence of events which led Hope to bring home to her Aunt Ella's a young man of whose existence she had not been aware at nine minutes past two that afternoon,—to bring him home solely from duty and out of courtesy to Miss Jones, she explained so many times to Ella, that this discriminating woman was forced to hide her tell-tale eyes from her foster daughter.

Ella was like a mother hen with a chick who has suddenly shown some new interest in life. It was the first time Hope in her more mature years had seemed to be thrown out of her calm poise at masculinity. And dragging him home as though responsible for him! While she helped Stena add a dainty dish or two to the dinner, she nursed her surprise and a certain sense of worry.

But during the dinner hour, Ella admitted grudgingly to herself that he was thoroughly likable. And it *was* something to know he was Miss Jones' cousin.

When he was leaving, he told Hope that he would stop again on his way back from his trip,— a promise that did not seem to antagonize her, Ella thought.

On Thursday it seemed nothing short of dishonest not to speak about him immediately to Miss Jones but he had asked her not to do so for the reason that he wanted to surprise her by dropping in at the college again in a few days. On Monday of the following week, whenever Hope heard a noisy approach in the hall, she grew slightly chilly and showed a tendency toward flushing at the cheek bones. But two days of the week went by, and he had not come back.

On Wednesday afternoon, as she went down the steps of the training school and rounded the building to the north, she nearly collided with him—the returning relative of the Head.

"Oh . . . !" She was genuinely distressed. "Didn't I tell you? I *thought* I did. Miss Jones goes over there *every* Wednesday afternoon," she explained earnestly.

"Does she?" Mr. Richard Jones was apparently torn between the intensity of his surprise and the depths of his mental pain.

"Every Wednesday," repeated Hope.

"I see . . . persistency . . . perseverance . . . stick-to-itiveness. It's in the blood."

To mitigate Mr. Jones's disappointment over the unintentional misunderstanding, Hope took him home again.

"Well, Stena," Ella said, upon glancing out of a window, "here comes our nice young man again. It isn't going to be *every* Wednesday, is it?"

CHAPTER XXIX

APRIL flung one more lovely week over the campus. On Wednesday afternoon Hope stood before her desk calendar and absent-mindedly drew two distinct circles around the two previous Wednesday dates. Then, with sudden alarm, she rubbed them out so vigorously that there were only smudgy holes left where the figures had been. When she looked up from the calendar, she saw Mr. Richard Jones standing in the doorway.

"My cousin . . . ?" He was beaming cheerfully. "Is she here?"

"You know she isn't," said Hope coldly.

"But you told me she went Wednesdays."

"This is Wednesday." There were icicles on the statement. "You know it is."

"Is it?" He walked over to the calendar and ran an investigating finger up the columns. "Why, so it is," he admitted amiably, and then asked curiously, "What made those two holes in your calendar?"

"Days that were wasted," said Hope evenly, "so wasted that I cut them out."

Quite suddenly, Richard Jones was not flippant. "They were not wasted." He was all seriousness. "They were delightful . . . so lovely that I came back to have one more of them before we have to take my cousin with us." And then, as quickly, he returned to his former lightness. "The year's at the spring . . . the horse at the curb . . . my face is all clean . . . your hair is all curled . . . God's in heaven . . . all's right with the world."

Hope had to laugh at that, and knew there was not a particle of use in trying to trace the various processes by which her mental equipment was assuring her that it was her duty to entertain him once more for the sake of Miss Jones, in spite of his flagrant fabrications.

So eliminating all analysis, and looking only at results, one might have seen the two, fifteen minutes later, driving through a woodsy road where the sun flecked the rubber-tire tracks through dancing shadows. The drive ended at the one college café, the Mellow Moon—the first of the many eating places which a generation later were to be found on every corner.

It was while they were dining that they heard a shrilly triumphant, "Miss Thompson . . . oh, Miss Thompson!"

"Somewhere a voice is calling," said Richard Jones, "tender and true."

The voice was the voice of the perfect female

child, and with its insistent decision and two forceful hands, she was dragging her parents to the table nearest the beloved teacher.

Hope spoke to the obedient parents, made a pedagogical-sounding remark to her adoring pupil, and then turned to discuss the critical question of dessert with Richard Jones.

"I'd love a piece of pie," she said wistfully, "but I can't have it."

"Can't? Why the 'can't'?"

"Because this energetic creature across from me"—she spoke very low—"watching my every movement, is the personification of all my work. She is the symbol of my career. I teach her to scorn fried potatoes and laud oatmeal . . . to eschew pie and chew prunes. I know that's an awfully low type of humor, but I couldn't help it. I ask you, then, could I sit here, under her eagle eye, and order pie . . . and let her see all my theories come tumbling down?"

Richard Jones grinned his interest.

"But if I ever leave . . ." she threatened.

Mr. Jones sat forward. "Yes? When you leave? You mean when you marry?"

"Every woman teacher who marries must leave the faculty," said Hope definitely. "There is a ruling to that effect. But it does not necessarily follow that, inversely, every one who leaves, has married. As I was saying . . ." She was a little confused. "Oh, yes . . . if I ever leave, I shall do just that . . . recklessly, before them all . . . the student teachers . . . your cousin, the Head . . . the perfect female child . . . all of them. I shall order the richest pie I can get . . . and eat it in their presence. It would be symbolic. It would be a gesture of freedom. It would be signing an emancipation proclamation. It would be snapping my fingers in the faces of the gods."

The little student waitress came up for the order.

"Prunes," said Hope to her resignedly, "stewed prunes."

It was when Richard Jones was leaving Ella Bishop's home in the evening that he quite brazenly came out with the declaration that he wanted to dine with Hope again the following Wednesday. And Hope, with one fleeting assurance to herself that there was no more comforting bit of philosophy than that one might as well be hung for a sheep as a lamb, said she would expect him.

On Monday, May took the nice spring weather by the hand, and the two fled precipitately, leaving behind them cold, rainy, disagreeable weather.

And then on Tuesday, the Head came into Hope's office. "This terrible rain!" she began in her ponderous way. "I'm glad I'm all through with the Maynard lectures."

Hope's heart missed a beat. So Miss Jones was through with her Wednesday trips. The perfect tête-à-têtes would cease. So she might as well speak of him now.

"A young man cousin of yours . . ." she had to busy herself among her papers to hide the agitation of her face, "was here looking for you."

"My cousin? Well . . . I haven't seen him since he was in his teens. How time does fly. And to think he's going to be married,—to a girl named Daphne Dunham. Isn't that euphonious?"

Hope's heart crashed head-on against the stone wall of the news. But her mind was saying stanchly: "People have more than one cousin. No doubt she has a dozen."

But Miss Jones was going placidly on. "He is the only cousin I have, and I do hope he is getting a lovely girl. He's a dear boy . . . but something of a philanderer, they tell me. Now that he's to be married, though, I'm sure he'll settle down."

Hope's heart seemed scarcely able to move in the midst of its wreckage. All that it could think was that to-morrow was Wednesday,—the day that Richard Jones was to come again.

Then her mind began to take charge of the situation.

"You've been taking your dinners at the Mellow Moon, haven't you, Miss Jones?"

"Yes, excepting of course those evenings I've been at Maynard. Why?"

"Oh, I just wondered. I'm dining there to-morrow night with a guest. I thought perhaps you'd join us."

Miss Jones thanked her, said not to wait if she was not there by six-thirty. And the day's work had begun.

All the rest of the day and Wednesday morning it rained. And all Wednesday Hope went doggedly about her work.

In the late afternoon, swathed in a brown rain-coat, with her dark hair tucked under a cap, she was splashing through the damp, dripping campus toward home.

With the swishing sound of a water-soaked raincoat, some one was coming rapidly behind her. She stepped aside, but a masculine hand closed over her own hand that held the umbrella.

"My cousin . . . ?" He had the nerve to laugh at that—this modern Claudius who could smile and smile and be the villain still.

"Your cousin . . ." She forced herself to laugh too. "Your cousin has gone to the county commissioners to report your weakening men-tality."

There was a blazing fire in the grate at Aunt Ella's when they arrived. Hope left the villain standing in front of it, looking after her, when she mounted the stairs to dress. She wished he hadn't looked like that—clean-cut and attractive—standing there so easily in front of the fire.

In her room she put on a brown dress, decided she looked ghastly, and changed it for a crimson one. When she came down, the two made their way under the dripping elms, over the slippery walks to the Mellow Moon. Two students, the homely blonde and the fat girl with glasses, smelling romance, left their seats in the far end of the room and came to take places at the next table.

"Miss Thompson . . . oh, Miss Thompson," broke forth an adoring sound.

"Ha!" said Richard Jones. "There's the voice that breathed o'er Eden."

"Why don't they ever eat at home?" commented the object of the adoration, irritably, as the perfect female child pulled her pliant parents to the other adjoining table.

The vacant chair turned against their own table seemed to eye Hope like a silent accuser. Miss Jones had said not to wait if she had not arrived at six-thirty. So the two ordered, ate and conversed—the last activity being somewhat handicapped by the close proximity of many ears. Hope was more nervous than she had ever been in her life.

And then she saw Miss Jones come in.

"Look, Mr. Jones," she said in a small voice that sounded flat and unnatural.

"At the what?"

"Don't you see her?"

"Which 'her'?"

"Your cousin . . . over there by the door."

"Oh, is my cousin over there? I thought you said she went every Wednesday."

"She did . . . but she's finished."

"Then so am I. Listen, Hope Thompson. There's something I want to explain to you before she comes."

"Oh, don't try to explain." She was looking at the heavy figure of the Head, who had stopped to speak to Professor Cunningham. "I know all about it."

"I should have told you." He was all seriousness. "I've just let things drift carelessly along . . . and happily . . . from week to week. But you won't let it make any difference with us, will you?"

Any difference! Hope smiled. She was thinking that Napoleon might have asked it of Josephine when he divorced her.

When Richard Jones saw the tremulous smile that was meant to be cheerful, he said quite savagely: "I'm all kinds of a cad to let you hear it from some one else. Who told you?"

"Miss Jones . . . your cousin. She said Miss

Dunham was a lovely girl." Miss Jones was now talking to the football coach and his wife, half-way down the room. "And I congratulate you."

"What for? Who's lovely?"

"Miss Daphne Dunham . . . your fiancée."

"My what?"

"Fiancée." And then, quite didactically, she explained: "The girl you're engaged to."

"Good lord." He was gazing in deep amazement toward the chatting group. "I'm not engaged to anybody . . . Daffy-down-dilly, or any one else . . . not for a few minutes yet anyway. I don't know where you got that, but it's immaterial just now. Listen, Hope, listen closely." He leaned nearer to her across the college café table. "I'm not the Head's cousin . . . nor her uncle . . . nor her grandfather. I never saw her before and I don't care a tinker's dam if I never see her again. I never heard of her before the day you first talked to me. I'm terribly sorry to tell you this here . . . and now. Can you hear me? These two human phonographs over here are recording it all."

The blonde girl and the fat one with glasses scarcely moved a spoon, so anxious were they to catch the conversation.

"You mean you haven't been her cousin?"

"Not any of the time . . . not even Wednesdays." He grinned.

235

"But you said you were."

"Oh, no, I didn't. You came out in the hall looking as sweet as a peach and as cold as a peach ice. I said: 'My name is Jones and I'm looking up my cousin.' And you said, 'Oh, you're Miss Jones's cousin'; and thawed out and acted cordial. My cousin is a little freshman. Her name is Bartholomew—Mary Bartholomew. But when you insisted that Miss Jones was my cousin . . . even though the woods are full of Joneses . . . and looked at me like that . . ."

"Don't be talking about it. She's coming this way."

"Yes . . . I'm going to talk about it. I'm going to be talking about it after she gets here, if you won't listen now. Would you have gone out to dinner with me if you had known I wasn't the Head's cousin?"

"Most certainly not."

"Don't you see . . . I had to? There was nothing else to do. The minute I saw you I knew you were the girl for me."

The girl-for-him gasped.

"I love you . . . and I want you to marry me and leave school. You'd have to, you know. You said there was a ruling."

Miss Jones came up. There were introductions.

The little student waitress came up too.

"Go right on and order," said the Head in her supervising way, "while I look over the dinner card."

"Prunes and cream, Miss Thompson?" asked the little waitress familiarly.

Like needles to two magnets, Hope's eyes turned to the eyes of Richard Jones. The eyes of Richard Jones were twinkling . . . and then the twinkling changed to something less mischievous.

"Or pie, Hope?" He asked it gently—so gently that, instead of a prosaic item on the menu, it sounded like the first few lines of an old love poem.

Hope looked across the table china at the impostor. Over at the next table the homely blonde and the owl-eyed fat girl strained their aural organs to catch every word. Across the other aisle the perfect female child bent worshiping eyes upon her adored teacher.

Then—quite deliberately Hope made the gesture. Quite definitely she signed the proclamation. Quite distinctly she snapped her fingers in the faces of the gods. For even as she spoke to the little waitress she was smiling across the china toward the junior member of Blake, Bartholomew, and Jones.

"Pie . . . " she ordered recklessly, "the

chocolate pie with the whipped cream and marsh-
mallow icing." And, instead of a prosaic item on
the menu, it sounded like the rest of the lines of
the old love poem.

CHAPTER XXX

SO Hope was to be married, and Ella knew the joy of witnessing another's happiness. Europe? She had no thought for it now—the Bridge of Sighs was but a plank across a stream, the Louvre might have been filled with circus posters, for all she cared.

She began buying things for Hope,—cloth for sheets one day, bath towels another. Good sense told her that she was spending more money than she should have done. "No, you keep your own money, Hope. It will come in handy. Don't forget this is probably the last thing of the kind I shall ever do for you."

So they shopped together, and Ella knew she was having as much excitement out of the expeditions as Hope. "I'm not so generous," she told herself honestly. "I'm really rather selfish, getting as I do such joy out of buying the pretty things."

There was a blue serge suit to be made by the local tailor,—a long skirt stiffened with buckram and a short stiff jacket with large banjo-shaped sleeves. There were fourteen yards of soft green crêpe de Chine to be purchased and ten yards of taffeta for the underdress. Then the wedding dress itself of soft white with dozens of yards of narrow lace to be used on the skirt which was ruffled to the waist. All summer Ella forgot pedagogy in her vicarious motherhood. All summer she purchased and planned and sewed. Her mother tried to help, but she muddled the patterns, sewed in the wrong sleeve, and Ella or Hope or Stena had to rip out and do it all over.

And sometimes in the summer as Ella worked, she thought of the dress upstairs in a chest,—the shimmering white dress with the pink rosebuds and the blue forget-me-nots in silken relief,— which had no hem, and into which the sleeves had never been sewed. But more often she thought only of Hope and the happiness that was hers.

Dick came twice during the summer and Ella, living the romance of the two young people, felt romantic too.

The wedding was in October—at the home. Ella wanted a church wedding with bridesmaids and the new pipe-organ playing and ushers from Hope's college classmates, but in that particular thing Hope seemed to be more sensible than Ella. "Oh, Aunt Ella,—*no*. Think of the expense and the fuss,—and the sort of—oh, I don't know, the *straining*."

Ella gave in. "I suppose you're right. But it's only once in a lifetime." In her heart she knew

240

that she was wanting a wedding so lovely that it would take the place of two,—Hope's own and the wedding that had never been.

So it was planned to be small and in the home. At that it turned out that Ella could not draw the line for guests. Over and over she sat with a paper and pencil and tried to eliminate all her friends to some semblance of a crowd of medium size. Faculty members, townspeople, janitors, students who had been in Hope's classes— In despair she gave up, and Hope took the responsibility of choosing a few of the ones closest to her.

"But, Hope—they're all my friends."

Old lady Bishop nodded over her quilt-block. "Yes . . . Ella . . . her friends . . . she was always friendly . . . like Pa . . . I don't know . . ." Her voice trailed off uncertainly.

So Richard Jones came for his bride and they were married on an October day with the campus trees green and gold and scarlet, with the haze of the Indian summer clinging to far horizons like the ghostly white smoke of long-dead campfires. Professor Wick, who had been an ordained minister, performed the ceremony, his new suit surprisingly immaculate and his bushy whiskers trimmed to an almost immodest closeness. President and Mrs. Watts were there, and Professor and Mrs. Cunningham and the Schroeders and the Fondas and the Wittinglys. Miss Jones was there taking all the credit for the match, and Miss Boggs, singing "Oh, Promise Me" with a bit of a smirk for having been chosen over Miss Honeycutt, and Chris and Hannah Jensen, a little stiff in their new clothes. Stena in a hardanger apron bossed the Minerva society sisters who served the refreshments, and old Mrs. Bishop came outside her bedroom door for the ceremony but vanished afterward like a little old frightened doe.

And then the young people were gone in a merry shower of rice and good wishes, and the guests had departed, and Ella and Stena and old Mrs. Bishop were alone. Life seemed suddenly to slump for Ella, and to have no meaning.

All winter only the thought of her postponed trip abroad gave her any renewal of keen interest. With the expense of the wedding over, she was saving every cent for the coming summer's outing.

Her one worry was her mother. She seemed more frail and gentle, and what worried Ella more than her apparent weakness, she possessed a vague dreaminess, at times a fairly definite unconcern over what went on about her. So seldom now did she inquire for college news, spoke more and more often of the past. Once or twice she seemed a little sly to Ella about her small activities of the day. All Ella could ever get from her in answer to the question of how she felt, was that she was tired, and maybe her head hurt a little.

If Ella could have known the mental wanderings of the gentle old soul, she would have been filled with an agonizing sympathy. For many afternoons when Ella was in school and Stena upstairs in her room, old Mrs. Bishop stole into her bedroom, closed the door and lived in a little world of her own.

With trembling old hands she would take from its wrappings in her closet the light blue silk dress of her girlhood, slip it over her head and pat it into place lovingly. Then she would open her lowest bureau drawer and bring forth a white lace scarf of dainty weave. This she would drape laboriously around her shoulders with stiffened arms and fasten with a hair brooch.

To the onlooker the effect would have been ludicrous: the incongruity of the thin old neck and wrinkled face rising above the low-cut lustrous silk gown that had been made to enfold a winsome maiden. But to old Mrs. Bishop the picture must have seemed eminently satisfying. She would gather the gleaming folds in her little knotted blue-veined hands and walk about the room with slow mincing steps.

Then she would sit by the window in her dainty old dress and try to remember. It gave her a feeling of stability, a connection with life which she did not always seem to have. She could not explain to her daughter. Ella would not know what she meant, for no one could understand. But sitting there alone in the soft old dress she seemed to be able to leave her body. For a little while she would wait, and then the strange thing would happen. She would rise out of her physical self and join her young husband and the friends of her youth. All the magic of health she could feel,—all the joy of living. She could look back at herself sitting there so old and tired in the chair and laugh at herself. She could talk with the one she loved, and move about in a world peopled with all her friends of the early days. It was a lovely experience. She waited each day for the time to come—that witching hour—grew to long impatiently for it, was childishly cross when Saturday and Sunday, with people about, kept her from her rendezvous.

Some uncanny sense of time gave her the cue to return to normalcy. "It's time to come back," some unseen thing would tell her. Then she would return to meet her tired body, become merged with that feeble old person who was herself. She wanted no one to know about it, was stealthily careful to move about quietly as she put the loved things away.

Then she would emerge from her bedroom, fatigued in mind and body.

"Did you have a goot rest?" Stena would ask.

"Very nice," old lady Bishop would answer with averted eyes.

By spring, when her mother seemed no worse, Ella began making definite arrangements for the trip which was to mean so much to her. Sometimes looking at the gentle little woman whose life was so confined, her heart smote her. "If it were not for you, Stena, I wouldn't think of going," she would say. "Are you sure she will be all right?"

"S'e vill be no better an' no vorse dan if you are here. I'll vash her an' iron her an' cook her and s'e vill be no different. You go an' forget dat mamma."

The last of March the others who were to go had settled definitely on the tour. Professor and Mrs. Schroeder, Professor and Mrs. Wittingly and Miss Hunter comprised the group. It was a congenial crowd and in the decision of joining them that Friday Ella felt a thrill of pleasure permeate her whole being. All afternoon her thoughts had wings as active as those of the pigeons in the tower.

It was rather late when she left her classroom. The March wind blew her long skirts about her all the way home. Fine particles of dust seemed permeating her eyes and nose. A snow fence across one corner of the campus had stopped a

low brown pile of loam and sand and subsoil,—
spring's dust blizzard with dirt for drifts.

When she went into the house Stena was set-
ting the table. The dining-room looked cozy
and inviting after the encounter with the distasteful elements.

"Where's Mother?" she asked.

"S'e hasn't come out of her room," Stena said.
"Not since her nap."

Ella felt a vague uncomfortableness even
then; so much so that without removing her
things she went at once to her mother's room.

Over in the big chair by the window she sat,—
dressed in the blue silk dress she had saved from
her bridal things. She was laughing softly and
speaking to some one. Ella looked about hastily.
Her mother was talking to some one not there.

"Mother!" Ella's heart contracted in a spasm
of deep dread, fear of some unknown terror, the
thing she had vaguely suspected the last few
weeks.

But old lady Bishop only laughed vacantly into
the shadows. She had forgotten how to come
back.

CHAPTER XXXI

THIS was a new trouble—a real one—one of those that swoop down with dark smothering wings and engulf one in the blackness of despair. Ella had their own physician in, then a mental specialist out from Chicago. There was, of course, nothing to do but to care for the frail little body left behind when the mind went on its long journey into the land of shadows.

She was gentle, sweet, docile,—wanted only to move about her room with its familiar objects. Ella tried taking her out into the other rooms with the thought that the change might brighten the mental outlook. But at the doorway of her bedroom, she clung with her bird-like little hands to the casing, whimpered like a child, and looking up at Ella, shook her head with a pitifully frightened, "No, no."

When Ella, scarcely seeing for the tears, led her back to the haven of her room, the old lady sat happily down in her chair by the window and began rocking and humming a cracked and weird little air that had no melody.

Ella gave up her trip. To Stena's scolding she said, "No, I can't, Stena—not now."

"But s'e doesn't care. S'e wouldn't *know*,—and I take shust the same care as if you vas here."

"Yes, I know that, Stena. That part would be perfectly all right. I'd trust you every minute. It's just that I have to be here, too. She might . . . Stena, she *might* suddenly get all right. What if I wouldn't be here? What if she got all right for just a little while,—and then . . . wasn't again? Don't you see,—I *must* be here."

"Vell, I suppose so. But you plan and safe your money . . . and den a big disappointment . . . it seem not right."

Ella turned away. "I'm not a child. I've had disappointments before."

Eventually she settled down to her work with renewed energy. Her mother's condition would never be changed, the doctors told her, so there was no use to forego any of the many activities outside her classroom work. Her mother's little body was well cared for by the faithful Stena who kept her clothed in immaculate aprons and white lace caps for which she crocheted endless trimmings. Other than that the old lady was no care, had no desire but to sit and rock and sort her colored quilt-blocks and hum her weird and cracked little song that had no melody.

Ella was in her late forties now, but so gradually that she could not have told how it came about, she found herself active socially with girls many years younger. Going to the same social functions, belonging to the same organizations whose personnel from year to year remained women of about the same age, she gradually slipped back at intervals to younger groups. No one ever gave her age a thought. Wit and humor and lively spirits are of no age,—and a woman who holds them all with no conscious effort is ageless. The Minerva literary society, and an English club,—the P. E. O. sisterhood, Altrusa and D. A. R. all were her fields of activity.

Hope came to visit one summer in 1909, sweet and matronly and rather more modish than in her teaching days. Two years later in the early spring she came home again, and Ella had a new concern—the coming of Hope's child. Sam Peters came over one March evening just at dusk to tell Ella if she ever needed help—in the night or any time—not to hesitate to call him.

It was the last of March when Hope was taken sick. There was a wild wind in the night. How queer, thought Ella, dressing hurriedly. A wild wind in the night! It tore around the house with malignant fury. Wild winds and birth,—they seemed always to go together. With amazing clarity the night of Hope's birth came back. She even remembered the street lamps going out and the blackness of the night, so that involuntarily she hurried over to the window and looked out. Electric lights at the intersections of the streets swung crazily on their long wires but held their glow. And now there was a telephone with which to summon aid—no need for Hannah either, with the trained nurse ready to come at the call.

Like a soldier on duty, she summoned the nurse and the doctor, comforted Hope, called Stena to make a fire in the kitchen range, went into her mother's room to see that she was covered and sleeping. The old lady slept like a child, unaware that a new life was coming, equally unaware that an old life was ebbing,—slept and dreamed little queer dreams and smiled in her sleep.

Ella thought she could not stand the strain of the long night and the day that followed. With sympathetic nerve tension, she lived the hours with Hope. That other time it had not touched her deeply. Great bitterness had so mingled with whatever sympathy she might have possessed that the one counteracted the other. But this was Hope,—like her own flesh and blood.

Dick arrived soon after the noon hour,—in a noisy new automobile, with chain drive and carbon lights.

Ella did not go to her classes. It was one of the few times in her life in which she put anything ahead of her school work. The nurse moved quietly up and down stairs. The doctor came, went away, came again. Stena went about her homely duties on exaggerated tiptoe and with guttural whisperings. Dick would not come down to eat. Ella sat by the kitchen range, all her heart upstairs with her foster daughter, and thought of many things. Old Mrs. Bishop, combed and immaculately clean in her white apron and lace cap, rocked in her room and hummed a cracked and weird little song with no meaning.

It was not until late afternoon that a high shrill wail came from above. It rang out so suddenly in the hushed atmosphere which had just preceded it that it brought Ella from her chair to her feet.

"There!" shouted Stena, and sat down limply with her gingham apron thrown over her head and burst into tears.

The baby was a girl, plump, healthy, well-formed. Ella moved in a daze as one thinking he is living over something that has happened precisely the same way before. All her thought was for Hope. Crazily, she kept feeling a superstitious fear that the whole thing would repeat itself,—that Hope would come out from a coma, flutter the lids over her blue eyes,—die. She stood transfixed with the thought, could not move for the paralyzing fear.

"Is she . . . ? How . . . ?" She could not say the words for the dryness of her throat.

"She's going to be all right." The nurse was cheerful. In the clutches of her paroxysm of fear, Ella imagined too cheerful.

But Hope was to be all right. Life to Ella swung back then to a normal thing of gratitude, work and interest in her fellowman.

Dick left in a few days, to come again as soon as possible. Ella went back to school. The house took on a routine which revolved about the new-comer. Once Ella took the little thing in its dainty blankets in to her mother's room.

"See, Mother." She held the blue and white covering back from the round red face.

The old lady stopped rocking and bent forward to look inquiringly at the wee mite. "A little baby!" She spoke so naturally that the tears sprang to Ella's eyes.

Why, she seemed all right! *Oh, Mother, hold on to it,—hold on to your understanding.*

"Yes, Mother. Isn't she cunning?"

"*I* had a baby once," she said proudly.

Oh, yes, Mother, try to remember that I am your baby.

Then, less sure, she stared at Ella. "Did I . . . didn't . . . I have a baby . . . once?"

And while Ella, tear-dimmed, could only nod,

she started rocking and humming a cracked and weird little song that had no melody.

At the end of the month, Dick came for Hope, a pretty matronly Hope, all anxiety for the welfare of the bundle she would let no one else carry. Gretchen, she called the baby. "Gretchen Jones. I like the quaintness of it," she explained.

"Well, Aunt Ella,—once more I have to thank you for seeing me through." She was saying good-by, now. "Do you suppose I'll ever, *ever* be able to repay you for all your kindnesses to me all my life?"

"Oh, that's all right, dearie." Ella was too tender at the parting to talk.

"I know,—when you're an old, old lady you can come and live with us. Can't she, Dick?"

"Sure, she can. That *will* be a way to repay her. Sure."

"You're nice children, and I thank you," said Ella Bishop. But she knew that not when she was an old lady, or ever, must she thrust herself into the privacy of this little family.

CHAPTER XXXII

FOR nine years, old Mrs. Bishop rocked in her room, sorted her colored quilt-blocks and sang the cracked and weird little song that had no melody.

There were those who said Ella's devotion was Quixotic, that a long desired trip abroad would have harmed no one, the old lady least of all, that Stena's attachment to the invalid was so strong as to be marked, and under those circumstances Ella was free to go any summer that she wished. But she refused to go. "She might get sick . . . and there's just a possibility she could get all right for a little while—she almost did, once—and want me. If I were on the other side of the ocean I couldn't get here."

But she continued her many activities in the community. Mrs. Bishop did not miss her, and more than ever Ella was the mainspring of the machinery of a half-dozen organizations,—some professional, others merely social. The college itself was mother to a host of organizations,—each department fostering its kind, while some of general character were broader in scope. Among the popular ones was the *Schillerverein* sponsored by

254

Professor Schroeder. He who entered its portals must forget the English language, express himself only in German, no matter in what depths of unintelligible jargon he might laughingly flounder. German songs, German speech, German refreshments,—the members of *Schillerverein* steeped themselves in a Germanic atmosphere.

In these educational circles with which she was so closely identified all these years, Ella had seen many new ideas and methods come to light, some to stay definitely, some to disappear like the dew of the morning. She had seen the rise and fall of the Pollard method and the Speer method and a dozen others. Vocational instruction now was emphasized everywhere. For a time it looked as though it was to be everything. "They're swinging the pendulum too far the other way," she scolded. "To make a wobbly horse-radish grater is now considered of far more importance than the king's English."

School and home—home and school—she moved energetically between the two, never forgetting one for the other.

In those nine years Hope made three or four visits home, bringing her little daughter,—a lovely dark-eyed child with creamy-satin skin of almost Spanish-like beauty. She came when the child was two and four and six. Life was pleasant for Hope with a devoted husband, her beauti-

ful child, and a good income. And then life was
no longer pleasant. The war hounds were un-
leashed, and their far-off frightful barking heard
in the tiniest village of every state.

This threatening clamor sounded even more
harsh in its contrast to the hitherto peaceful life
of the college. War clouds hanging above the
campus became of far more consequence than the
fluffy masses of haze floating across the blue
which Professor Fonda had always thought so
important.

Attendance at *Schillerverein* fell off from forty
to twenty,—to a half dozen. Few wanted to be
associated with so Germanic a club. On a certain
Friday night, Professor Schroeder waited an hour
for a possible attendant, took the basket of
kaffee-kuchen which Mrs. Schroeder had sent,
turned out the lights, and walked slowly down
through the campus,—like an old man.

Hope came home the next year, a frightened
tearful Hope, with little seven-year-old Gretchen
who could not understand why it was anything but
grand for Daddy to have a uniform and high
leather puttees and to get a long ride on a big
ship.

One after another the college boys left. The
draft was on. Recitation rooms thinned out, took
on a feminine appearance. When Professor
James of the English department left, Ella took

over his classes. She plunged into Red Cross work, collected food, clothing and funds. She taught conscientiously all day, remembering always that Hope would be waiting to see her at the Red Cross headquarters to tell her the latest news. And so, Ella Bishop, with no husband of her own to follow in tortured imaginings, must then be as torn in her emotions as the others.

Professor Schroeder's classes fell away to almost a negligible attendance. There had grown up on the campus a vague spirit of hostility toward him,—a tendency to refer to him as the Hun. The courses on Faust and Schiller were dropped.

Sometimes Ella ran into him on the campus, walking along under the elms that reminded him of his linden trees. Unless with Professor Fonda, he walked a great deal by himself these days, his huge shoulders drooping, his former long stride slackened to a slower pace. No longer did he greet her with his jovial "Hail, blooming youth." Always he stopped almost timidly to see whether he was to be received warmly or with the cool nodding of an averted head. His deep-set eyes looked hurt, tragic.

To Ella he presented a pitiful result of a foolish and unreasoning hostility. Sensing her sympathetic understanding he sometimes sought her out as though he wanted to talk to one with less animosity than the others. Miss Bishop seemed always a mother confessor to the people with whom she came in contact. In her presence they dispensed with all subterfuges, became themselves.

"How can I deny loving my fatherland?" he would break out. "Cannot they believe that I love my America more?" And sometimes shaking his leonine mane sadly: "Music and literature—they have no nationality. Wagner . . . Goethe . . . Schiller . . . what have they to do with it?"

Watching him go down the campus walk, Ella felt a sisterly tenderness toward him, realized that a patriotism which knew no reasoning at the moment was crucifying good old George Schroeder.

Dick came back from the wars wounded, and it seemed for a time after his release, so long was it before he felt strong, that instead of Ella making her home with the young people as they had suggested, they would be living at the old house on Adams Street.

But the physical wound cleared, if not the memory of the experience, and Dick and Hope and little Gretchen, nine now, were back in their own home.

The Red Cross shop was closed. Restrictions on food were lifted. A memorial was built on the campus to the boys who never came back,—a campanile with its clock faces looking toward the four winds of the world and its chimes playing every hour. Professor Schroeder's department was consolidated with the department of Romance Languages. The war was over,—all but the hideous after-effects which could never be called "over" while the generation lived.

Life went on in the old home much as before. Stena washed and ironed and cooked and cleaned, put a fresh tissue-paper flower under the picture of the pale young man every spring, and took care of the little old lady who was like a fragile China doll.

Ella took the supper tray into her mother every evening and stayed to see that she was happy and comfortable. On an evening now in May, with the tulip buds showing a gleam of color through green slits, and the spirea bushes bursting into white foam, she took the tray to her mother's bedroom, placing it on the walnut bureau until she could arrange the little table for her.

Old Mrs. Bishop sat in her chair by the window, her head on a stand in the crook of her arm like a child, sound asleep. Ella pulled up the tea-table and then bent to waken her, raising her head gently so as not to startle her.

But old Mrs. Bishop would not waken.

Ella stared for a moment at the dainty face, waxen-white under its snowy lace cap.

259

She was gone, smiling faintly, gone to seek her lost mind in the shadows.

Ella stooped and picked up the fragile little body in her own strong arms and sat down in the old rocking chair for a few moments before she called Stena. And as she rocked, she wept wildly, deep sobs shook her, and some of the tears were for all the sorrows that she had been compelled to bear in her life, and some were for the long years in which she had not known a real mother, but some of them were merely for the loss of the cracked and weird little song that had no melody.

CHAPTER XXXIII

AFTER her mother's death, Ella thought she ought not to keep Stena. But Stena was as frightened over being turned out as old Mrs. Bishop had ever been.

"I'm sisty-two," she said, "and dat's too old to fin' a new place. I safe my money—vy can't I keep my room and shust stay vidout vages?"

It touched Ella that Stena did not want to leave. And sometimes she had been so impatient about her. But Ella Bishop always paid her obligations, so they settled on a new scale of wages and Stena stayed on.

The longed-for European trip could not be taken for awhile after the war, and when conditions had cleared and groups of the faculty were turning their faces toward the old world once more, Ella had the one severe illness of her otherwise healthy life, which made such inroads into her savings, that she put aside the dream as unfeasible until she had caught up with her finances.

In coming back from her illness, she lived through that experience which comes only to humans who have gone into the Valley a little way and returned to the sunlight. With the memory of the shadows still fresh within her, the world took on new coloring, sweeter sounds, more fragrant odors. Never had she known tulips so brilliant, robins' songs so lovely, lilacs so sweet-scented. It was as though the misty shadows which for a day or two hung about her, in lifting, had cleansed eyes and ears and nostrils until they functioned with renewed acuteness.

The school was a huge unwieldy thing now. Ella sometimes laughed to herself to think of those old days when the faculty was a big family, holding reading circle meetings, or having a picnic together, with a half-dozen baskets containing the refreshments. A faculty family picnic now, for sheer size would have looked like the county fair, a faculty reading circle in its circumference would have encircled the athletic field. She missed the old familiar camaraderie at times, clung a little to the Wattses and the Wittinglys, the Fondas and the Schroeders. New people came in almost every year and occasionally an old familiar face dropped out. Professor Wick and Professor Carter died,—not long afterward, Professor Cunningham. Sometimes Ella thought of sandy-haired Professor O'Neil dismissed for his monkey talk and his daring statements about a new social order and wondered whether he would now be considered even slightly radical.

Old Central was now carrying out its name in

truth, for it was almost in the exact center of the great sweep of buildings which rose on all sides. It looked worn and shriveled, and, covered with heavy ivy vines as it was, gave the appearance of a shrunken old woman peering out from under her green shawl. Ella had moved from her old classroom into Corcoran Hall. It had given her a queer feeling to leave the inner office in the tower room and the pigeons with their eternal "coo coo," "although when you stop to think of it," she had admitted, "these present ones are about forty generations removed from their ancestors I first knew."

Surveying the school as one disinterested, she could see a hundred changes. "For better or for worse?" she asked herself. "More often better," she acknowledged, "sometimes not so good."

Before the turn of the century a new element had crept into the college,—a national sorority. Nine girls, by some secret process of selection, having been given a charter, had become Kappa Kappa Gammas, rented the old Banker Van Ness home and proceeded to establish themselves as Midwestern's social *élite*. Another had followed and another,—and others. Kites, keys, crescents, anchors, arrows, all jewel-set, sparkled now above the hearts of Midwestern's fair ladies,—and triangles, shields, scimitars, serpents, and swords, all flashed now on the lapels of Midwestern's brave men. Dinner dresses and tuxedos, evening gowns and spike-tails had followed in their wake until now there was not a corn-fed lass who did not have a dress which was held on by a mere shoulder strap,—not a corn-fed boy but knew, if he did not own a full-dress, where one could be most cheaply rented.

"Poor old Minerva society," Ella would say, "once 'the four hundred' of the campus!" and would add with a dry bit of sarcasm, "Just to think that we were merely studious and fun-loving and literary—no Minerva sweethearts or queens chosen for their shapely legs or general kissableness!"

Dancing, instead of being the misdemeanor it once had been, was now a part of the social fabric of the school. Student pressure and changing public opinion had removed the bar. Where it had once been a reproach to mention the pastime, now faculty members took their turn as patrons and patronesses of the classes and fraternities sponsoring it. Where it had once been thought the height of daring to slip away to Maynard and dance, now it was an unheard-of procedure. Once a sin, now a social virtue. "O the tempora of the times. O the modes of the customs," Ella sometimes flippantly juggled the words.

Miss Bishop was a favorite chaperon. "The first hundred years I enjoyed it," she confided to

Sam Peters. "But the same music, flowers, young people, the second hundred it gets to be something of a nuisance. I've been the fifth one so many times . . . have read the item so repeatedly: '. . . chaperoned by Professor and Mrs. Hess, Professor and Mrs. Alderslot and Miss Ella Bishop,' that when prizes are given for the campus's best running fifth wheel, I'll get it."

In truth, there was no faculty member so called upon for a thousand things by the student body as Ella,—to chaperon, advise about decorations and refreshments, making over dresses and having tonsils removed—to aid in writing theses and wording applications for jobs—a confidante for those financially embarrassed and to lovelorn swains.

And now every year a student or two found shelter under her own roof. Every year she gave a little financial aid to some one of them who otherwise could not have finished.

She had a sly way of finding out things she wanted to know. "You will hand in a five-hundred-word article on 'My Ambitions.'" Or "For Monday, a brief paper on 'Characteristics I Admire.'" All these she perused herself. No hired reader of human type articles for Miss Bishop.

Although particular about the mechanics, she admitted to herself that she really cared more for the contents than the commas, gave far more thought to the spirit than the spacing. More than one young chap revealing in an assignment his tendencies to a display of temper quite surprisingly found himself in Miss Bishop's office freely discussing self-control with her. Many a young girl admitting in an English paper envy of her better-dressed classmates found herself later in that room laughing with Miss Bishop over the story of the prolonged life of the old Scotch plaid dresses and emerging with a clarified outlook on the subject of clothes.

President Watts was now seventy-seven, his long shambling legs moving a little more slowly, but his active mind as keen as ever. Ella wondered sometimes whether it would be possible for other figures so picturesque to come after these: Wick, Carter, Cunningham, Wittingly, Schroeder, Fonda,—the ones from the old days. It never occurred to her to add another picturesque figure: Miss Bishop.

And then Professor Fonda died, as though having looked long upon the heavens he had suddenly become one with the moon and the clouds and the Milky Way. After his death, Ella's heart went out to old Professor Schroeder who seemed more lost than ever without his comrade. Once at Commencement time, now 1929, he stopped to talk to her under the elms grown old along with these two. When he shook his big head sadly, it was as though a hoary old lion tossed his mane.

"Fonda's gone on and my work has gone. The labor of nearly a half-century swept away," he said mournfully, but with no bitterness. "Where are they all now—those students I taught and loved?

> *"Sie horen nicht die folgenden Gesange,*
> *Die Seelen, denen ich die ersten sang?"*

"You'll have to translate, Professor Schroeder, I never studied it, you know."

"That's right,—you did not know my Goethe in the language in which he is loveliest. You have missed much. It is:

> *"They do not hear my later measures,*
> *The souls to whom the first I sang."*

He stopped and looked out over the campus,—the wide rolling green and the great buildings, the hoary old trees and the campanile erected to the memory of the World War boys who had gone from his Midwestern to meet in combat the boys from his Heidelberg. Then he said quietly as though she were not there:

> *"I thrill and tremble, tear on tear swift follows;*
> *My stoic heart grows wild and soft,*
> *What I possess as things remote I see,*
> *What I have lost becomes the real to me."*

267

He stood for a few moments, deep in thought, and then saluting her in courtly old-world fashion, turned and walked slowly down the green sloping campus.

CHAPTER XXXIV

IT was that very afternoon when the letter about Gretchen came from Hope. Gretchen had just graduated from High School—eighteen now, it simply couldn't be possible—and once more Hope was turning to Aunt Ella in time of trouble. "And to whom else could I go, Aunt Ella, but my port in all storms?"

Dick was having trouble again, a result of the old wound,—she was going to Hot Springs with him, and would it be at all possible for Gretchen to come to Aunt Ella's and go to school? They had always planned to send her east but finances were just too low, with Dick's hard luck about his health—

Already, even before finishing the long letter, Ella had mentally refurnished the south bedroom in ivory and yellow to go with Gretchen's Spanish-like beauty. Already she felt younger, gayer, to think of the lovely girl there in her home. It would be like having Hope all over again.

Life took on a new lease for Miss Bishop that summer. And when Hope wrote that her daughter would be there in time for the rushing parties, and she wished Aunt Ella would see that everything went off as well as it could, Miss Bishop began mentally looking over the sororities with appraising eye.

Driving to the station in her coupé, she felt a genuine thrill of excitement over the coming of the young girl. It had been three years since she had seen her and some periods of three years are much more important than others—from fifteen to eighteen for instance.

When Gretchen came down the steps of the Pullman, Ella drew in her breath at sight of the sheer loveliness of the slim thing who wore her clothes like a manikin. Tall, olive-skinned, with geranium-colored lips, Gretchen was the possessor of a cool little air of detachment which might have passed for hauteur if she had not been so friendly.

Dear, dear, Ella thought, picturing to herself in a swift mental flight, her own entrance to school and that of Hope:—her own sturdy body in its plaid ruffled dress and brass buttons, its heavy square-toed shoes, laced up to the calves of her legs, the mop of hair piled high on her head in its intricate criss-cross braidings,—Hope's shirt-waist and long pleated skirt, and ugly stiff sailor hat. "Clothes have improved, if nothing else," she admitted to herself.

Gretchen settled comfortably in her pretty room and if Ella chanced to be a bit disappointed over

the nonchalance with which the girl took in the
new artistic furnishings, she put the thought aside.

Gretchen's attractive looks and her connection
with Miss Bishop proved to be a ticket of admis-
sion to almost any social organization with which
she cared to affiliate. Ella did her best to subdue
an overwhelming pride in the striking appearance
of her charge and the admiration which followed
in her wake.

"I love to look at a pretty girl, and not having
been irresistibly beautiful myself, I appreciate it
all the more," she said to Sam Peters, who pro-
tested immediately against the disparagement of
herself.

Gretchen was indeed lovely, "a perfect model
for the girl on the magazine cover," Ella thought
to herself. She introduced her to a few young
people, and no more labor on her part was necessary, for the modern lovely girl quite capably
looks after herself.

Gretchen became, then, one of the most rushed
of the rushees, and when the breakfasts, luncheons,
teas, dinners, and evening parties of that hectic
week were over and the fraternity shouting and
the sorority tumult had died, she was returned to
Ella's home on Adams Street by a victorious group
of Kappa Alpha Thetas in a sixteen-cylinder car.
Ella was still up in her room and called to
Gretchen to come on in and tell her all about it,

wondering idly as she did so whether she would ever get too old to care about such things.

The girl came in, slim and lovely and poised. Evidently all the rushing had not moved her to abandon that cool little air of detachment. As she related the events of the evening, Ella was thinking: "I know the kind. She's the type for whom people fall over themselves. She demands much without even realizing it. And she gets it.

"This is the way of it the wide world over—
One is beloved and one is the lover;
One gives and the other receives.

Gretchen will be the beloved,—the one who receives. As far removed from Amy in method as can be,—but nevertheless a modern sophisticated version of her."

Gretchen wore her Theta pledge pin. It was apparently characteristic of her that at no time had she let her emotions run away with her mental processes. She had thought it all out carefully, she told Aunt Ella,—chosen wisely, she thought, and well. "I was not going to let any of them sweep me off my feet. Perhaps I really had the best time at the Pi Phi house,—the girls were awfully attractive,—and the Delta Gammas were thoroughbreds, but some way I felt that Kappa Alpha Theta would land me in the end where I want to go."

"And where do you want to go, Gretchen?" Ella was amazed at the freshman's viewpoint, was remembering her own green, country enthusiasm when she entered the new school, Hope's naïve, bashful girlishness. "Yet I don't know why I should be surprised," she thought. "This isn't the first modern-day freshman I've known."

"Oh, well," Gretchen laughed lightly, "maybe I can tell better where I *don't* want to go, and that's into a schoolroom to teach."

No, she wouldn't. The Gretchens do not usually choose the teaching profession.

"I've thought this all out, that since Father had his illness, he can't begin to do the things for me that he would have. Mother is sweet and anxious for me, but worried over Father and rather helpless. So it's up to me to make the most of my opportunities and push my way along,—meet the right people, make the friends who will be of most advantage. . . ."

Ella found herself blinking a little as at a flashing light. "Friends . . . of most advantage," from the mouths of babes. She had never thought of friends that way,—almost laughed aloud to think of some of her oldest friends,—old Sam Peters, Chris and Hannah and Stena. Dear, dear, —friends of most advantage!

So Gretchen, slim and lovely and cool, went her freshman way, more worldly wise than Ella.

CHAPTER XXXV

AS time went on Ella realized how nice it was to have Gretchen there. It brought the sorority young people to the house,—made life flow on about her in a gay bright stream. Even though she was tired and went to her room, it was not unpleasant to hear the rise and fall of the merry chatter below. Yes, it kept her young in soul and mind,—was a magic cord that bound her still to youth. And she herself had never quite relinquished that youth, never quite outgrown being one of the crowd, was not above swinging into the rhythm of the life of Gretchen's friends. As the time she found the three kinds of fudge sitting about her kitchen cooling on platters, and left the hastily scribbled note in Vachel Lindsay style propped up against a kettle:

Do you remember ages ago
The time
The kitchen
Was filled
With cocoa?
There was brown fudge on a purple platter
And pink fudge and white fudge
And pale tan fudge on a whitish platter.

274

Miss Bishop

Years on years I but half remember
Man is a glutton for sweets they say
Through May and June and then dead December.
Who shall end my dream's confusion?
Life is a pink and brown and white illusion.
I remember, I remember
There were sugar and chocolate and nuts and eggs
There were kettles down from all the pegs
Bending one to another
From north and south
They infinitely echo in the red caves of my mouth.

This half-way meeting of flippant youth kept her, too, a part of that youth, made the fleeting years find her not dimmed in eye, dulled in men‧tality nor cold in heart. Only the body turned traitor, only from the physical was toll demanded by the years.

Her hair was snow-white now, and she kept it beautifully groomed. Her carriage always erect, her head always held high, one saw little by which to count her years. It was only in the privacy of her room that she admitted to fatigue. She grew more and more fastidious about her person, her skin, her nails, her clothes. "You can get away with careless grooming when you are young, but not at my age," she would think. She wore a great deal of navy blue and white, navy blue school dresses offset by immaculate white collars and cuffs,—frilled ones that melted into the white of her hair and softened her aging face and hands.

For evening she chose white, a lace with which her hair vied for snow whiteness. And she was not above deepening the pink of her cheeks. She looked modern, smart, aristocratic, she who had been but a plain girl, with only nice eyes and a cheerful smile for her assets.

During the winter, she realized that as well as she thought she had understood her freshman girls before Gretchen came, she was having a better opportunity now to see them at close range through the girl. Not that they could all be classified like so much animal life under observation in the laboratories, but the viewpoint of many, naturally was the viewpoint of Gretchen.

And to study her and the changes that had taken place in all young femininity, Ella sometimes called up pictures of herself and of Mina Gordon, Emily Teasdale, Janet McLaughlin, and of the others who had constituted the feminine population of the college in that long-gone day. Individuals would always differ as long as the world lasted, but just wherein lay the general difference? She thought of Evelyn Hobbs gently fainting away one evening when a strange man opened the door of her room at the boarding house. She could visualize Gretchen's hauteur under like circumstance and her possible: "Just what's on your mind? Whatever it is, kindly step out and take it with you." She remembered the silly titterings and heart palpitations with which the Minerva girls always greeted the masculine contingent at those long-gone Friday afternoon programs, the customary vehement denials from a girl of that day that she so much as liked a young man until her wedding invitations practically were issued. Physical courage, honesty, figuratively looking life straight in the eye,—these attributes were the modern girl's.

And just as she had decided entirely for that modern girl, Gretchen might breeze in and so casually observe that Papa Rigdon (all professors were papas to her) "must hold the theory, Aunt Ella, that every unmarried woman like you should mingle socially a great deal with men to receive a missing stimulus," Ella would grow pink behind the ears and vote mentally for the old femininity which surrounded itself at least with a semblance of reticence.

The end of Gretchen's freshman year was the fiftieth anniversary of Ella's old class. But no one made any move to celebrate it. Professor Schroeder's health had broken—he was at home behind closed blinds, waiting for—he knew not what—perhaps "to pierce the ether's high, unknown dominion—to reach new spheres of pure activity." Janet McLaughlin and Emily Teasdale were dead. Professor Fonda was sleeping out in

Forest Hill, above him a simple stone with the carving:

> *We have loved the stars too deeply*
> *To be fearful of the night.*

"We'll just let the fiftieth reunion go," Ella thought a bit morbidly for her usual gay self, "and plan to have a reunion . . . Sometime . . . Somewhere."

Gretchen went home, but only for the summer. The plan now was for her to take all four years at Midwestern. Ella would not accept anything for the girl's board. Hope and Dick were having his illness to combat and she insisted that she could help them to the extent of keeping their daughter.

Gretchen's sophomore year saw her back at the old home on Adams Street, cool and unperturbed over a rush of dates, and intensely interested in dramatics. Tolstoy and Shaw and Oscar Wilde were her daily diet and she openly discussed delicate points of attack which made even Ella, used to modern youth, feel a bit embarrassed. It made her smile, too, to think of "dramatics" at Midwestern in her own student days, a scene from "Merchant of Venice" in Minerva Hall with the old calico curtain pulled aside by two perspiring supers signaling frantically to each other, and a plump Portia in a wild costume composed of President Corcoran's wife's black silk dolman and

Irene Van Ness's little brother's velvet pants. Now a play was the last word in attention to detail, a perfection of scenery, props, and costumes.

It was toward the last of her sophomore year that Gretchen was cast as Lady Teazle, and, as always, on this Saturday morning she was living her part at home, discussing details of hairdress, costume and jewelry of the times.

Ella was vaguely aware that the prospective Lady Teazle had been rummaging about upstairs half the morning but it was not until she heard her give a squeal of delight and call, "Oh, Aunt Ella, I look like a million dollars," that it came to her just what the girl had been doing.

When Ella came to the foot of the stairs she looked up to see Gretchen, slim, graceful, her brown eyes glowing, starting slowly downward dressed in Ella's wedding dress.

The new-old thing with its bunches of flowers on the white of the silk, turned now to a deep ivory, looked surprisingly not old-fashioned on the girl. Queer as it was with its panniers and its countless yards of pleating, it had merely the appearance of a lovely quaint party dress. Her prettily molded arms were bare, and in her hand she held the long sleeves.

Ella watched her slow descent, fascinated, as one looks at a natural phenomenon over which he has no control, a transfixion of gaze at the on-coming of a storm. Her mind seemed numb, unable to function. She wanted to call out, to warn her, to tell her to go back out of her sight so that she would not have to witness the painfully embarrassing scene of seeing her aunt in distress. She wanted to cry for the desecration. And then she wanted to laugh for the deference. For the girl was saying: "Where did the *darling* thing come from?" and, "Oh, *could* I wear it? I'll be the perfect Lady Teazle."

One graceful hand slipping along on the bannister, she made the slow descent.

"Am I not *perfect?* Isn't it the answer to a maiden's prayer? May I wear it? What does the sweet old auntie say?"

Pictures tumbled about crazily in Ella's head, the bald-headed man who sold her the material wishing her much joy, the standing for hours while Mrs. Finch pinned the uncut goods about her,—the first overwhelming sight of herself in the dressmaker's glass. Emotions came surging over her that she had thought long dead,—the crushing sensations of wild despair, of hurt pride, of righteous anger. For a brief moment she felt them all with poignant reality. How queer life was. Only yesterday she had been trying on the lovely thing at the dressmaker's. And to-day, with snow-white hair and slowing step, she was watching another young girl, looking like a Gainsborough, come down the stairs in the shimmering gown.

"You're stunned speechless at my gorgeousness, aren't you?"

Delbert was long dead. Amy was long dead. And yet here was the dress. Things lasted longer than people. She, too, would die and the dress would still lie in the trunk, all the bouquets of flowers crumbling to dust,—all the little pink rose-buds and the blue forget-me-nots falling into nothing.

"What's the answer, sweet pumpkin?"

"Why, yes—you may wear it."

Gretchen held out the sleeves,—long and narrow, gathered in mousquetaire fashion into their seams.

"Look—how funny! They were never sewed in,—and the hem is only basted. It almost looks as though it had never been finished."

Old Miss Bishop stood looking at the lovely freshness of Delbert Thompson's granddaughter in the old-ivory silk with the bouquets of raised flowers.

"No," she said simply, "it was never finished."

CHAPTER XXXVI

ELLA'S trip abroad became one of those mirage-like visions that appear on the horizon but vanish as one draws near. "I do hate to think of going in a wheeled-chair," she said to Stena, "but if I wait much longer, it will lie between that and being carried on a stretcher."

Stena scolded. "You do too many t'ings for odders. One t'ing one year for somebody . . . one t'ing anodder. Now look—dis year! Dis house wasn't goot enough for G'etchen." Stena could never get her tongue around that combination of "gr."

"Oh, yes, it was, Stena. It was just natural for her to want to live at the sorority house a year. I would, too, if I were young. And next summer for sure I take my trip. Miss Hunter is going again and Professor and Mrs. Alderslot, and believe me, so am I."

Stena grumbled. "I vait 'til I see you on de boat."

For Gretchen was at the Theta house in her junior year. She had lived happily at Ella's for two years but after coming back in the fall of her third year, she had gone straight to the point. She wished she could stay at the sorority house the rest of the college course. She knew it was quite impossible, that it would be more expensive, realized there was no use crying for the moon, but did not believe in beating around either bushes or truth, and that was that.

Ella had thought the matter over for a few days, had come to the conclusion that there was argument on Gretchen's side, and decided, Ella-like, to see that the girl had her chance. "I'm supplying the extra money," she wrote to Hope, "so I believe you will agree that it can be done. You know there is something about living in the midst of things on the campus that beats staying with an old Aunt Ella over on Adams Street."

Gretchen was too honest to protest. "I think you're a luscious old peach. I suppose I ought to be noble and say I couldn't think of accepting the offer, but I'm crazy to do it, and will take you at your word that you really want me to."

So Gretchen moved out, but came dutifully back at intervals to report. Ella enjoyed her cool appraisal of the girls, their dates, the house mother, wondered as always at the methodical way in which she went about cultivating people who would be most helpful to her. Stanch in her loyalty to modern youth, she would not admit that they were deteriorating in any sense. "They're brighter,— maybe not quite so stodgily thorough as they used to be,—but keener. When I look back on the first students here of which I was one, standing bashfully around, waiting to be pushed into something, I'm ashamed of all of us. My modern students,—they do 'go places and do things' as they say."

Gretchen had accepted many and sundry dates from the moment she arrived on the campus, but they had always been fraternity boys, and so in the winter of this junior year when she appeared at Ella's with a tall red-haired young man from away whom she introduced as Mr. Jack Burdick, Ella was moved to later inquiry.

He was living in Chicago now—was a salesman —she had known him when she was in high school —he came from a wonderful family—he was in town on business and just dropped in to call.

"He looks older than to have been in high school with you," Ella suggested.

"Oh, he wasn't in school *with* me. That wasn't what I said. I knew him when *I* was in high school."

Something struck Ella, as peculiar intuitions will do,—a fleeting thought of a bit of evasiveness on Gretchen's part, so that when old Stena came in later to say she had just seen Gretchen with her red-head again in a "svell car," Ella was vaguely troubled.

And when Gretchen failed to speak of the visit, although mentioning less important trivialities, all of Ella's accumulation of knowledge of young people told her that something was not quite right. She wanted to inquire from Hope, but Hope was at the Springs again with Dick and she would not trouble her. "Besides, she's my girl temporarily and it's my problem. I'll see it through myself."

Ella, herself, saw them two weeks later, slipping through a winding drive of the campus in the big roadster, and when later Gretchen failed to mention him, she felt that she must act. She pondered a long time on the procedure. With Hope it would have been so different,—Hope was like her own, brought up in her way, with her own ideals. There was something of Amy in Gretchen,—she must be looked after,—but how to go about it with this lovely, slim young girl who was modern, cool, detached. There seemed no element of childishness about her.

She approached it with lightness as though it were of no consequence.

"I saw you with your Mr. Burdick, Gretchen, but you passed up your decrepit old aunt with hauteur." That was the best way, you could not preach at these young moderns.

"Oh—so! Spying, Aunt Ella?" She laughed, certainly not spontaneously.

"A-huh! Hiding behind trees on the campus just to see you pass by."

There was a long pause, as though she pondered. And then the girl said: "I'm afraid I've got it bad, Aunt Ella, the old malady, love."

"Why, Gretchen, really?"

"Really."

"Of course, it was to be expected,—but you're young . . . and just your junior year this way. You've no . . . plans, yet, have you?"

The girl gave a short dry laugh and shrugged a lithe shoulder. "Scarcely, not as long as . . . well, I would say 'as long as Jack has one perfectly good wife,' but she's neither good nor perfect." Coolly and a bit defiantly she looked unflinchingly at the older woman.

Ella thought she must take hold of something to steady herself. Oh, why was life so hard? Life was meant to be happy without deep problems to solve. This past year had seemed singularly free of complexities and here was one of the utmost seriousness staring her in the face.

"Oh, Gretchen—no." It was a wail of distress, so deeply did she feel it.

"Yes, Aunt Ella—yes!" It was a cry of challenge to an older generation. Then suddenly Gretchen broke, cried a little wildly. All her coolness was gone, her poise shaken. The little tale she related was so old, that Ella, herself, could have told it instead of listening patiently, sympathetically to every broken word. Jack had been in town first on business,—that part was true,

—he had called because he had known her,—they had driven around, he had come again and again, —now it was the real thing. His wife didn't understand him, she didn't care for him, was a card shark, gone all the time, but he was afraid he'd have difficulty in divorcing her, his business being wrapped up with his father-in-law's.

Such a sordid little tale from the lips of the lovely young thing! Ella's heart bled for her, for Hope who would be distressed, for Dick whose pride Gretchen was, for all young things who have to face life as it is.

The problem took all of her thought. She did not know just what to do. A hundred girls she had talked out of foolish ventures, a thousand times she had assisted with advice or material aid. This was different. Gretchen was so close to her, so nearly her own flesh and blood, so coolly independent, so modern. Oh, why had this come up just now? Life had been uneventful the past few months, which meant entirely peaceful. She wasn't so young as she once was,—why should she have such problems confront her at her age?

It was two weeks later upon coming home from acting as chaperon at the Sigma Nu spring party that she found Gretchen and Jack Burdick alone in her home, Stena's hour for retiring coinciding exactly with the time the parties usually began.

She talked pleasantly with them for a time, handling young people wisely these days including as it did the condition of mind in which one approached them.

When the young man was helping Gretchen slip on her short fur jacket to leave, Ella said carelessly: "Why don't you stay here to-night, Gretchen? Won't you be too late for the house?"

"Yes, I think I will be; it's not hard to get *out* of," she grinned cheerfully at Jack Burdick, "but not so easy to break into. I may, Aunt Ella, I may come back, but I may not."

Ella had a sudden uprising of wrath toward the girl. Augmented no doubt by her physical weariness, a great anger seized her that this slim young thing could have the audacity to defy the conventions, could be standing coolly there with a young married man of her acquaintance, saying, "I may do this" or "I may not." She wanted to shake her, to spank her, to put her in her place with sudden vehement force. For a moment she had a violent antipathy toward all modern young people with their cool way of appraising every one and everything. She had a wild foolish brainstorm of wanting to do something about it, of forcibly bringing back the old days when young people were ruled with an iron hand by parents, by teachers, by society. Standing there in her spring party dress, sleepy, weary in body and soul, old Miss Bishop staged a mental revolution that, could it have been let loose upon an unsuspecting world of young people, would have found them all locked behind heavy doors, subsisting on bread and milk until they might come to their senses.

Then the king of reason as suddenly called a halt on the stick-and-stone throwers of her mind, all the violent revolutionists dropped their missiles, and she was herself,—a modern teacher, handling modern young people wisely and well.

"I think I *must* know, though, whether or not you are coming, Gretchen," she said soberly.

The girl dropped her eyes from the serious ones of the woman. "I'll be back in less than a half-hour."

Ella paced her room. Something must be done. To-night. This could not go on. She was responsible for this impossible situation. When the girl came upstairs Ella called her at once into the bedroom and went directly to the point.

"Gretchen, I think you'll agree with me that this can't go on. It's dangerous, not only dangerous to you both but a cause of anxiety to your father and mother and to me. It will end in your sorority pin being taken from you. It will interfere with your work, put a cloud on your reputation, and *never,* as long as you live, bring you one moment of genuine happiness."

"Happiness?" the girl broke out. "That's what I'm looking for! That's what Jack Burdick is looking for! That's what we *all* want, isn't it? If Jack Burdick can give me my happiness . . . if I can give Jack Burdick some happiness . . . having none in his home . . ."

"Happiness," Ella said grimly, "gained at the expense of some one else ceases to be happiness. I know that if I know no other thing."

"Just *how* do you know, Aunt Ella?"

How? What was the girl saying? Was she thinking her Aunt Ella did not know these things?

"Forgive me, Aunt Ella, if I hurt you." The cool velvety voice went on. "I don't mean to, in any way, you understand that. But I'm frank, you know, and so won't attempt to camouflage my meaning. Tell me, Aunt Ella, honestly how can *you* know anything about it—how *can* you,—an old maid school teacher tucked away with your books here at Midwestern—how have *you* ever been able to understand *life?*"

Ella Bishop looked at the lovely slim girl standing there at the doorway in the arrogance of her youth.

A dozen answers rose to her lips, a thousand thoughts flew to her brain. They beat with throbbing rhythm against the chambers of her mind as the pigeons beat their wings against the windows of the tower in Old Central.

She felt angry, insulted, robbed of some gift. Why, she would tell this disdainful girl—this modern young woman who thought the present generation had a monopoly on all the emotions—she would tell her that she, too, had been red-blooded, warm, vital,—that all her emotions had known life. That she, too, had known love and desire, and been violently swayed by them both. Love and desire, they had both been her own. But love had gone its lonely way. And desire. . . .

Suddenly all her anger left her and she felt very old.

. . . and desire shall fade, and man goeth to his long home.

With all the self-control at her command, she stilled her trembling lips, and laughed, a little ruefully, but it passed for laughter.

"Oh, I don't know about that, Gretchen," she said with studied calmness. "Life to an unmarried school teacher hasn't necessarily been *all* participles and subordinate clauses and term papers."

CHAPTER XXXVII

IT was time now to make preparations for the trip if she intended going. Ella wondered why she kept thinking of that insidious "if she intended going." Of course she was going. But having Gretchen so constantly on her mind, she seemed to have lost interest in making plans. Sometimes she thought she would tell Gretchen about her love for John Stevens,—it might have an effect on this apparent infatuation of hers for the young married man. But to what effect? Modern young girls were not Elsie Dinsmores upon whom the telling of a story with a moral would have the slightest result.

In fact she could visualize her merriment, in fancy hear her flippant remarks: "What, you, too, Bruty! Why you sly old vamp, whoever would have thought it of you,"—and more of that sort, with specific references to Cleopatra or Helen of Troy or more probably Greta Garbo.

No, her pitiful little secret was not to be the mark of Gretchen's gay shafts.

Something more must be done, something to get her away—something to take the place of this youthful infatuation—

And so Ella faced the truth of that subtle suggestion which her heart had been trying to tell her mind. If Gretchen could go abroad with the other five sorority sisters who were going,—spend that wonderful summer in London and Paris and Rome—

"Oh, no," her mind was protesting. "I couldn't do that much for her,—not *that*. I've always wanted to go. Time after time I've given it up. I owe it to myself. My life doesn't have to be one of entire self-denial. I've given up things all my life."

She seemed to plead with some one not to consent to her doing this absurd thing. But just as surely as she had satisfied herself that it was all Quixotic, all a foolish sense of altruism, just as surely would she find herself insisting that she must do it.

"She's not even my own flesh and blood," she would protest to this argumentative conscience of hers.

"She's your Hope's little girl, and she's in danger."

"But I can't go about saving people from their own foolish sins. If she would slip into a silly love for this man here and now, she would do a similar thing any time and anywhere."

"It's a crucial age. She's young. If you can get her through this time . . ."

"No, I'm going to give myself this trip. I've planned it for years. It's a reward of merit for . . . for everything."

"You're old,—with your work all behind you. You would merely sight-see and soak up some information. She's young,—and has all her life . . . perhaps a career before her."

"But *I* came through such an affair . . . by myself." Back she would go in the dual character she was playing. "*I* couldn't run away. No one helped me . . . or sent me abroad. *I* had to fight the thing out here."

"Maybe you were stronger in character . . . in fact, you certainly *were*. Isn't that why you should help—now—some one younger and less strong?"

After dinner she phoned for Gretchen. She felt an overwhelming joy, was consumed by that exhilarating sensation she always experienced when about to give happiness to another.

"I'm really not unselfish at all," she told herself when she put down the receiver. "I like to do things like this so well that I enjoy giving myself the thrill of it. In reality it's one type of selfishness."

Gretchen came, her graceful figure with its gliding walk crossing the lawn to the side porch where Ella sat in the fresh spring evening.

"Did you want something special, Aunt Ella?"

"Yes."

"I rather gathered so."

"How would you like to go with your sorority sisters on the European trip, Gretchen, with Madame Volk and her music students?"

"How would I like to crash the pearly gates and purloin Gabriel's horn? But what *is* this—an examination in fiction plotting?"

"Something on that order. I'm rather thinking, Gretchen, that you can go."

"Using what for money?"

"American dollars."

"Whose?"

"Mine."

The color slipped away from the girl's face. "Aunt Ella, you . . . you don't mean that."

"Yes, I do, Gretchen."

"For me to go with you?"

"No . . . I'm not going."

"Oh . . . I see. I thought there was a catch somewhere." She stood up, her slim figure graceful against the new green of the rose vine. "And you not go." Her throaty voice was the embodiment of sarcasm.

"But if I choose to send you in my place?"

The girl laughed shortly and shook her lovely head: "I see through you like cellophane. In fact, Aunt Ella, I shall now tell you the entire workings of your mind. You're worried about me and Jack

Burdick. You think if you'd get me away . . . abroad . . . it would wear off . . . 'it' meaning love to me—infatuation to you. To that end, you're willing to give up your trip. You're an old smoothy,—in fact you're probably the noblest soul that ever trod over campus dandelions,—but I just couldn't let you be *that* noble . . . not to-day, Miss Bishop."

There were always forces to be met in Gretchen which had never been Hope's. Hope had been entirely feminine, pliant and lovable,—easily molded. Gretchen's mind was that of a frank boy's, going directly to a point.

It pleased Ella that the girl showed so little tendency to be grasping; she had accepted much in the past without demonstration, but evidently she felt this was carrying it too far, and with no further controversy expected to close the subject.

But in the days that followed, Ella, with much argument and explanation had her way, and Gretchen left with the girls after Commencement week. Stena was in such a state of disgust that she would scarcely talk to her mistress whom she characterized as "too voolish to be vidout a guar*deen.*"

"After all, Stena," Ella said, "it's awfully nice to know you can sit on your porch all summer . . . no summer school . . . no tramping around Europe . . . just relax and rest."

And when long interesting letters came from Gretchen with the tang of the salt sea in them and the breath of Scotland moors, Ella insisted that the girl was seeing more with her young eyes than she herself could have done,—which elicited only a portentous snort from Stena.

When Gretchen came back from the trip for her senior year, she kissed Ella warmly. "Never as long as I live can I forget what you did for me. What can I ever do for you in return?" She stood, slim and lovely and glowing, some inner light lending warmth to her usual aloofness.

"It's payment enough to see you so happy, Gretchen. It is much better than having gone."

"Would it recompense you, just partly, say the first down payment if I told you your little scheme that I saw through all the time worked to perfection—that I'm cured . . . and not a little disgusted at the Gretchen of last spring?"

"It finishes the payment." Ella, too, glowed with happiness. "Account settled in full."

"But don't be hasty and give too much credit to the mere separation, Aunt Ella. I could have gone over foolishly thinking I loved him, and have come back foolishly dittoing. But it's because of a new man—the grandest old thing you ever knew. First I met him going over . . . then he was in Paris with . . ."

"Oh, Gretchen," Ella was laughing. "Out of the frying pan into . . ."

"But *what* a fire! His name is Smith, . . . not so hot maybe to think of that Jones-Smith headline when the announcement comes out, . . . but wait until you see him, . . . Ronald Smith. And is he good looking? He's tall and broad and 'andsome and well-to-do and *not married*." She gave an exaggerated little squeal of rapture and kissed Ella again.

Old Ella Bishop was very happy. So much so that she hated to say the thing that was on her mind, that owing to the cut in salaries which every one was having to take she thought perhaps Gretchen would have to give up living at the Theta house and come home.

"Oh, *that!*" The girl waved it aside as a mere triviality. "I intended to. Since I've lived there I've stalked my prey,—so it's home again, home again for me. And I suppose it would never occur to you, you clever old virgin . . . well, anyway you're a virgin . . . that I'd rather have my grand Ronald . . . Mr. Smith to you . . . come to see me here this year in the privacy of this little living-room than in the middle of the arena at the K.A.T. house?"

Ella was almost ready to turn out her light that night when Gretchen came to the bedroom door in her gaudy pajamas. Looking up from her book, she was struck anew with the charm of the girl's loveliness.

"Aunt Ella, I almost forgot to tell you something awfully odd. After we got back home, in one of his letters Ronnie said he had found out that his grandmother was an old schoolmate of yours."

"She was? I wonder who?"

"Her maiden name was Van Ness, Irene Van Ness."

"Irene . . . was . . . your . . . Ronald's grandmother?" It sounded forced from her, like a thing unbelievable.

"Oke. She went to school here when you did, he says."

A whirl of thoughts went about in Ella Bishop's head with dizzying effect after Gretchen had gone. "Ronald Smith is Irene's grandson." She said it over to herself with bewildered patience.

When Amy Saunders came to town and left grief and trouble in her wake—when she married Delbert who should have married Ella herself,—Gretchen, here, was to be born of that line later. When Chester Peters went away because of a mad infatuation for Amy, Irene who loved him, married another—this Ronald Smith was to be born of that line later. Was it possible, then, that all the suffering and humiliation of that early day *had* to be, in order that Gretchen and Ronald might have this very beautiful love for each other? Oh, no, that was a foolish thing. One could scarcely put it that way. Fate never went to that degree. And yet—it would not quite leave old Ella—the thought that out of all that misery and suffering of a long-gone day, two generations later had grown a lovely romance,—like the white lilies that cover stagnant pools in the tropics.

CHAPTER XXXVIII

AND then very suddenly old President Watts died—one Friday night, with all his engagements marked on his desk calendar for the following week.

The blow came with unforeseen force to the old faculty members who had worked with him for years upon years.

"It's one of the most peculiar relationships in the world," Ella thought, "that relation of the superintendent of a public school to his teachers, or the president of a college to the women faculty members. He is like a husband or father in every sense but the family life. I knew President Watts almost as well as his wife knew him,— every mood, everything that irritated him, everything that gave him happiness, his ideas on practically anything one could mention. I could read his mind, detect his reactions to various incidents. I went to him for sympathy and advice and criticism. I could console him and scold him and encourage him.

"I think there are no finer friendships in the world than these, utterly devoid of sentiment, but completely abounding in understanding. I could feel not much worse at his loss if he *had* been my husband."

She dreaded thoroughly the advent of a new president, watched the papers, questioned any one who might have information. Two or three local men were suggested, heads of departments, but when the news was announced, he proved to be from a college in another state,—Melvin Bevans Crowder.

When he came, it was noticeable that he was extremely young, efficient, progressive. Tactful, too, for that matter, as he made no changes to speak of that first year. But with capability and diplomacy he was molding the school to suit his plans, instituting innovations and gradual changes.

When Ella drew her salary now with its twenty per cent cut, she looked a little ruefully at the check with its diminished figures. "Reduced pay," she said, "in some jobs would call for reduced effort on the part of the jobber. But I don't know how any teacher can have the heart to take it out on her students when they are so entirely without blame for conditions. The next generation has the big task of pulling the country back to normal times,—so I suppose the least we teachers can do is to inspire our young people to as high ideals as we can. In other words, I guess the teacher is the last one to let outside conditions affect her work."

Ronald Smith, the magnificent, came from Ohio several times during the year to see Gretchen. It gave Ella a warm sense of pleasure to witness their happiness. "All my life I've been looking on at these things instead of participating in them and I can't see but that it gives me about as much joy," old Miss Bishop said.

Ella Bishop had lived past many inauguration days in her three score and ten years, but never one before that had for its immediate and personal effect the closing of her bank and leaving her with no pocket money. She made light of it along with most other patriotic citizens until the day for the bank's opening came, when Sam Peters came over to see her. Sam was showing his age more than ever this spring,—looked the old man he really was, with his thin parchment-like face and slim trembling body.

He had heard bad news and as usual had come across the street to tell it to Ella himself—to try to protect her against the storms, as he wished he might always have protected her.

He sat down now in her pretty living-room, his cane between his bony hands.

"Did you have money in the Bank of Oak River, Ella?"

"Why, yes, Sam. Almost all I had. Why?"

"I hate to tell you, Ella, but they say uptown

it's to open only on a restricted basis, virtually liquidated."

Cold hands were clutching at Ella's heart and throat. Money—she had not given enough thought to it in years gone by. Now, what was Sam saying?

"How do you mean, Sam?"

"You'll be asked to sign what is called a waiver, —give up a certain per cent of your deposit,— fifteen, twenty, thirty, whatever seems necessary. Then they will open up and you will be allowed to draw probably one per cent per month of the rest."

"One per cent, Sam? Twelve per cent a year only."

"Yes."

"But, Sam, that would take . . . years to get it?"

"Yes." He twisted his cane nervously between mummy-like fingers.

"But, Sam,—I'm not as young as I used to be." It was the first time she had allowed herself to admit old age to any one. "I thought . . . I hadn't expected to work much longer."

"It's hard luck, Ella. I'm more sorry than I can tell you."

She got up and walked around the room, straightening a pillow, touching book-ends. "I suppose I haven't thought enough about . . . old age, Sam. It always seemed so far away,—and the present so full of important duties."

"You're not old, Ella. Except for your white hair you don't look a day older than . . . almost when you started to teach." Love is not blind— it merely sees that which another can not.

She stopped in front of the little old man. "Do you know, Sam, I'll tell you what I had told no one, not a soul. I had expected next year to be my last. Just this spring I made up my mind that I'd teach only one more year. But now,—one per cent per month . . . for years." She sat down a little heavily like a tired old woman. "That will squelch *that* plan right now." Then, —"I know what I'll do, Sam." She was suddenly alert, the old Ella. "I'll teach three or four years more and give a thought to nothing *but* money. I'll just reverse my attitude. It will come first. Gretchen is graduating. I'll cut out entertaining students from this day on, every bit of help to any one, and think only of myself. You just *have* to be selfish in this world sometimes, don't you, Sam?"

She talked on rapidly, enthusiastically, while little old Sam Peters sat and twirled his cane.

"Three years more, Sam, instead of one. That's my deadline. I'll save every cent but the smallest sum for actual living. Then I won't have to worry. I've been too easy, I know,—too ready to think there was no end to salaries. I can think of a dozen things I've done that I shouldn't. But you'll see from now on, Sam. I've had my lesson."

Old Sam Peters stood up. He looked out of the window at the pale March sunshine on the dirty snow of the hedge.

"As a . . . what you might call, last resort, Ella . . . there's always my . . . house and name . . . and anything I have."

A mist sprang to her eyes and she put out her hand. "You're so good to me, Sam. I wish . . . I wish it *could* have been."

Old Sam Peters pressed her hand. "That's all right, Ella. You couldn't help it."

"And we've been good friends, Sam."

"Yes . . . we've been good friends."

He went a little shakily down the steps, through the hedge, and across the street to the yard with the rusty old deer.

CHAPTER XXXIX

IN spite of the short distance to the college Ella drove it every day this spring. With jealous care, Chris Jensen always fought for her rights. No one could run over Miss Bishop while Chris was around if the correction lay within his power. As when, in parking the car as near the entrance to Corcoran Hall as was possible, she happened to mention to him that she usually found the car of a student or of another instructor in her chosen place, old Chris immediately set out to right the great injustice to his favorite. Getting no satisfaction from the superintendent of grounds or the new President Crowder that any special privileges could be shown, Chris stubbornly painted a small sign: "Miss Bishop. Do not park here." And slyly planted the sign half under a bridal-wreath bush near Corcoran Hall. When called to his attention by an irate assistant, the superintendent of grounds passed it off with: "Oh, let the old codger leave it there if he gets any satisfaction out of it."

"The only annoying feature about it," Ella said to Gretchen with the humorous twinkle of her old eyes, "is that I ran into it and split the 'e' off, so it now reads 'Miss Bishop. Do not park her.'"

It was only two weeks later that Ella received the note. Chris brought it to her, clumping along in his heavy work shoes up the walk between the hedges. When she saw him coming it occurred to her that she had not noticed how he had aged the last year. One grew used to another through the years, and seeing him that way every day, she had not been able to notice the change. Why, he was old, Chris was,—an old man, his broad shoulders stooped, his arms swinging limply at his sides, his massive head drooping forward so that his iron gray hair hung over his forehead. His step, too, was slow and not quite steady.

She went at once to the door to meet him. "Are you hanging me a May-basket, Chris?" She spoke lightly, gayly, as she often did. It was one thing that had endeared her to those who did manual labor about the campus. "That Miss Bishop,—she's nice to everybody, ain't she?" one workman might say to another.

"Not like that Miss Rogers who acts as though she was smellin' something," might be the answer.

But to-night old Chris would not joke. He delivered the note with dignity and left with no word, clumping along down the walk with shuffling gait and loose swinging arms.

Still standing outside the door as Chris had left her, Ella read the note.

It was from President Crowder—brief, gracious, explanatory. There were to be several changes in the faculty and he thought it much better that she know about the change in her own department before the board met. Delicately veiled, with the kindest of motives, it suggested that she might prefer to get in her resignation prior to the board's action.

Stunned, she could only stand and peer through her eyeglasses at the words of the surprising message. Not quite able to absorb the enormity of the thing that had just descended upon her, her mind darted away from the paper in her hand to the thought that it was Chris who always brought her bad messages. "He's like Eris whom the Greek gods used to send with messages of discord," she thought whimsically. "Just change the 'Ch' to 'E' . . . his name ought to be Eris Jensen . . . instead of Chris."

Then her mind came back to the full import of the note,—and she groped for a porch chair.

For a long time she sat there on the porch in the deepening twilight,—the letter in her lap. Anger toward President Crowder shook her body so that it trembled uncontrollably. In a moment the anger gave way to wounded feeling. A deep sense of hurt pride enveloped her whole being. She had been *asked* to leave,—subtly, delicately, —but what mattered the method? In another year or so she had intended going of her own volition. It made no difference now what she had intended,—she had been *told* to leave.

And then the hurt quite suddenly gave way to fear,—a cold and unreasoning fright. She had not made enough provision for the future. In the years that were gone there had always seemed so many who needed her help. Life had sped along so quickly. Yesterday she had been young with all the years of her life unlived. To-day she was old with not much to show for those years of service to the college and community. Service was such a vague immaterial thing,—you could not handle it nor show it to your friends nor exchange it in the market place.

Because this was true she had gone her blithe way, putting from her the thoughts of old age. And suddenly here it was. Would it be a still harsher thing, dependent old age? That pitiful little one per cent which would be meted out to her! Would the small savings be ample to cover all?

By a system of arithmetic as old as the science itself she worked her problems. Her small income made the dividend,—the possible number of years she might live became the rather pathetic divisor,—the quotient resulted in a pitiably small sum which must henceforth cover all expenses. The meagerness of it frightened her. Old age seemed to have developed horns and cloven hoofs, to have taken on a demon-like leer. For the first time she felt genuine panic,—for the first time seemed thinking of herself. Hitherto she had brushed away all her troubles with humor and sane philosophy,—but all her bravery could not hide the Thing that confronted her to-night. The tissues of her courage seemed as weakened as the tissues of her body.

"On a pinch, I could go to the old people's home," she said to her frightened self. At the thought a cold hand seemed clutching her heart. She had visited that home once. It had been pleasant and comfortable, almost luxurious because of various bequests. But the old ladies who had been there sitting on the big porch aimlessly watching the world go by, alien souls, women from whom the glow of living had died,—old ladies with knitting and palsied heads and loose artificial teeth. Quite hastily she put her hand to her mouth and smiled at the inadvertent gesture. At least if she found it necessary to go there eventually she would see plenty of things to amuse her. Pathetic rôles were not meant for her.

Over and over in the deepening dusk she worked on the problem of what to do with the remainder of her life. That potential trip abroad was a huge joke now. Why had she not saved more for herself? Why had she seemed always to have others on her hands?

If worse came to worst she could take a pay roomer or two, do private tutoring. Again and again she tried with courage to work out her problem, so much harder than algebra.

"Let X equal the unknown quantity," she said to herself.

But there was no answer, not in the back of the book or anywhere. Not until God closed the book would old Ella Bishop find what X equaled.

CHAPTER XL

ON Monday morning she drove over to school, turning in at the north gate just in time to see Chris wave an assistant librarian's car away from his chosen spot for herself.

"Little upstart," he was muttering, "hasn't been here but eight or ten years. Thinks she can pick out her . . ."

"Chris . . ." Ella said suddenly when she was out of the car. Why not tell Chris first of all,— wasn't he the only one left with her from the old days? "Chris, I'm through teaching. I'm resigning to-night."

"Vell . . . dat's funny, Miss Bis'op. You and me bot'. I'm quittin', too. Only I ain't got to resign like you on paper. Just tell old Long-legs I'm t'ru,—and dat's all dere be to it,—just *t'ru.*"

Ella looked at the old man bent over there by the snow-white blossoms of the bridal wreath, no whiter than the locks of hair straggling down on his forehead.

Then he straightened and for the fraction of a moment old Ella Bishop's bright blue eyes caught the watery blue ones of the old janitor. For the fraction of a moment they saw eye to eye and heart to heart. Suddenly, with no words, each knew about the other. Each knew the other had been let out.

"Aw, I ain't carin', Miss Bis'op," the old man broke the embarrassment of silence. "Don't you care, neider."

"No, I'm not either." She spoke lightly. "Not at all."

"Neider am I," old Chris repeated stoutly. "Not a bit. Not a mite."

If Miss Bishop secretly entertained thoughts to the effect that both the gentleman and the lady did protest too much, she kept them to herself.

Suddenly he burst out: "Maybe I *am* old, but I don't feel so. I'm strong," he spoke belligerently as though Miss Bishop had indicated otherwise. "Strong as an ox. See dat." He rolled back a blue denim sleeve and displayed flabby old muscles. "Anyways," he added a little ruefully at the sight, "it don't take no great shakes of strengt' to clap erasers 'n dust 'n chase de trainin'-school kids out o' Old Central."

He turned his head away. Miss Bishop understood. English department or janitor work. What difference did it make?

It was the next night that she picked up the *Daily Clarion* and walked over to her favorite chair under a bridge lamp. It was a lovely evening. She could hear all the Maytime sounds

314

of the college town,—cars slipping by, the chimes from the campanile ringing out the hour with rhythmic announcement, a group of fraternity boys shouting unmelodiously: "The Girl in The Little Green Hat." She could smell all the May-time odors that so associated themselves with preparation for Commencement, fresh paint next door, lawns after the late spring rains, honey-suckles outside the window.

For a moment she held the paper idly, remembering her own part in starting the crude little sheet a half-century before. Then she recalled that this was the issue which would announce the changes. It startled her to see it in black and white: *Miss Bishop Resigns.* She felt a justifiable pleasure in the paragraph referring to her long career, a genuine gratitude toward President Crowder for handling the situation so adroitly. He had saved her pride if nothing else.

She read on down: ". . . Among other changes for this year, the student body will say good-by to Old Central. Those who return next fall will find it listed among the missing. Razing of the old building will begin the morning after the Alumni banquet which will be held this year for sentiment's sake in the old auditorium."

It moved her unaccountably. She and Old Central—both would be listed among the missing. And old Chris—she must not forget him. He, too, had been associated with Old Central since its beginning.

And if Ella Bishop sat idly for a long time with the paper in her lap, let no one enter into the hushed inner chamber of her thoughts.

After a time she arose and took a light wrap from the hall closet, calling to Stena that she was going out for a walk by herself. Once outside, she turned up the street toward the Jensen's little house across from the campus. When she tapped at the door, there was a muffled tread in the hall and old Chris himself came, shading his weak eyes with his hand.

"Good evening, Chris."

"Vell . . . Miss Bis'op." He took a sooty old pipe out of his mouth and gave an apologetic glance at his blue and white socks quite free from inhibiting shoes. That was the way Miss Bishop had affected him for several decades.

"Chris, they tell me Old Central is to come down at last." To her surprise, she had to make an effort to keep her voice steady. She had not realized that it was meaning so much to her.

"Yes, dey do say so." At the risk of a conflagration old Chris was pocketing his pipe. "Come on in, Miss Bis'op."

"No, no thanks. You still have a key I suppose, Chris?"

Old Chris nodded. "Yes, ma'am," he added.

"I wonder if you will let me take it. It's so nice to-night, I'd just like to go over the old building for the last time in a sort of 'We who are about to die, salute you' attitude."

Old Chris had never heard of the *Morituri Salutamus* but he recognized fully the emotion in Miss Bishop's voice.

"You will laugh at me for being so sentimental," she said apologetically.

"No, I von't," old Chris shook his heavy gray head. "I von't laugh at you. It's got me a-feelin' blue, too. I know every crack in de plaster 'n every knot in de woodwork."

He shuffled back into the dark interior of the cottage and brought back the key,—a huge affair, like a key to some ancient castle.

"Good night, Chris, and thank you. If you see some one prowling around Old Central, don't shoot or send for the campus policeman."

Ella Bishop walked up through the campus under the elms. The moon was full and there was the heavy scent of syringas in the air, snatches of music came from Fraternity Row, and laughter from the steps of Alice Wayland Hall. It had the smell and feel of all the long-gone Commencements.

In front of Old Central she paused and looked at it with appraising eye. In the moonlight all discrepancies in the old building were hidden.

One could not see the cracks in the brick under the ivy nor the settling window-frames nor the slight sagging of the steps. It looked sturdy, unyielding. It seemed holding up its head proudly. Like Miss Bishop.

She turned the huge key and pushed the iron latch which had clicked to three generations. Softly she stepped into the shadows of the hall. It was stuffy and chalk-scented,—but friendly, as though it welcomed her home. She had a swift feeling that the old building wanted her to know it held no grudge about her leaving, and smiled at the foolishness of the thought.

She crossed the hall and mounted the stairs, her hand slipping along the bannister which was as smooth as old ivory from the polishing of countless human palms.

Straight to her old classroom she passed, a large room with its rows of recitation seats, half in the moonlight, half in the shadow. She was not just sure what it was used for now, but had a faint impression of manual training projects on a bench by the window.

Toward the front of the room where the instructor's desk stood, Ella Bishop walked softly as people do in the presence of the dead. A composite picture of all the classes she had ever taught seemed before her. Personalities looked at her from every recitation seat but she did not realize that in point of time they were sometimes fifty years apart.

There was Frank Farnsworth, indolent, mischievous, even stupid in English courses because he did not care for them, wanting only instruction in business administration. Why did she remember him? There was Anna Freybruger. She was a missionary, some one had told her. Over there sat Clarence Davis, a congressman now. Here laughing Esther Reese, a happy wife and mother. She summoned them back out of the shadows, not mature nor successful, but young freshmen, needing her guidance.

Slowly she circled the room, recalling a dozen events of the olden days. Queer how easily they came back to-night.

Then she turned toward the tower room, opened the door and stepped in. Once it had been her Gethsemane. On a day she had come in here full of happiness and the joy of living. When she went out, some of her had died. The part that had lived she had dedicated to young people, warming her cold heart at the fire of their youth, putting into her work all the love and interest she would have given to a husband, home, and children. Here she had said good-by to John Stevens, her love and admiration for him unbesmirched.

She crossed the little room, opened one of the windows and sat down by it. The May breeze, sweet with the smell of Commencements, came in and touched the soft tendrils of her white hair.

Memory went back on the road of the years. She tried to sum up the results of the journey. Nothing,—but age and near poverty. Foolishly, she had thought the teaching itself would compensate her for all of her devotion to the task. A deep bitterness assailed her. It was not right nor just, to give all and receive nothing. She had been a fool to think that if you gave your heart the service rendered would be its own reward.

Across the boulevard the sorority houses were lighted to the last window. Cars were at the curbing. Young people came and went. How unnecessary she was now to this newer college life. Once she had seemed indispensable. Slow tears came, the more painful because hitherto she had met life gallantly with high hopes, deep courage, boundless faith.

Ella Bishop raised her face to the May sky as though to hold intimate conversation with some one. How foolish she had been to think that by binding herself to youth she could retain her own light spirits. That early dedication of hers to the lives of her students was all Quixotic. That old idea of carrying a torch ahead to show them the way to unrevealed truths had been all wasted effort. Every waking thought she had given to them, watched her every act and decision that she might be a worthy example.

There were instructors who heard recitations and then left their responsibilities hanging like raincoats in their lockers. She had not been able to do that. She had given the best that was in her, not only that her students' minds would further unfold, but whenever they needed assistance for those other sides of their lives, the physical and the moral. A suggestion of eye-strain in a student and she had not rested until the matter was rectified. A knowledge of recurring headaches and she had not known peace until the source was traced. And then that other thing which she had noticed among the newcomers, that elusive thing which was neither all physical nor all mental nor all moral, that subtle thing which crept into the lives of youth. How she had pondered over it, questioned and advised. Many a mother, less motherly than herself, had not known the danger, or having known, had lifted no hand to guide. All this she had done for her students,—and what was her reward? Old age and poverty. And perhaps later,—loneliness. For youth not only must be served, but after that it forgets. Tears came again. And some were for lost youth and some were for advancing age, but some were for a faith that was shattered.

There was nothing now to look forward to —but death. Death! How little thought she had ever given to it! So full of living,—her hands so filled with duties,—she had existed only from day to day, doing the hour's tasks as well as she could.

She pictured herself lying dead—out in Forest Hill by her mother—under the leaves—

Suddenly a pigeon flew against the bell overhead and it tapped, so that in a great whirl of beating wings all the pigeons flew from the bell tower, their bodies almost brushing the windows. Startled, she jumped up and looked furtively behind her. She had that queer suffocating feeling that one has when he is conscious of a frightened sensation. Usually placid, she realized her heart was pounding wildly. All at once the familiar old building was cold and forbidding. It was as though there were soft foot-falls, phantom whisperings. The ghosts of all her yesterdays seemed haunting the place. Was her brain addled? Had she played too long with her memories? Was she slipping mentally like her mother? All her poise was gone. She wanted to fly as from a tomb.

It seemed almost a physical impossibility for her to return through that shadow-laden classroom.

She gathered herself together and crossed the

office to the classroom door. Eerie rustlings, low murmurs, faint mocking laughter played tricks with her imagination. The bell tapped faintly. The pigeons swirled past the window again.

In a perspiration of nervousness, she crossed the moonlighted floor of her old classroom, passed through the upper hall, down the long stairway with its bannister polished by a thousand hands, and hurried out into the clear air of the night.

She crossed the campus and went home, tired in every portion of her body, every bone aching, every nerve tingling with fatigue. At home she went straight to her room with an intense longing to get quickly into the cool depths of her bed. She took off each garment wearily, stopping once or twice to cast longing eyes toward the haven of her couch with a half-formed decision to drop onto it as she was. With extra effort at control she finished the task and slipped into the welcome comfort of that familiar port of rest.

Getting under the quilts was like crawling under leaves, she thought vaguely. Either one meant rest. Rest for a tired teacher. What difference did it make—quilts or leaves? There was peace under either. To let your tired mind and body sink into the blessed comfort of them,— quilts or leaves,—to let them cling softly and gently to you, easing the ache and the long, long weariness.

What difference did it make? Leaves . . . or quilts . . . ? Quilts . . . or leaves . . . ?

CHAPTER XLI

"YOU know, Gretchen, I think I'm not going to the Alumni banquet this year." Ella Bishop was sitting in front of her dressing-table and speaking over her shoulder to the girl in the hall. She had tried to make her voice casual, matter-of-fact, but she had a feeling that it quivered and cracked "like the old woman I suppose I might as well admit I am," she thought.

"Not going? Why?" Gretchen, attractive as always in a white sport outfit, came to the door.

"Oh, I just thought I wouldn't this year—leaving as I am. . . ." She said it so lightly that she was highly pleased with herself. "And as long as Old Central is to come down—you know it just wouldn't be good taste to consume food in your own mausoleum."

"Oh, Aunt Ella, what a terrible thought."

"And anyway I've been to a thousand. My word, Gretchen, some time I'm going to sit down and figure the hours I've spent at them, and the words I've heard going to waste in the ponderous speeches that have been made. Now, for instance . . . let's see . . . I began going in 1880 . . . this year would make fifty-three times . . . no, fifty-two . . . I escaped one, anyway, the year I

325

was east. Fifty-two Commencements . . . say three hours each allowed for sitting at the tables,— one hundred and fifty-six hours . . . that's . . . wait a minute . . . over nineteen working days of eight hours each." She was enjoying her bit of irony.

> *"The hours I've spent at them, dear heart,*
> *Are but so many words to me,*
> *I count them over, every one apart,*
> *Their ora-tor-ee! Their ora-tor-ee!"*

She laughed at her own light humor,—had complete control of herself now. "For nineteen full working days have I listened to flowery rhapsodies or ponderous advice. As for the energy expended, it has been immeasurable."

"Oh, but you *must* go." Gretchen was earnest in her vehemence. "The very fact that you *are* leaving, Aunt Ella, is the biggest reason for being there."

"I suppose you're right. Who am I to shirk?" she answered in the same light vein she had been employing. "Twenty full days would end the whole thing with a flourish, make it an even number, and one can always go into a sort of coma and think of other things if the oratory proves too powerful an anesthetic. And, anyway, I'll have perfect peace and freedom for they haven't asked me to talk this year."

It was rather an important Commencement, what with its being Ella's last while a faculty member, and Gretchen graduating. Hope and Dick came in time for the festivities, Dick never quite rugged since the war and so never quite the success he might have been, Hope heavy and sweet-faced, and both wrapped up in pride for their lovely daughter. And Ronald Smith came, driving through with his grandmother, old Mrs. Irene Van Ness Hunt, wrinkled and sallow, and looking so much older than Ella that one could not imagine they had been girls together. But she had a whole rumble seat full of bags containing gay lace dresses and high-heeled pumps, and every time she shook her sprightly old head, a different pair of long earrings jangled against her magenta-colored cheeks.

Ella housed them all but Ronald who stayed at the Phi Psi chapter house.

The night of the banquet they were all going together over to Old Central, which, lighted from top to bottom, was making merry on the eve of its own private Waterloo.

Every one was ready quite on time but Gretchen who seemed slower than usual with her dressing. Ella was groomed and ready long before the young girl, a full half-hour before Ronald came to join the group. Always punctual, she could not tolerate the careless way in which the young people seemed to regard time.

"At least, let's be there when the fruit cocktail is eaten," she called up the stairs, and added more for her own pleasure than the waiting group: "I can visualize the whole thing from that well-known cocktail to lights out. I could even stay at home and hear in my head every word that will be spoken."

Old Miss Bishop looked nice. She had on her white lace dress and black velvet evening wrap. Her snow white hair was beautifully groomed and even the inevitable black velvet band at her throat which she wore this last year served not only its pitiful little duty of covering those tell-tale shrunken neck tissues but of accentuating the loveliness of her hair and the pose of her head.

There were so many cars parked around the campus when they arrived that Ella said: "An unusually large attendance, it looks . . . that will be on account of sentiment for Old Central. We really shouldn't have been late."

She hastened the pace of the group a little, but Ronald and Gretchen, strolling exasperatingly up the curving walk and around the Administration Building toward Old Central, called to them not to be in such a hurry. Ella was thinking sentimentally that the lights of the old building looked familiar and friendly sending out their message for all to come to the festivities with no thought that to-morrow night and other nights they would not beckon.

One of the big busses that had replaced the old jangling street car disgorged a few people who slipped in ahead of the little group of six. Otherwise, the campus was deserted.

"We're the *very* last," Ella complained. As though Ronald and Gretchen had not used skillful maneuvering to see that this was so.

Old Chris stood in the lobby, almost unrecognizable in his best suit and large shining shoes. His massive gray head was held a bit stiffly above his low loose collar, and his wide bony shoulders drooped heavily under the weight of their years.

As these last comers entered he pulled on the rope dangling through his big gnarled hand. High above them in the old belfry the bell rang, and with a great whirl of wings the pigeons flew out.

"Pretty nigh de last time," he said to Ella as she passed. "Don't it sort o' get you?"

She nodded wordlessly.

Just inside the door of the old auditorium they paused. Something was unusual, Ella was thinking. Not for years had there been such an enormous turn-out. She caught a fleeting vision of rows upon rows of tables, a multitude of people seated at them, flowers, class banners, whitecoated waiters, overflow tables in adjoining rooms.

The bell might have been a signal, for the orchestra broke into "Pomp and Circumstance." Something was happening. The diners were rising as one man. All faces were turned toward the group at the door. President Crowder and the chairman of the board were coming toward them. They were offering Ella their arms, one on her left, one on her right. Ronald was slipping off her velvet wrap. Gretchen was whispering: "All for you, sweet pumpkin."

Applause broke, wild and unrestrained. In a daze Ella took the arms of the two men and together they walked the full length of the huge room.

Together the president and the board member opened a double gateway of ferns and escorted her to a chair at the head of the long sweep of tables. The chair was rose covered, and when they pulled it out and seated her in the sweet-smelling bower, Miss Bishop looked like a white rose herself. The president and the board chairman seated themselves at each side and the great audience sat down. There was an orchid corsage at Ella's plate,—and quite trivially it came to her that she had never worn an orchid in her life.

It was all very hard to comprehend. Her mind felt numb, callous, incapable of concentrated thought. A drowning person must feel so. "It isn't true," she kept thinking. "I'm moving about only in dreams. This thing hasn't happened for me. I'm an old woman, worn out, poverty stricken, shelved, with nothing to show for my life."

Conversation broke on all sides with a humming noise of pleasure. All of the people closest were leaning toward her speaking to her. But she seemed without emotion, as though the years had wrung her out, hard and dry, like an old dishcloth. She spoke and smiled mechanically and made futile stabs at her fruit cocktail. What had she said once about a fruit cocktail—something sarcastic? It must have been years ago.

In that same numb and callous way, she finished the courses with the others, not quite understanding, never quite comprehending the thing that was happening.

The dining over, the toasts began. They were all for Miss Bishop "who has given a lifetime of service to the upbuilding of this school," or "who perhaps more than any other faculty member of the half century has had a deep and lasting influence upon all students."

Presently she seemed to come out of her stupor. In a great sweep of understanding, this thing that was happening suddenly did seem true. She was being honored. This was for her. All her old students appeared to have returned. Never had there been such a huge reunion,—not in the whole history of the college. They had come back to honor Old Central—and her.

They toasted her, told jokes on her, teased her, praised her. A United States senator admitted that if it hadn't been for Miss Bishop he might still be saying "have saw." A prominent minister said that next to his parents, Miss Bishop had influenced his life more than any other human. A millionaire merchant, who had arrived in his own plane, told the audience that when mothers were lauded, not to forget one of the very best of them all, Miss Bishop, *mother of students*. A mechanical engineer said he had done a little figuring and found that if Miss Bishop's influence for good upon her hundreds of students could be computed and turned into—

There were cries of "Technocracy" and good-natured banter.

It was the new president who said that in the brief time he had been here he had come to realize that Miss Bishop was one of the chief representatives of the real spirit of the school, courageous, progressive, high-minded, *human.*

The last of the speakers was the chairman of the board who said it had been one of the happiest tasks of his life to journey two hundred miles in order to present his old instructor, Miss Bishop, with the highest degree that had ever been given by the college,—a D.M.H.S.,—Doctor of Mind, Heart and Soul.

Through it all Ella Bishop sat quietly, poised, head up, facing the great throng whose eyes were all upon her. And the wine of new life flowed through her veins.

Sitting there while the speeches went on, sweeping around her, like waves about some little island of her own, her mind was a swiftly changing kaleidoscope of thoughts. They darted hither and yon, those thoughts, like white-hot bits of steel flying from the anvil of her mind, struck by the hand of God. She seemed endowed suddenly with some great power hitherto unknown to her, a prophetic vision to see life as a whole. Little pieces of her life swept together, small incidents tumbled into shape, so that a completed pattern visioned itself before her in one compact unit. The whole mosaic of her life spread out in front of her. For a few moments it hung before her mind as a tapestry might have been displayed before her mortal eyes.

Once in her youth she had started to weave a tapestry at the loom of life with a spindle of hope and dreams,—and the center of the fabric was to have been a little house in a garden and red firelight and the man she loved and children. But the threads had been broken and the spindle lost, and she had woven another. And now for these brief minutes everything was understandable. Every decision she had made was thread of the loom, every incident in her life was a silver or scarlet or jet-black cord woven into the warp and woof of the fabric. And surprisingly the black threads were necessary to throw into relief the figures of the weaving.

For a few moments she had a complete vision of things as they are. An occult power was her own for that brief time. Some unknown force seemed saying: "Here is the work of your life. Take one swift look. It is not given to many to see the completed whole. This is what you have woven from the threads God gave you."

Ella Bishop dropped the lids over her eyes for a moment in abject humility before the loveliness of the scarlet and blue and gold of the weaving.

Never before had such understanding been given her; vaguely she sensed that never would it be again. All rancor concerning the forced resignation was swept away in a flood of understanding. She was closing her work before her faculties dimmed, singing her swan song on a high clear note. To-morrow she would be an old woman. To-night she was ageless. Yesterday she had merely mumbled the words that life was eternal. To-night she knew it. She feared nothing now . . . poverty or old age or death. None of them existed. There was no end to the soul of her . . . to the real Ella Bishop . . . here or anywhere . . . not while all these people lived . . . or their children . . . or their children's children. The remembrance of her in men's hearts would not be for anything she possessed,—but for what she had done.

Something was tapping at her memory,—some long forgotten dream of her youth. Suddenly she remembered,—that early dedication of her life. Why, she must have . . . almost without realization . . . by doing her simple duty from day to day . . . she must have given some of the living flame that glows more brightly as the ages pass.

She had nothing to fear,—here or beyond. Out where Professor Fonda lay sleeping the stone said:

> *We have loved the stars too deeply*
> *To be fearful of the night.*

The stars had been Albert Fonda's deepest love. Her own love was the students to whom she had given her life. This, then, could be her own confidence and faith at the end of the journey:

> *We have loved humanity too deeply*
> *To be fearful of the dead.*

The last speech was over. The great assembly was calling for her. She must say something. This was her last opportunity. She must stand and tell them what she had just discerned,—that every thread of life's weaving must be strong, every fiber firm. True to the dedication of her life she must tell them of this knowledge she had just acquired.

Old Miss Bishop rose. The applause was deafening. Before she passed from their lives she must teach them one thing more . . . these men and women she loved. But how could she approach it? What could she say? She looked over the vast sea of faces. No, it was too late. You cannot teach a great truth like that in the space of a few moments. You may only accomplish it, little by little, day by day, over a long period of time. If she had not done so by example and precept in a half-century's teaching, she could not do so now. And perhaps she had. God knew.

She stretched out her arms to them all, with superhuman effort stilled the trembling of her lips. "The book is closed," said old Miss Bishop. "Hail and farewell."

And the affair was over.

They crowded around her, congratulating her, pressing her hand, giving her merry messages. When they left, group by group, she had a dozen dinner dates and out-of-town week-end invitations. Not that old indefinite "Come to see me, sometime, Miss Bishop," but "to-morrow night at seven" and "next Friday on our silver wedding anniversary."

Every group which left put the same question: "Are you ready to go now? We'll walk over to your car with you." And as many times she answered: "Thank you. I'm not quite ready."

Even when Ronald and Gretchen and the rest of the party came for her it was the same. It was Gretchen who intuitively sensed it. "Come on," she whispered to them all. "I believe she *wants* to be the last one."

Just inside the hallway with its cracks in the scarred walls, old Ella Bishop stood, erect and smiling, and bade the great throng of students good-night. Like a mother she watched the last child break the tie which bound it to home.

For a few moments then she stood alone watching the shadowy figures move across the campus under the giant trees,—north—south—east—west —down the four roads of the world.

Then she walked firmly over the worn threshold and closed the doors that had swung to a thousand youthful hands.

The bell tapped and the pigeons with a great rush of beating wings flew out of the tower.

Old Chris turned out the lights.

(7)

THE END